THE KING OF MACAU

BOOKS BY JAKE NEEDHAM

THE JACK SHEPHERD SERIES

DON'T GET CAUGHT
THE KING OF MACAU
A WORLD OF TROUBLE
KILLING PLATO
LAUNDRY MAN

THE INSPECTOR TAY SERIES

THE GIRL IN THE WINDOW
THE DEAD AMERICAN
THE UMBRELLA MAN
THE AMBASSADOR'S WIFE

OTHER NOVELS

THE BIG MANGO

THE KING OF MACAU

A Jack Shepherd Novel

Jake Needham

Half Penny Ltd
Hong Kong

E-book edition ISBN 978-616-335-908-7
Trade paper edition ISBN 978-616-7611-37-2

English-language publication history

First edition, e-book: Half Penny Ltd, Hong Kong 2014, ISBN 978-616-335-910-0
Second edition, e-book: Half Penny Ltd, Hong Kong 2016, ISBN 978-616-335-908-7
Third edition, trade paper: Half Penny Ltd, Hong Kong 2016, ISBN 978-616-7611-37-2

JACK SHEPHERD IS a lawyer, but he doesn't much like to admit it. He left the sour life of a Washington lawyer far behind and now he works by himself in Hong Kong. He no longer lobbies government agencies, negotiates for corporations, or shows up in court. From his little unmarked office on Hollywood Road, he works quietly to solve the problems his big-money clients don't want anyone else to know they have.

One of the world's largest casino operators discovers a massive money-laundering scheme targeting its casino in Macau and they ask Jack Shepherd to shut it down. Macau is a tiny place on the South China Coast that is the biggest gambling center on earth. It is also a stronghold of Chinese organized crime, which makes it a dicey place for a white guy to go around asking too many questions.

Shepherd is in Macau ducking Chinese gangsters and searching for the source of the black money swamping the casinos when he is sucked into a bizarre caper. A man who knows the most secret schemes of the North Korean government has found out that Shepherd still has high-level connections in Washington. He wants Shepherd to slip him out of Macau and get him political asylum in America, maybe with a nice beach house in Hawaii thrown in for good measure.

Soon Shepherd is tumbling headlong through this modern-day Casablanca on the South China Sea, a bubbling caldron of gunrunners, money launderers, hustlers, gangsters, gamblers, con men, and spies. He joins forces with the daughter of a shadowy old man everybody calls the King of Macau to outwit the Chinese gangsters and shut down the black money flow. At the same time, he has to battle a gaggle of North Korean hit men to try and bring his defector in alive.

Move too fast, and he'll lose control of everything. Move too slow…and Macau just might kill him.

WHAT THE PRESS SAYS ABOUT JAKE NEEDHAM

"Tight and atmospheric, Needham's Jack Shepherd novels are thrillers of the highest caliber, a perfect combination of suspense and wit that will satisfy even the highest of standards. Jake Needham is a man who knows Asia like the back of his hand."
– The Malaysia Star

"In his raw power to bring the street-level flavor of contemporary Asian cities to life, Jake Needham is Michael Connelly with steamed rice." **– The Bangkok Post**

"Jake Needham is Asia's most stylish and atmospheric writer of crime fiction." **– The Singapore Straits Times**

"Needham certainly knows where a few bodies are buried." **– Asia Inc.**

"Jake Needham has a knack for bringing intricate plots to life. His stories blur the line between fact and fiction and have a 'ripped from the headlines' feel…Buckle up and enjoy the ride."
– CNNgo

"What you will not get is pseudo-intellectual new-wave Asian literature, sappy relationship writing, or Bangkok bargirl sensationalism. This is top class fiction that happens to be set in an Asian context. As you turn the pages and follow Jack Shepherd in his quest for the truth, you can smell the roadside food stalls and hear the long tail boats roar up and down the Chao Praya River."
– Singapore Airline SilverKris Magazine

"For Mr. Needham, fiction is not just a good story, but an insight into a country's soul." **– The New Paper**

THE KING OF MACAU is dedicated to the memory of Ray Ransome, who left us much, much too soon.

Karl Marx wrote that history repeats itself
the first time as tragedy,
the second time as farce.
And the third time, he might have added, as North Korea.

– Fareed Zakaria, The Washington Post

Don't matter how you do it,
just do it like you know it.

– Jerry Jeff Walker

1

ONCE UPON A TIME…

Wait, I shouldn't begin that way. You're going to think this is a fairy tale. And this story is anything but a fairy tale, although I admit there are things here that might at a glance make it sound a bit like one.

It does, after all, take place in an exotic land you may not believe is real. Take it from me, Macau is real. It is a centuries old city-state occupying a tiny spit of land on the South China coast. Its name is sometimes spelled as Macao, and there's your first clue about the place right there. When people can't even agree on how to spell its name, you ought to know right up front that you're pretty much fucked if you think you're ever going to figure it out.

All of Macau taken together doesn't add up to more than a dozen square miles, but it is still the biggest gambling town on earth. It already has thirty-three casinos including the massive Venetian Macao, the largest casino in the world, and new casinos are constantly under construction. Macau is closing in on $50 billion a year in gambling revenues, several times the gambling revenues of all of Nevada combined. The place is Las Vegas on steroids, and that's no fairy tale.

But there's something else, too.

AT THE HEART OF this story is a man many people call a king, although Macau was never actually a kingdom, and Ho Hung Sun was never a real king.

After four hundred years as a Portuguese colony, the Portuguese sailed away in 1999 and Macau became a Special Administrative Region of China. At the time, Ho owned all the gambling casinos in Macau. Every single one of them. A bit of every dollar thrown on Macau's tables and fed into its slot machines ended up in the pockets of Ho and his family, and all that money made Ho Hung Sun, who always introduced himself to westerners as Stanley Ho, nothing less than the king of Macau.

The power Stanley Ho's gambling monopoly gave him over Macau was simply more power than the Chinese government was willing to allow anyone to wield in their new Special Administrative Region, but even the Chinese moved cautiously around Ho. It wasn't until 2002 that they finally came to an accommodation with him and began granting new gambling licenses to big international players like the Las Vegas Sands, the Wynn Resorts, and MGM Mirage.

Although Stanley Ho still operates about half of Macau's casinos, his power is not what it once was. Like King Lear, the king of Macau is old and knows his kingdom is slipping away.

But that is not the end of this story. It is really only the beginning.

Because here's the thing…

Stanley Ho has a beautiful daughter, and her name is Pansy.

IT DOES SEEM RICH material with which to contrive a modern-day fairy tale, doesn't it? An exotic land, a once powerful king now grown old, and the king's beautiful daughter.

Of course, there is still something missing. We need a handsome prince to ride in on a white horse and save the king's beautiful daughter.

That, more or less, is where I come in.

NOW I'M NOT BAD looking, although calling me handsome might be stretching a point or two, but I haven't got a horse, not one of any color, and sadly I'm no prince. I'm only a lawyer. At least that is what I say when someone asks me what I am. The whole truth is rather more complicated than that.

I don't research points of law or figure out tax codes or go to court. I solve problems. The sort of problems most lawyers don't want to know about.

When people are being polite, they call me a troubleshooter. I've never been sure what that actually means, but I have to admit I rather like the sound of it. I find the trouble and I shoot it. Neat, huh? If things were only that simple.

This is what I really do: I fix the shit nobody else wants to touch. I work by myself, I keep a low profile, and I don't get personally involved. I'm like a surgeon. I show up, cut the son of a bitch, patch him up as well as I can, and I'm out of there.

I am being glib, of course, something I have been accused of more than a few times in my life, generally by a woman. The things I actually do to earn a living aren't nearly that straightforward. Here's what I mean…

I GOT AN EMAIL from a man named Gerald Brady. He said he wanted to see me about a matter of considerable importance. I had no idea who Gerald Brady was and I learned nothing from doing a quick Google search other than that Gerald Brady was a far more common name than I imagined.

Mr. Brady asked me to meet him the next day at the MGM Hotel in Macau, and he demonstrated his bona fides by having a courier deliver a bank check for ten thousand dollars within an hour after his email appeared in my in-box. Even better, it was ten thousand big dollars, the American variety, not Hong Kong dollars. That was pretty persuasive so that afternoon I made the one-hour jetfoil trip across the Pearl River delta to Macau and checked into the MGM, where a very nice suite was waiting for me exactly as Brady said it would be.

I had no idea what he wanted to talk to me about, of course, but I doubted very much it would involve writing a memo on some point of corporate law. People don't call me when they want a memo. People call me when they have a problem they have to fix, a problem that scares them so badly they can't talk to anyone else about it. People call me when there isn't anyone else they *can* call.

My name is Jack Shepherd.

You should keep that in mind. There might come a time when there isn't anyone else you can call either.

2

THE FIRST SHOT WENT wide and the second shot went high, and I have absolutely no idea where the third shot went.

By the time I heard it, I was flat on my belly behind a black Rolls Royce that someone had fortunately left parked in the driveway right where I was standing. The concrete smelled of rain and the car smelled of wax, and the silence that followed the three shots was so complete I could have counted the tiny ticks from the car's engine cooling in the night air.

I could have, but I didn't. I was too busy trying to figure out what was happening. And more important, whether it had anything to do with me.

I had been in Macau for only a few hours. Surely I hadn't pissed anybody off that quickly, at least not enough for them to want to shoot me.

Then again, I'd been wrong about things like that before.

WHEN THE SHOOTING STARTED, I was just standing there looking at the early February fog filling Macau's narrow streets. The thin, wispy light made the whole place feel even more romantic and mysterious to me than it usually did. The upper half of the Grand Lisboa Hotel, a golden-hued monstrosity of a building that was supposed to resemble a gigantic lotus blossom, was gone, lost in the grey-white shroud lying on the city. Wrought iron balconies, cobblestone alleyways, flickering streetlights, and the indecipherable Chinese characters of the road signs were all rendered in feathery soft focus by the gauzy billows of fog. It was like walking into a black and white movie. I felt like Robert Mitchum waiting on a misty street corner for Jane Russell to appear.

I had spent the last hour or so killing the evening by strolling around the casino at the Wynn Macau. The brightly lit rooms, the crowds of Chinese gamblers, the haze of smoke over the tables, and the brittle anticipation breathed in and out by a thousand gamblers in near perfect synchrony had held me for a while, mesmerized by the great world of vice and dissipation. But I'm not a gambler myself, at least not when it comes to casinos, and I felt no personal tug from the tables, so after a while I lost interest and walked out through the Wynn's east entrance with the vague idea of having a nightcap at the Lisboa Hotel's justly famous Whiskey Bar.

Then I heard the sound of the shots ricocheting off the concrete and I wasn't Robert Mitchum anymore. I was just a middle-aged guy trying to dig a hole in a driveway.

THE SHOOTER, WHOEVER HE was, started firing again and I gave up the thought of risking a glimpse over the hood of the Rolls before it was completely formed. I could tell from the sound of the reports that the shots were coming from a handgun, probably a nine. At least the little creep wasn't wielding an AK-47 on full auto like some LA gangbanger.

I heard five more shots. None of the bullets hit the Rolls, and I counted the pings as they ricocheted off the driveway. Either the gunman was the world's worst shot or he couldn't bring himself to put holes in a Rolls Royce. That's what I'd bet on. In Macau, wealth and its display were about the only things most people thought worth defending.

When I heard the rumble of a big bike revving hard and moving south toward the harbor, I figured that had to be the shooter beating it out of there and I resurrected the idea of taking a glance out from behind the Rolls. I pushed myself to my knees and did a quick head fake over the hood. Since that didn't draw any fire and I didn't see a shooter, I lifted my head and took a long look around.

Nobody was down and there wasn't any sign of damage. All I could see was a lot of people running around like idiots. Macau was getting back to normal already.

SUDDENLY I REALIZED I wasn't alone there behind that Rolls Royce.

A middle-aged man dressed in a dark grey suit and a white shirt without a tie was sitting on the ground and leaning back against the car's rear door. He looked Chinese, with a square face and a head so large he made me think of a bobble-head doll. The man was serenely smoking a cigarette and he looked as if he had merely chosen the driveway behind the Rolls as a convenient place to relax and grab a smoke following a hard night at the tables, rather than as a shelter from flying bullets.

The man saw me looking at him and smiled politely. "It's a real nuisance, isn't it?" he said.

A nuisance?

"You needn't worry," he continued while I was still thinking about his choice of words. "They probably just wanted to scare somebody."

"They sure as hell scared me."

"They almost never hit anyone. I doubt they even mean to."

"Are you saying this sort of thing happens all the time?"

The man looked me over more closely. "I took you for a local," he said. "Where do you live?"

"Hong Kong."

He nodded his head very slowly as if that fully explained my ignorance about life in Macau, but he didn't say anything else.

“Are you telling me attacks like this are common here?” I asked him again.

“It happens,” the man shrugged, looking uncomfortable now.

“I thought the gang violence ended when the Portuguese left and the Chinese took over.”

“All that ended when the Chinese took over was anyone talking about the violence.”

The man pushed himself up and brushed at his trousers with his open hands.

“You said they probably wanted to scare somebody. Who are you talking about? Who is ‘they’?”

The man dropped his cigarette and ground it out under the toe of one impeccably polished wingtip, but he stayed stubbornly silent.

“You mean the triads, don’t you?” I pressed. “You’re telling me those were triad shooters we were ducking.”

“I velly solly,” the man murmured. “I no speakee English.”

He shoved his hands in his pockets, trotted quickly up the steps, and disappeared into the lobby of the Wynn.

I WAS STILL ON my knees behind the Rolls Royce, and I felt pretty silly about that, so I got up and looked around. There were some people here and there who might be described as appearing anxious, but appearing anxious was pretty much the usual state of most people in a gambling town like Macau, and no one really looked like they had just survived a barrage of gunfire.

Near the end of the driveway two Chinese men in dark suits were punctuating their conversation with animated gestures. The loud, harsh cadence of their Mandarin made them seem as if they were about to start swinging at each other. I doubted they were. Mandarin is an angry-sounding language at the best of times. I remembered somebody once telling me that Mandarin isn’t a spoken language at all. It’s a screamed language.

Back in the other direction, a black and cream colored taxi was unloading two women and a man who could have been almost any nationality. The man was badly dressed in long black shorts, flip-flops, and a wrinkled t-shirt, but the two women were costumed as if they were going to a ball. One was in a long silver sheath that glittered in the light, and the other was wearing a short purple dress that displayed her legs to maximum advantage. I glanced at the man's face as they passed. He looked as smug as someone who had hit the daily double. Which, in a manner of speaking, I guess he had.

I looked out toward *Avenida 24 de Junho* where the shooter's bike roared away not two minutes before, and I watched as a young woman in a short yellow dress and red heels puttered past on a sea-blue motor scooter that looked like a Vespa. I doubted it actually was a Vespa, but rather almost certainly a Chinese copy. The woman was slim and small-boned with tightly cropped hair and a dazzling smile, and I wondered briefly if she was a fake, too, a sort of Chinese knock-off of Audrey Hepburn.

Then I stopped wondering about the people around me and started wondering about something far more important.

I started wondering what I was getting myself into there in Macau.

3

I DIDN'T SLEEP WELL that night, probably because being shot at makes you pretty jittery. Or maybe that's just me...

After tossing and turning for a few hours, I woke around dawn to murky grey light creeping past the heavy wine-red drapes in the bedroom. For a minute or two there I couldn't even remember where I was, but then I did, and I sat up, found the phone, and called room service for toast and scrambled eggs. And coffee. Lots and lots of coffee.

I showered, shaved, and dressed in khakis and a white shirt while I was waiting for breakfast. I pulled out a lightweight blue blazer, but I didn't even think about putting on a tie. I stuck with the uniform I had settled on some time ago for first meetings with new clients. The jacket said I was a lawyer, but I figured the open-neck shirt added that I wasn't anything like the rest of those pompous pricks.

Breakfast arrived and I ate the eggs and toast and drank coffee out in the living room while I watched the New York market wrap on CNBC. When it was over, I shut off the television, poured the rest of the coffee out of the pot, and unfolded the copy of the South China Morning Post that had been left outside my door. I read for a while and was wishing I had some fresh coffee when, at exactly nine o'clock, the suite's doorbell rang. I folded up the paper and opened the door.

"I'm Gerald Brady, Professor Shepherd. Welcome to Macau."

"Call me Jack, huh? I haven't been Professor Shepherd for quite a while."

We shook hands and Brady nodded slowly. Something close to a smile slid over his face and was gone. I was left with no doubt Brady knew the story of my hasty and slightly undignified exit from the academic life. At least now I wouldn't have to tell it myself.

"I'm a vice president of MGM Macau, Jack. I'm in charge of security for the company."

I guess that explained why I had such a nice suite.

When I stepped back and invited Brady in, a room service waiter wheeling a cart followed closely behind him. The cart was covered with a crisp white tablecloth and held a silver urn, a silver tray with a cream and sugar service, and two cups. The cups rattled against their saucers as the waiter pushed the cart across to the two love seats upholstered in dark green velvet that faced each other across a large glass coffee table.

"I hope you don't mind," Brady said. "I had some coffee brought up."

"I never mind coffee."

Brady and I sat opposite each other on the two love seats while the waiter fussed about, drawing us coffee from the urn. I examined my prospective client while the waiter worked. He was wearing an obviously expensive grey suit with just a bit too much sheen to it, an expensive gold watch that was just a bit too chunky, and an expensive haircut that was just a bit too perfect. Brady's face also had that curious perma-tanned look everyone associated with Las Vegas and Hollywood. I had always wondered why chemically induced tans inevitably come out as an odd shade of color never seen in nature. How hard can it be for a nation that has sent men to the moon to come up with a cream that turns people's skin brown instead of orange?

After the waiter finished, he bowed slightly toward Brady and slipped out without hanging around for somebody to produce a tip. It was obviously good to be vice-president.

I took a sip of coffee. It was a lot better than the room service coffee I'd had for breakfast. Maybe the executives at the MGM got classier coffee than the guests.

"Is this a corporate matter?" I asked to get the ball rolling. "Your email left me with the impression that it was personal."

"I don't like to be too specific in emails. You never know who's reading them, do you?"

I thought I knew who was reading my emails and, hysterical claims aside about how NSA is watching us all, I was pretty sure it was the people to whom I sent them. But then I wasn't running security for a major casino in Macau. Maybe that was a whole different deal.

So I nodded, drank some more coffee, and waited. When in doubt, I have always believed, drink more coffee. And wait.

"YOU COME WELL RECOMMENDED, Jack."

"By who?" Or was it whom?

"He asked me not to mention his name."

Okay, I thought, *at least that narrows it down a little.* Brady said 'he', so both of my ex-wives were out as the source of my testimonial. Not that I was hugely surprised by that.

"Why did he tell you not to mention his name?"

"I don't know. You'll have to ask him that."

"Which is hard to do if I don't know who to ask, don't you think?"

Brady gave a tiny nod that appeared to concede the point, but he said nothing else.

I thought about that for a moment. Then I put my coffee cup down, leaned back on the love seat, and laced my fingers together behind my head.

"Okay, Mr. Brady. I'm listening. Why am I here this morning?"

BRADY RAMBLED ON FOR at least ten minutes while I listened and drank coffee. I didn't really mind because it was good coffee, but the story Brady told was pretty simple and needn't have taken nearly that long.

The casino at the MGM Macau had recently experienced an unusual spike in its drop, the gambling industry term for the total amount of money the punters throw on its tables and push into its slots every day. I nearly went to sleep while Brady explained how they recognized the spike was unusual and not merely a matter of business getting better. I was willing to assume Brady, since he was head of security, recognized unusual when he saw it. I didn't really need for him to persuade me.

The bottom line was that Brady suspected the MGM casino was being used for large-scale money laundering. Only he didn't know quite how or, naturally, by whom.

"I understand, Jack, you're pretty good at getting to the bottom of things like this."

I was, so I didn't say anything. I think modesty is tedious, and false modesty is downright obnoxious.

"We want you to find out what's going on. If we're being used to launder money, we want you to find out who's using us and what the source of the funds is."

"That's all you want?"

"That's all."

Brady didn't seem to realize I was joking, and I didn't bother to tell him that I was. When you have to explain irony, it's no longer particularly ironic, is it?

"Do you have any suspicions?" I asked instead.

"Of course. We always have suspicions."

I said nothing and, after a moment, exactly like I knew he would, Brady told me exactly what those suspicions were.

"The triads aren't as powerful in Macau as they once were," he said. "But they're still very much here."

"So you think this is triad money?"

"It's certainly a possibility that has to be considered."

I gave him a look.

He cleared his throat.

"I guess it's a fairly strong possibility," he murmured.

MOST WESTERNERS THINK OF the Chinese triads, if they think of them at all, as something out of a Bruce Lee movie. Just a bunch of crazy Chinese guys, mostly fictional, and even a little comic. The truth is that there's nothing fictional about the Chinese triads. And absolutely nothing about them that is even slightly comic.

The triads have been established in Macau for at least four hundred years. The Sun Lee On, the Dai Huen Jai, the 14K, and the United Bamboo are the biggest players, but there are others, too. They're all involved in drug trafficking, extortion, kidnapping, loansharking, smuggling, gambling, prostitution, and most every other form of criminal activity that anyone has been able to think of.

Officials in Macau routinely deny that the triads are active there, but nobody even pretends to believe them. Macau is the biggest gambling city on earth. It floats on an ocean of cash. Get serious.

In the 1990's, Macau was a sanctuary for gangsters, gunrunners, pimps, corrupt officials, and spies of almost every nationality. It was a mixture of Chicago in the 20's, Shanghai in the 30's, and Casablanca in the 40's. The Chinese triads controlled the streets, and everybody else kept their heads down. Most locals were smart enough not to go out after dark.

Then, on December 20, 1999, the first day of Chinese sovereignty over Macau, heavily armed convoys of PLA troops rumbled over the border in trucks and armored personnel carriers. They were greeted with cheers by thousands of Macanese. The message was clear: the Portuguese had been hopelessly inept in dealing with the violence and lawlessness in Macau, but the Chinese would impose order because order was good for business.

I thought back to what my bobble-headed friend had said the night before when we were sharing the shelter of that Rolls Royce. He said that the Chinese hadn't stopped the triads at all. They had just stopped people from talking about them.

"SO YOU WANT ME to investigate the triads," I said to Brady.

"I didn't actually mean—"

"You said you wanted me to get to the bottom of a spike in your drop, you think is money being laundered through your casino, and you think it is triad money."

"We want you to find out the source of the spike in funds, Jack. Perhaps it's triad money, perhaps it's not."

"You know it's triad money, Mr. Brady. In Macau, what else could it be?"

Brady looked down at his shoes, which pretty much answered my question.

"There's no way I'm going to get involved with the triads," I said. "I was outside the Wynn last night when somebody plinked a few shots in my direction, apparently for grins. I'd hate for them to be serious about it next time."

"We're not asking you to get involved with the triads, just to—"

"You're asking me to finger the triads for washing dirty money through the MGM casino and to find a way to stop them from doing it anymore. How is that not involved?"

Brady looked away. He didn't say anything.

"Forget it," I said. "I'm not your guy."

"Will you talk to someone else before you make your final decision?"

"That is my final decision. I'm not going to change my mind."

"We paid you a substantial retainer for this meeting, Jack. It seems only fair to ask you to give us just a little more time. If you don't want the job at the end of the day, we certainly can't make you take it."

I had to admit that was a reasonable point of view. I could

always give Brady his ten grand back and go home to Hong Kong, of course, but the idea of returning money I had already been paid wasn't very appealing. The other possibility was that I could stick around a little longer and listen to somebody else try to persuade me to investigate the triads in Macau.

One way, I was out a fair amount of dough. The other way, I would have a few laughs.

"Who do you want me to talk to?" I asked.

I COULDN'T HELP BUT smile when Brady told me, although I tried not to be obvious about it. I knew who Pansy Ho was, of course. Anybody who read the business papers in Hong Kong knew who Pansy Ho was.

Pansy was a daughter of Stanley Ho Hung Sun, one of fifteen or twenty children the old man was willing to admit to, and she had become quite successful in her own right as MGM's local partner in Macau. Recently she had been keeping a low profile. Some of the gambling regulators in the US had begun pressing MGM Mirage to explain their involvement with Pansy in connection with MGM's licenses in New Jersey, Nevada, Maryland, and other places in the United States. It wasn't really Pansy who was making American gambling regulators nervous. It was her father.

Stanley Ho was at least ninety now and he had never been charged with any crime in Macau or anyplace else, but the stories about his supposed triad connections wouldn't die. Ho and his companies held an absolute monopoly over all the gambling in Macau for nearly two generations, and he still controlled a couple of dozen major casinos as well as Macau's whole transportation infrastructure. How could that be possible, people wouldn't stop asking, without, at the very least, Ho making a few deals with the triads along the way?

American gambling regulators are particularly sensitive to anything that smacks of organized crime, even if the crime is

Chinese, half a world away, and not actually all that well organized.

So Brady wanted me to meet Pansy Ho and talk to her about investigating the triads, huh?

That was worth hanging around for.

4

BRADY AND I WENT down to the third floor and were shown straight in to Pansy Ho's office, which caused me to feel uncommonly important. I was pretty sure that was the whole idea.

I was a little surprised to see that Pansy's digs were on the modest side. I suppose I expected something more Las Vegas, but what I found was an average-sized room that looked out on the Wynn Macau right next door. There was an antique wooden desk on one side and four wingback chairs upholstered in a bright red print sat around a mahogany coffee table on the other. Steve Wynn's driver probably had a fancier office.

"Professor Shepherd," Pansy said, coming around her desk and offering her hand. "Thank you for making time to see me."

They weren't going to quit with the professor stuff, were they?

"It's just Jack," I said.

While we were shaking hands I tried to look Pansy over without being too obvious about it. I could remember when men looked at women without risking indignation or a lawsuit, but that was a long time ago. These days, frank appraisal can get you in trouble. My guess was that Pansy was accustomed to appraising looks and wouldn't mind, but I was about to tell her to shove her job offer so I figured a bit of caution was probably in order.

Pansy was a petite, good-looking woman who wore her jet-black hair in a neat, no-nonsense bob. On her left wrist was what looked like a Cartier tank watch with a brown alligator strap, and on her right were three tortoiseshell bangles that click-clacked together when she moved. I remembered reading somewhere that Pansy was over fifty, but I would never have guessed it. In her crisp white blouse, knee-length Dolce & Gabbana tweed skirt, and gold spike heels, somewhere around forty was far more believable.

"I'm told you had a very distinguished academic career, Jack. Your expertise in banking and money laundering seems to be internationally respected."

"Who told you that?"

I saw Pansy's eyes flick to Brady, who remained expressionless. It was obvious that she didn't want to come up with a name, or couldn't come up with one so, being a gentleman, I took her off the hook.

"I taught international business at a university in Bangkok for a couple of years, that's true, but I'm not sure you could call my academic career distinguished. I got fired because the university didn't like the kind of people I hung out with."

The welcoming smile on Pansy's face never wavered.

"What kind of people were those?" she asked carefully.

"I represented Plato Karsarkis. He wanted me to get him a presidential pardon so he could go back to the United States. The university didn't particularly want to be connected with a notorious international fugitive," I shrugged, "so they sacked me."

Pansy nodded slowly and studied a spot on her desk that didn't seem to me to be all that interesting.

"Did you think Plato Karsarkis was guilty?" she asked after a moment, her eyes still on her desk.

It sounded as if this was going to turn into one of those 'how-can-you-represent-a-man-like-that' conversations. I hated conversations like that.

"To get a pardon you have to admit you're guilty," I said.

"Or at least you have to be convicted."

"As he was," I nodded.

"But do you think he was really guilty?"

I smiled. "You don't really expect me to answer that, do you?"

Pansy smiled right back, and it was a very nice smile indeed. Warm and ironic at the same time.

"Let's sit down," she said, gesturing toward one of the wingback chairs. "Shall we?"

THE THREE OF US made small talk about Macau while an assistant fussed around with another coffee service. I guess that's one of the advantages of being in the hotel business. You got all the coffee you can drink. When the assistant finally left and closed the door, Brady got straight to the point.

"Jack says he's not interested in our proposition," he told Pansy.

"I never heard your proposition," I corrected him. "We didn't get that far. What I said was that I wasn't interested in taking a job investigating the triads."

"I didn't ask you to investigate the triads."

"You asked me to locate the source of money laundering activity that you admitted might be triad related. It's the same thing. Any white guy who accepted a job like that in Macau would have to be out of his mind."

Pansy made little patting gestures in the air with her hands. And very nice hands they were, I couldn't help but notice. Her fingers were slim and tapered, and her nails were carefully manicured and finished in a deep red polish, a shade that fell about halfway on the scale between librarian and party girl.

"I think we're getting ahead of ourselves here, Professor Shepherd."

"It's Jack," I reminded her.

"Yes, okay, Jack. I understand you've been very successful in tracing funds for all sorts of people, including agencies of the US government. You've come highly recommended to us as an expert in international money laundering. All we want you—"

"Recommended by who?" I interrupted. "Or is it by whom?"

Pansy looked confused. "What?"

"You said I came highly recommended. I want you to tell me who highly recommended me."

Pansy looked distinctly uncomfortable, although I couldn't see why. It seemed to me to be a simple enough question, so that's what I said: "It's a simple enough question."

"Yes, I see that. But I can't tell you."

"You can't tell me who recommended me?"

"No."

"That doesn't make any sense."

"I can well understand how you might come to that conclusion, but he asked me not to use his name."

Still not one of my ex-wives, then.

"Why not?"

"You'll have to ask—"

"Never mind," I interrupted. "I've already had that conversation with Brady."

Pansy and Brady once again exchanged a look. This time I didn't even try to guess what it meant.

"PLEASE, JACK," PANSY SAID, "would you at least hear me out here?"

I nodded and she leaned toward me with an earnest expression on her face. I was sort of hoping she would stare deep into my eyes and place a hand on my thigh, but her eyes focused somewhere above my head and her hand stopped on my arm. I was left disappointed all around, but I nodded again anyway. It seemed to be the polite thing to do.

"I'm sure you've heard the stories about Dr. Ho," she said.

Dr. Ho? Not 'Dad' or 'my father'?

What Pansy chose to call her old man was none of my business, of course, but it did seem curious. And what was Ho a doctor of, anyway? I tried to imagine someone referring to Steve Wynn as Dr. Wynn and almost burst out laughing.

That was when I realized Pansy was staring at me. She appeared to be waiting for me to acknowledge that I had indeed heard the stories about her father before she went any further. I assumed she meant the stories about Stanley Ho being connected somehow with the triads, the nature of his supposed connection varying wildly from one story to the next. I had indeed heard those stories. Nearly everyone I knew had heard those stories. So I ventured a small nod, not entirely certain what Pansy might think I was agreeing to. But a simple nod seemed harmless enough, and anyway, it looked like the only way I could keep the conversation going.

The nod seemed to satisfy Pansy, whatever she thought it meant.

"I want to tell you that those stories are not true," she continued. "Dr. Ho has no connections whatsoever with the triads. He runs gambling casinos in the biggest gambling market in the world, so it is inevitable that criminals come to his casinos, but that does not mean he himself is a criminal."

"A lot of people say your father has cooperated with the triads and that was why he wasn't a suitable partner for a company like MGM Resorts in Macau."

"Yes, I understand that."

"They say you're MGM's partner here only because your father can't be."

"I understand that, too. But what do you say?"

"I don't say anything. I have no idea."

"We all have fathers," Pansy snapped. "Even you, I suspect."

That was true, of course, but I doubted it would be polite to point out that, as far as I knew, nobody had ever thought my father might be an organized crime boss.

"Would you like to be held responsible for everything your

father has ever done, Mr. Shepherd?"

I noticed that Pansy hadn't exactly addressed the question on the table. I also noticed I was no longer Jack. I wasn't even Professor Shepherd. Now I was plain Mr. Shepherd.

"You've been in Asia for a long time," Pansy continued while I was still contemplating the significance of my abrupt demotion. "You of all people must understand that triads are a fact of life here, particularly in Macau. People who say Dr. Ho cooperates with criminals do not live in this part of the world and so they do not understand how this culture works. But that does not stop us living our lives."

I didn't even want to try guessing what *that* meant.

WE TALKED ON FOR another ten or fifteen minutes after that, or rather Pansy talked and I listened. I found that an occasional nod on my part was enough to keep things going. When Pansy was done with her pitch, she leaned toward me again and that earnest expression returned to her face.

"So do you understand what I'm saying, Mr. Shepherd?"

"I do."

"If triad money is being laundered through the MGM and it is not stopped immediately, I will be blamed for it."

"You probably will be."

"That will be seen as validating all the old stories about my father and I will become a personal liability for MGM."

"Yes, I think you're right."

"American gambling commissions have the power to shut down casinos if they suspect they have any kind of connection at all with organized crime anywhere in the world. To save their other assets, MGM will cut all ties to me if stories begin to circulate that triad money is being laundered through this casino. Getting to the bottom of this quickly and quietly may mean my personal survival."

"I can see that."

"I cannot allow that to happen."

"You certainly cannot."

"So you'll help me?"

"No."

Pansy's head jiggled slightly as if she had been riding a bicycle down a perfectly smooth roadway and unexpectedly hit a speed bump. Which, in a manner of speaking, was exactly what she had done.

"What?" she asked. "Why not?'

"The way I see it, there are only two possibilities here."

I held up two fingers. I felt a little stupid doing it, but I did it anyway.

"Perhaps this isn't triad money at all, in which case you don't have the problem you're obviously so afraid you have, and you don't need me."

I paused and now it was Pansy's turn to nod. She did.

"Or it is triad money, in which case a lone white guy running around a Chinese city trying to pin down its source is going to feel like a rabbit in a pen full of hunting dogs that haven't been fed."

I figured I was due for another nod from Pansy at about that point, but she remained motionless.

"It's a no-win deal for me," I finished, even without Pansy's nod. "I don't get involved in no-win deals."

"Please reconsider, Mr. Shepherd. I really do need your help here."

"Never kick a cow turd on a hot day. Harry Truman said that. Words to live by."

"What?"

Pansy looked confused again, as well she might have. So for the second time I did the gentlemanly thing and took her off the hook.

"Look, why me?" I asked. "I can recommend any number of people who can do the same job for you, people who live in Europe or the US and don't have to worry about the triads getting pissed. I live in Hong Kong. I don't want to sound like a sissy, but I really don't want to piss off a whole army of violent gangsters who can easily find out where I live."

"I don't want someone else. I want you to do this."

"Why?"

"I trust you, Mr. Shepherd. I think you are an honorable man."

Pansy had only met me a few minutes before, but somehow she had already detected at least one of my many personal virtues that so many people seemed to miss. Of course, I didn't believe for a moment that my supposedly remarkable character was the real reason Pansy wanted me to do the job, but I paused briefly to savor the concept regardless.

"You will be very well paid, Mr. Shepherd."

"I'm sure I would be, but I'm not going up against the triads at any price."

"Oh really? I got the impression a minute ago that you were blaming Dr. Ho for doing exactly the same thing you are doing now: choosing not to go up against the triads."

"That's a different situation."

"Is it?"

No, it really wasn't all that different. Pansy had me there. So I shut up. I have always believed the first rule of life is this: when you find yourself in a hole, stop digging.

"Is there anything I can do to get you to change your mind?" Pansy asked after several moments passed in silence. "Anything at all?"

"I doubt it, but you could try telling me who recommended me to you and we could see how things work out from there."

Pansy's eyes flicked quickly to Brady, whose sphinx-like expression never wavered.

"I can't do that," she said. "I just can't."

"Then, Ms. Ho, may I say it's been a pleasure."

I stood up and extended my hand.

Pansy looked at it for a moment as if it were some kind of foreign object, but finally she rose slowly and took it. Her hand felt tentative and yielding as we shook.

"And if you're ever in Hong Kong with nothing to do," I added to lighten the moment, "give me a call. I can show you a place that makes the best tacos in Asia."

To my surprise, Pansy smiled broadly at that and her grip became noticeably firmer.

"I might do that, Jack," she said. "I really do love tacos."

Pansy pronounced it 'tack-o's', but I didn't bother to correct her.

Damn, I thought to myself, *a beautiful woman who owns about half of Macau wants to have tacos with me? That's pretty darn cool…*

5

AFTER I LEFT PANSY'S office, I probably should have tossed the few things I brought with me into my bag and headed straight home to Hong Kong. But I didn't.

Truth be told, I wasn't really all that busy right then. There was a jetfoil to Hong Kong every hour and I had a nice suite in the MGM that Pansy Ho was paying for, so what was my hurry? Even if you do have to duck a few bullets occasionally, Macau is still a pretty pleasant place to hang out for a while.

Most of the year the humidity on the south China coast is just plain nasty and walking anywhere is a damp, unpleasant experience, but the winter fog made Macau feel air-conditioned so I decided to take advantage of the nice weather to explore the laneways of the old city.

I cut through the casino at the Wynn Macau, took the pedestrian underpass beneath the broad boulevard called *Avenida da Amizade*, and surfaced again in front of the Grand Lisboa Hotel. The Grand Lisboa is Stanley Ho's crowning achievement. It is either an architectural marvel or an architectural monstrosity, depending on your point of view, and mine tended toward the monstrosity end of the scale. Soaring more than fifty stories over Macau, the Grand Lisboa is sheathed in golden glass and shaped like a lotus flower growing out of a silver and gold, egg-shaped dome. As a monument to wretched excess, it's world class.

After a half-hour's wander through the Grand Lisboa and another half-hour exploring its older and dowdier sister, the Lisboa Macau, I turned north along the commercial spine of the Macau peninsula, *Avenida de Almeida Ribeiro,* known to everybody in Macau as San Ma Lo. At Senado Square, the iconic center of Macau, I bought a Coke from a kiosk and sat for a while on a green wooden bench.

Senado Square looks authentically Mediterranean. Mosaic tiles form wavy black and white patterns in the pavement, and the low-rise buildings surrounding it are faced with ornate iron balconies and painted in pastel shades of pink, green, and yellow. On the other hand, the square is filled day and night with mobs of tourists and they are almost all Chinese. It is an oddly disorienting experience to sit in a Mediterranean city square completely filled with Chinese faces, so I finished my Coke, tossed the can in a trash barrel, and continued my stroll.

I passed St. Dominic's Church, the ruins of St. Paul's, the old city walls, and St. Augustine's Square, and eventually I emerged from the narrow, hilly streets at the edge of the inner harbor. The docks of the inner harbor were where the ferries from China used to tie up in the days when a trip to Macau meant half a day on a steam ferry with nothing to break the humidity except whatever breeze the sea might be willing to provide. These days, helicopters from Hong Kong and airplanes from everywhere have turned Macau into just another exotic stop on the international tourist circuit. In less than a generation, the place has been completely transformed. But transformed into what?

Sometimes people like to say that whenever something is lost something else is gained, but trading the fairy-tale old city of Macau for nothing more than a clutch of garish gambling casinos makes a sad joke of that old cliché. So much had been lost in Macau, and so very little gained.

When I'd had enough of exploring, I took a cab back to the MGM and treated myself to the luxury of an afternoon nap. Around seven I got up, showered and dressed, and headed out to dinner.

HENRI'S SITS WHERE IT has sat for generations, on a quiet residential street at the edge of the harbor not far from Government House. *Avenida da Republica* is overhung along most of its length with ancient oak trees that over the decades have knitted their branches together into a living canopy. It is a neighborhood that feels both tranquil and timeless.

When I got out of the cab, I stood for a moment and looked across the harbor to where ranks of powerful white floodlights etched the Macau Tower and the *Ponte de Sai Van* bridge into the velvety black of the night sky. The Macau Tower looked like a gigantic rocket ship all lighted up on its pad for a midnight departure to deep space, and the *Ponte de Sai Van* bridge looked like the last remaining connection tethering it to earth. A breeze rippled the leaves of the oak trees and in the near silence I could hear them murmuring. It almost seemed as if they were whispering something to me. It was all so beautiful it took my breath away.

The unassuming little two-story structure that houses Henri's faces the harbor from across on the other side of *Avenida da Republica.* The front of the building is covered in blue and white tiles, and the big windows are for some inexplicable reason outlined in garish green and blue neon. I crossed the road, but before I even made it to the front door the guy who runs Henri's bounded out and began vigorously pumping my hand.

"Welcome back, my friend," Raymond boomed. "Welcome."

Raymond and I really were friends, but Raymond called everyone 'my friend', partly because he thought everyone was his friend and partly because he had a lousy memory for names. He seated me at a window table and got me a Portuguese lager. He didn't bring me a menu because I never looked at one when I was at Henri's. Raymond brought me whatever he thought I ought to eat that particular night.

I sipped my beer and looked across *Avenida da Republica* to the harbor. There was very little traffic. Occasionally a nocturnal jogger glided past in the darkness along the water's edge, but not often. The local residents were mostly Chinese, and the Chinese weren't big on physical activity, particularly activity that didn't make any money. The empty streets and sidewalks gave Henri's a lost and abandoned quality I found terribly attractive.

Before I had finished my beer, a waiter delivered a platter of African chicken, another of grilled Macau sole, a small dish of curried crab, and a plate of steamed rice. Raymond brought over a bottle of wine I didn't recognize, pulled out the chair opposite me, and sat down.

He poured me a glass of the wine and, while I ate, we talked about nothing in particular. When Raymond realized he had drunk most of the wine himself, he went and got another bottle, and sat back down.

"Let's have a drink when you're finished dinner," he said.

"Isn't that what we're doing now?"

Raymond pulled a face and sloshed more wine into both of our glasses.

"I'm being subtle, Jack."

"No wonder I couldn't work out what you meant."

"I need to talk to you, man."

"I knew that," I said and wiped my lips with a napkin. "So go ahead. Talk."

"I don't want to spoil your dinner."

Uh-oh.

"You want to talk to me about something that's going to spoil my dinner?"

"It's just that I want to ask you a favor. It doesn't seem fair to buy you dinner and then ask you to do something for me in return."

Raymond was buying me dinner? Now I really was worried. This had to be something serious. I chewed thoughtfully at a piece of African chicken and waited.

"Okay, I'll tell you what I'm talking about," Raymond said, "but can I ask you about something else first? I mean, before the favor."

I waited a little longer.

"I heard you were a pretty important guy when you worked in Washington," Raymond said, lowering his voice theatrically.

I didn't know quite what to say to that, and I didn't want to laugh, so I said nothing.

"I heard you got involved in some important things, even if you can't talk about them now," Raymond went on, entirely undeterred by my silence. "That you knew some really important people."

"I wasn't a spy, Raymond, if that's what you're trying to say. I was just a lawyer. Exactly like half the rest of the people who work in Washington."

"That's not what I heard. I heard you were connected all the way up to the White House. I heard you still are."

"You shouldn't believe everything you hear."

"Plato Karsarkis hired you to get him a pardon from the President of the United States, didn't he? He could have hired any lawyer he wanted, but he hired you. He must have thought you were connected. Are you? Connected, I mean."

"What is this all about, Raymond?"

Raymond pushed his wine glass a couple of inches to the left, turned it, and pushed it back exactly where it had been before.

"I have a friend."

In my experience, any story that starts with 'I have a friend' almost always ends with some embarrassing revelation about the teller.

Raymond caught the look on my face and said, "No, really. This is about a friend of mine. He has an immigration problem."

"I don't know anything about immigration law, Raymond."

"He's an important guy. He wants asylum in the United States."

"Political asylum?"

Raymond nodded.

"Someone from Macau thinks he is entitled to political asylum in the United States?"

"He's not from Macau. He's just…well, visiting."

I thought about that for a moment.

"What you're telling me, Raymond, is that some Chinese guy you know looted the treasury of the province where he is a minor bureaucrat, gambled it all away in Macau, and now wants political asylum in the States so he doesn't have to go back to China where they'll probably shoot him."

Raymond shook his head. "I know a few guys like that, too, but that's not what this is about."

"Then what is this about?"

"So you'll take my friend's case?"

"I already told you, Raymond. I don't do immigration law. But you bought me a good dinner, so I ought at least to be polite enough to listen to whatever you want to tell me."

"Would you at least talk to my friend?"

"Look, Raymond, I don't see—"

"He's right here in Macau. It won't be any trouble for you."

I sighed. "Who is he?"

"I can't tell you."

I shook my head. First Pansy wouldn't tell me who recommended me to sort out MGM's money laundering problem, now Raymond wouldn't tell me who this friend was he wanted me to talk to. This seemed to be my day for people refusing to tell me things, even when it didn't make much sense that they wouldn't.

"So can you meet with him, Jack?"

I knew I ought to simply say no and let it go at that, but Raymond was a friend and a nice guy and what harm could it do to talk to somebody for him?

"Look, Raymond, I'm going back to Hong Kong tomorrow, but the next time I'm in Macau you can invite your friend to dinner and I'll—"

"No, that might be too late. It's got to be right now."

"I just told you I'm going back to Hong Kong tomorrow."

"There's a jetfoil every hour. You can meet him in the morning and go back right after that."

I felt trapped. It was either talk to whoever this guy was or disappoint Raymond, and I didn't much like disappointing my friends. Then, too, there were all those great plates of African chicken and endless refills of my wine glass to think about…

"Come on, Jack. Please?"

I hesitated again, finally nodded. "Okay, Raymond, I'll talk to him, but I really don't see what I can do for him. I know absolutely nothing about immigration law or filing applications for asylum."

"You won't be sorry, Jack. I promise you won't."

I already was sorry, but I didn't tell Raymond that.

"I'm staying at the MGM. Ask him to come there at—"

"No," Raymond jumped in quickly. "He can't meet you there. Let me work something out and I'll call you."

"Can't meet me at the MGM? Why not?

"He's concerned about security."

"Security? Who are we talking about here? The Premier of China?"

"Something like that."

I took a close look at Raymond's face, but he wasn't smiling. Obviously, smile or not, he had to be kidding, but now I was becoming intrigued in spite of myself.

"I appreciate this, Jack. I really do." Raymond stood up and pointed to my empty dinner plate. "You want something else to eat?"

I shook my head.

"Okay, I'll set something up and call you first thing in the morning," he said, and with a wave he wandered off to talk to the guests at another table.

I finished my wine wondering what I was getting myself into. When I was done, I stood up and dropped some Hong Kong dollars on the table for the waiter. No reason he should lose his tip because of Raymond's unaccustomed fit of generosity.

I gave Raymond a wave across the room and headed out into the night.

6

I CROSSED THE ROAD to wait for a taxi going in the direction of the MGM. The fog had thickened while I was inside Henri's, and the bright lights of the Macau Tower were now an indistinct glow in the grey mist shrouding the city.

"I thought you were never going to stop eating."

I looked around to see who it was who had spoken, and if they were speaking to me, but all I saw in the darkness and the fog was a silhouette of someone sitting about thirty feet away on the low brick wall that separated the roadway from the harbor.

"I'm out here waiting for you," the voice went on, "and I've had no goddamned dinner, and what do I have to do for an hour? I have to sit here and watch you through that window while you fucking eat."

That was when I realized it was somebody talking to me, and in the next moment I also realized exactly who it was.

"You could have come inside and joined me, Pete," I said. "There was plenty."

"Nah…" Pete drew the word out like he was thinking about what he had missed. "That would have been a really lousy idea."

I took my time about it, but I walked over and sat down on the wall next to Pete Logan. He had short, dark hair, small eyes, and thin, narrow lips. He couldn't have looked more like a cop if he had been wearing a baseball cap that said COP on it.

"I suppose there's absolutely no point in asking how you knew I was having dinner at Henri's," I said.

"None at all."

"Then should I get straight to asking you why you're sitting out here waiting for me?"

"Wouldn't get you anywhere either. I'll tell you when I'm good and ready."

Pete Logan was a cantankerous son of a bitch who had been the legal attaché in the American Embassy in Bangkok for a couple of years. I had always thought legal attaché was a terrific title. It sounded sort of old world to me and invoked visions of cutaway coats, red sashes covered with medals, and formal parties in enormous, gold-trimmed ballrooms. Sadly, as with a lot of titles, the reality of it is far less than what it sounds like. Legal attaché is simply the State Department's designation for the resident FBI man posted in an American embassy.

And that's what Pete was: a special agent of the FBI posted in Bangkok. At least, that's what Pete said he was. Sometimes I wondered a little. Pete had a habit of turning up right in the middle of all kinds of strange stuff and offering lame explanations as to what he was doing there. Was he really a CIA guy operating under FBI cover? Frankly, it wouldn't have surprised me one bit.

Pete and I had some history together. A lot of history, actually. We had been on the same side a few times, and we had been on opposite sides a few times, but through it all we had remained friends, although it admittedly had been touch and go there once or twice. Like the time a few months ago when Pete arrested me for a murder that he knew full well wasn't actually a murder. He even did it right in my hospital room, when I was lying in bed nursing two bullet wounds.

"So, Pete, you want to go into Henri's, grab a couple of beers, and talk?"

"Yeah, I do, Jack, but there's a problem with us going in there together."

"What's that?"

"I don't want anyone to connect you to me."

And that was when I figured out who it was who had given my name to Pansy Ho.

PETE DIDN'T SAY ANYTHING else for a while. Then he glanced sideways at me and grinned. "I guess I really ought to tell you—"

"That you were the one who set me up with Pansy Ho? Yeah, I got that, but why didn't you want her to tell me it was you who had recommended me?"

"I'm not involved in this. Can't be. I'm not even here talking to you tonight."

"You look to me like you're here."

"But I'm not. Nowhere near here. You must be mistaken."

"Huh," I said, "imagine that."

"So...you going to thank me for fixing you up with Pansy or what?"

"I'm supposed to be grateful to you for getting me into this?"

"You don't think she's good looking?"

"Yeah, I think she's good looking."

"And she's a billionaire."

"I know she's a millionaire."

"No, man. I said billionaire. That's with a B and nine zeros."

I realized Pansy had some serious coin, but it hadn't occurred to me it might rise to quite that level of seriousness. Still, I didn't want to admit to Pete that I was impressed so I didn't say anything.

"I introduce you to a beautiful woman who's a billionairess and you sit here looking like you want to piss all over me, Jack. What's up with that?"

"I don't think billionairess is an actual word."

"Who cares? Don't be a pedant."

"Okay then, let's get this over with. Thank you, Pete. You have my everlasting gratitude. Happy now?"

"No, actually I'm not. Why didn't you take the job?"

"How do you know I didn't take the job?"

Pete just looked at me.

I shrugged. "Pansy wants me to find out if the triads are laundering money through her casino."

"Yeah. So?"

"Look, Pete, I was standing outside the Wynn last night minding my own business and some guys cruised by on a bike and plinked six or eight shots in my direction. I don't think they were even shooting at me. I'm told they were just some wild and wacky triad guys having a little fun."

"And your point is…"

"I'm a white boy in a Chinese city. I'm already too damned visible to those guys for my own good. I'm sure as hell not going to do anything to make myself even more visible."

"What makes you think the shooters were triad?"

"You figure it might have been a couple of Swedish tourists out celebrating a birthday?"

"I never thought of you as a pussy, Jack."

"Learn something new every single day, don't you, Pete?"

Pete Logan sighed heavily and pushed himself off the wall. He stood looking at me for a minute with a tired sort of expression on his face, and then he jerked his head in the direction of Government House.

"Let's take a walk," he said.

"I thought you were hungry."

Pete gave me a baleful stare, pointed into the fog, and said, "Walk, pussy."

AVENIDA DA REPUBLICA WAS deserted. By the time Pete and I had walked fifty feet away from Henri's, we were completely enveloped in fog. I was almost inspired to trot out my best

Humphrey Bogart imitation, but Pete didn't seem to be in the mood for jokes so instead I fished around in my pockets until I came up with a Montecristo No. 3 and my cutter.

"Do you have to smoke one of those things right now?" Pete asked. "You look like you're sucking on a turd."

"This from a man who eats at Mexican restaurants."

I cut my Montecristo, found a box of wooden matches in another pocket, and lit it. Puffing the cigar into life, I rolled the first mouthful of sweet, pungent smoke around in my mouth for a moment before I let it go. It was always the first mouthful of a fine cigar that tasted the best, although the other mouthfuls weren't bad either.

We walked along together for while without saying anything. Me enjoying my Montecristo, and Pete...well, I had no idea what Pete was doing there other than walking. Then he cleared his throat and I figured I was about to find out.

"I want you to take the job," he said.

"I'm not going to take the job."

"Take the job."

"What's going on here, Pete? What are you trying to get me involved in?"

"Take the job. You owe me."

"I owe you?"

"Sure. I got you out of jail a few months back, didn't I?"

"Pete, it was you who put me in jail in the first place. And for something you knew damn well I didn't do."

Pete shrugged, but he didn't say anything.

"Why is the FBI interested in Pansy Ho anyway?" I asked.

"We're not interested in her."

"So it must be her father you're interested in."

"Are you crazy, man?" Pete chuckled. "I'm not going to fuck with Stanley Ho. It would take bigger balls than I have to go after Stan."

Pete stopped and pointed across the harbor to where the brightly lit shape of the Macau Tower loomed through a break in the fog. The tower was a slim concrete spear shooting over a thousand feet into the night sky.

"Did you know people bungee jump off that thing?" Pete asked. "They say it's the highest bungee jump in the world. I saw a clip on YouTube once of a guy doing it on a bicycle. Now why do you suppose anyone would want to bungee jump off a thousand-foot tower on a bicycle?"

I had no idea why anyone would want to bungee jump off anything, let alone off a thousand-foot tall tower while riding a bicycle, so I said nothing.

"You ever hear what the locals call that thing?" Pete asked, pointing to the Macau Tower.

I shook my head.

"They call it 'Stan's Boner.'"

The tower had a bulbous looking observation deck on top that I had to admit did give it a certain resemblance to male anatomy in full flight. It was unfortunate, but utterly unmistakable.

"Stanley Ho is about ninety and in a wheelchair," I said. "He's probably forgotten what a boner is."

"Doesn't matter. I still ain't fucking with Stan. He's the king of Macau, man."

"I never figured you for a pussy, Pete."

"Learn something new every single day, don't you, Jack?"

I let the silence hang between us after that and gave my full attention to my Montecristo. The only sound was the muffled impact of our feet on the concrete walkway alongside the harbor.

It wasn't long before Pete started talking again, exactly as I knew he would.

"WE'VE BEEN WATCHING THE money flows in Macau, Jack. This place is a fucking mountain of cash." Pete waved an arm in the general directions of where the bright lights of the casinos were lost in the fog. "Do you have any idea how much money passes over those tables out there?"

"More than in Las Vegas."

"A lot more. Six or seven times more. More than in the whole fucking state of Nevada, my friend."

"What's your point, Pete?"

"My point is that we live in a world in which cash has become a problem. Some of it's just cash, of course, a few bills that Mom and Dad have put aside to have a little fun, but more and more of it is something else altogether. It's the proceeds of government corruption, or drug sales, or arms dealing, or smuggling, or plain old thefts and swindles. Some of it finances bombings and killings and people who are trying to blow up airplanes."

Pete glanced at me to make sure I was listening. I was, but barely. Mostly, I was hoping Pete would get to the point before I fell asleep.

"Cash is a problem for people who have it because they usually don't want to admit they have it. So they try to put it into the banking system in a way that makes it difficult to tell where it came from. A casino is the perfect way to do that."

"You don't have to explain money laundering to me, Pete."

"I like to do introductions. They appeal to my sense of symmetry."

I puffed on my cigar and made a rolling motion with my right hand.

"Okay, here's the thing. A lot of money is laundered through the casinos in Macau. We understand that. There are thirty-five casinos already with more being built every year. And remember, Macau is a place with a population of less than half a million people. It's a river of cash with very few people sitting on the bank watching it. It's inevitable that a lot of dirty water is going to get mixed up with the river."

"That's a remarkable image for a cop to come up with, Pete."

"Yeah, I thought it was pretty cool myself."

"I'm going to try this one more time before I give up. What's your point?"

"About a month ago there was a spike in the amount of money moving over the table in Macau."

"Pansy's already told me that."

"Yeah, but it was a major spike, and it wasn't a one time thing. It's still happening. That worries us."

"How major?"

"So far…" Pete seemed to be adding something up in his head. "Ten, maybe twelve million dollars a month."

"Hong Kong dollars?" I asked, since Hong Kong dollars were the usual currency of Macau's gambling tables.

"Nope," Pete said. "US dollars."

I whistled slightly, impressed in spite of myself.

"If we don't do something to find the source and stop it," he went on, "we could be looking at a hundred and fifty million dollars of dirty money funneled into the international banking system over the course of a year. I need you to help me here, Jack. I need you to trace the money. I need to know where it's coming from, and where it's going."

We came to a corner and turned north alongside a wide boulevard. I took a last puff on my Montecristo, flipped the butt into the gutter, and glanced up at the blue street sign to find out the name of the street we were on now.

Avenida Doutor Stanley Ho, the sign said.

Of course it did.

7

"I ALREADY TOLD YOU, Pete. I'm not dealing with the triads. If I won't do it for Pansy Ho, the beautiful billionairess, I'm sure as hell not doing it for you. You're ugly and you're poor. Forget it."

"I thought you said billionairess isn't a real word."

"That's not the point."

"Okay, then try this on for a pretty good point. This isn't triad money. The triads are a big deal here, but not that big a deal. A hundred million dollars is out of their league."

I was so surprised at that I stopped walking and glanced back at the street sign that said *Avenida Doutor Stanley Ho*. I half expected to see it smirking down at me.

"Are you telling me, Pete, that you already know where the money's coming from?"

Pete didn't say anything. He had continued walking when I stopped and by now he was half lost in the fog. I didn't know if he was ignoring me or he hadn't heard my question, so I caught up with him and repeated it.

"Are you telling me you already know where the money's coming from?"

"No. But I know it's not the triads."

"How do you know that?"

"I just know, okay? Don't piss me off here."

Pete looked over and gave me a smile that had absolutely no humor in it.

"Look, Jack, you understand more about shit like this than anybody I've ever known. My job was to open the door for you. I've done that, and now I've had to come all the way up here and starve my ass off to get you to walk through the fucking thing."

"What are you talking about?"

"Who do you think tipped Pansy to the spike in money passing over the MGM tables?"

"It sounded to me like they had figured it out for themselves."

Pete gave me a long stare.

"Okay," I said when I saw Pete's face, "but why would the FBI have to tip MGM off about money hitting their casino? They must have some pretty sophisticated cash management systems in place. They would have picked it up before anyone else."

"They would have if all the money was flowing thorough MGM, but it isn't. To them, it would only look like they were having a few better months than usual. Which is what any business always expects to have, so they don't try too hard to explain it."

"You're saying this mysterious bubble of money is turning up at more than one casino?"

"It's spread pretty evenly across at least four casinos."

"So why only tip Pansy? Why not tip everybody?"

"Because Pansy is the most vulnerable. She scares easiest because the slightest hint of a triad connection to her would blow her personally right out of the water. I figured she might even be scared enough to hire somebody from outside to track down the source of the funds. So I floated your name and lied my ass off about how smart and reliable you are."

"I'm sure you did a hell of a sales job."

"Well…to tell you the absolute truth, it turned out to be easier than I thought. She'd already heard of you. Said you had a great reputation as a troubleshooter. She had to be thinking of somebody else, obviously, but I saw no point in correcting her."

Pansy Ho had heard of me? Said I had a great reputation as a troubleshooter? Even I was pretty impressed by that, but to Pete I only nodded matter-of-factly. *Of course Pansy had heard of me,* I wanted my expression to say. *How could she not have?*

"And you went through all of that…why? To save the FBI having to pay me?"

"Don't be stupid. I did it for the cover. You think I'd want everybody to know you've been hired by the US government to track down the source of a flood of money through Macau? Why would the FBI need some half-assed lawyer hiding out in Hong Kong for something like that?"

"But you do."

"Well…ah, yeah. We do."

"I'm flattered, Peter, but—"

"Look, man. Think about it. It's beautiful. All Pansy knows is that I tipped her about millions of dollars being laundered through MGM every month, so she hires you to get to the bottom of it. That gives you inside access to MGM so you can shut off the dirty money before anyone finds out about it. What she doesn't know is that some other casinos have exactly the same problem. If she thought her competitors were involved, too, she would never give you the kind of access you're going to get. Beautiful, huh? Fucking beautiful."

Oh, yeah, beautiful. Fucking beautiful.

PETE DIDN'T SPEAK AGAIN until we were almost directly in front of Government House.

"Then today," he said, "Pansy calls and tells me you've refused to take the goddamned job. You know what she asked me? She wanted to know if I could recommend anyone else."

"And could you?"

"That's not the point."

"In other words, you couldn't."

"I got on an airplane, came straight to Macau, got a couple of our local lads to track you down, and here I am starving my ass off and begging you to take the goddamned job. Does that answer your question?"

"I'm flattered, Pete."

"You sure as shit ought to be. Look, Jack, I know you're the best at this kind of thing so I need you. You happy now? Want me to say it again? You're the best! I need you! How's that?"

"My God, Pete, you must really need me if you're willing to debase yourself like that."

"Tell me you'll take the goddamned job and I'll figure it was worth it."

I stood looking at the front of Government House, a two-story Mediterranean structure the color of over-ripe raspberries. With its white shutters and white balustrades, it looked like a very large cake of some very peculiar flavor.

"Let me make absolutely certain I understand what you're saying here, Pete. You want me to let Pansy pay me to track down the source of this mystery money and tell the FBI where it's coming from. Is that right?"

Pete nodded.

"You don't think it would be unethical of me to give you information my client had paid for?"

Pete turned his head and gave me such a look of total amazement that I laughed right out loud.

"Okay," he said after a moment, "if it bothers you so much, think about it this way. You're an American citizen. If you happen on evidence of a crime under American law, you are ethically bound to report it to the appropriate American law enforcement authorities." Pete tapped himself in the chest with his forefinger. "That would be me."

"And would I happen on evidence of a crime under American law by looking into this money laundering at the MGM Macau?"

Pete pursed his lips and made a thinking face. "It's…possible."

THE SIMPLE TRUTH OF it was that Macau held an undeniable appeal for me. I had always been attracted to weirdness, and Macau is a free fire zone of weirdness. In a world floundering through the swamps of correctness, regulation, and regimentation, Macau is an outlaw. How can you not love that?

Macau for a couple of weeks? Working for a beautiful billionairess? Picking up some big money and being given license to dig into the financial records of one of the biggest casinos in the world?

"You promise me, Pete, this isn't triad money?"

"Have I ever lied to you?"

I just looked at him.

"Okay, Jack, I take your point, I do. But I'm not lying now. It is not fucking triad money."

"How do you know?"

"I…know. You have my word on it."

"What is it you're not telling me, Pete?"

"For Christ's sake, Jack, there's a ton of shit I'm not telling you. I'm not completely stupid."

"But you're telling me the truth about the money?"

"Yes."

"Not triad?"

"Not triad. Scout's honor."

I PRETENDED TO PONDER for a little longer, but that was mostly for show. I couldn't have Pete thinking I was a pushover, could I?

Later, when I looked back and asked myself how I had gotten into all this, I could take no comfort in ambiguity. I couldn't explain it away as coincidence or bad luck. I couldn't say it was all unforeseen or, even better, someone else's fault. It had happened right at that moment, and I had done it to myself. Everything that came afterward began when I agreed to do what Pete was asking me to do. Everything started the very second I spoke the words that Pete had flown all the way from Bangkok to hear.

"Okay, Pete," I said, "I'll take the goddamned job."

In spite of my misgivings, I have to admit I felt a slight buzz of anticipation the moment I caved in. There was stuff to figure out, secrets to learn, shit to fix. Perhaps even a few tacos with a good-looking billionairess thrown into the deal.

This, I told myself, *just might work out okay after all.*

8

THE NEXT MORNING AFTER breakfast I called Gerald Brady to tell him I would take the job. Brady wasn't in, so I left a message that we needed to talk about the specific terms of MGM's proposal. After that I went into the bathroom to shower and dress and, of course, the goddamned phone rang the moment I finished soaping up. I leaned out of the shower and grabbed the receiver of an extension helpfully mounted on a wall within reach.

"What?" I snapped.

There was a brief silence. Then: "Professor Shepherd?"

The voice was female, deferential, and slightly tentative. The woman sounded so nice that I immediately felt like a jerk for the way I had answered the telephone.

"I'm sorry," I said. "I didn't mean to be rude, but I'm in the shower."

The woman's tone may have initially been deferential, but she didn't acknowledge my apology and it didn't appear to bother her all that much that she had called when I was in the shower because she didn't acknowledge that either.

"Please hold for Ms. Ho," she intoned crisply, and there was a click.

I stood there, half in the shower and half out, dripping on the bathroom floor and listening to hold music that sounded like an accordion band playing the greatest hits of Barry Manilow. Where did telephone manufacturers get this stuff?

"Good morning, Jack."

Pansy Ho's voice cut off my cascade of internal rants before I could get too worked up.

"I hope I haven't called at an inconvenient time," she said.

"No, not at all. I just finished breakfast."

I'm such a pussy when it comes to good-looking women I even embarrass myself sometimes. I wonder if I would have responded the same way if Pansy Ho were short, fat, ugly, and poor. Actually I know the answer to that, and it isn't pretty.

"I understand you've decided to help us, Jack. I wanted to tell you how very pleased I am. Very pleased."

"It sounds like word travels fast around here. I haven't even talked to Brady. I only left a message."

"It's a small town and, to be completely honest, Gerald's office was told to notify me immediately if they heard from you. I hadn't given up. I was still hoping something might make you change your mind."

For a split second, I thought Pansy was about to ask me what it was that had changed my mind, and I didn't have a clue what I was going to tell her. But she didn't ask.

"I'm looking forward to having you around, Jack."

I was getting a creepy feeling I was being manipulated, but I wasn't completely sure to what end. If it was Pansy using her feminine wiles to get me to take the job…well, maybe that wasn't too bad. Yeah, okay, I am a pussy. I admit it. All right?

"Why don't you come down to my office right now and we'll get everything worked out?"

"I had assumed I was going to be working with Gerald."

"Oh…"

Pansy trailed off for a moment, which gave me the opportunity to kick myself. Hard.

"...that's okay, too, if you would rather."

I was being manipulated. Now I was sure of it. But I didn't actually mind all that much.

"I'll be down in fifteen minutes," I said.

WORKING OUT MY DEAL with Pansy was painless. She asked me what my billing rate was. I told her I billed a thousand United States dollars an hour plus expenses, and if I had to bring in any people to help me their fees would be on top of that. She said fine. I was a hell of a negotiator, wasn't I?

To be honest, quoting a rate like that always embarrasses me a little. I understand people aren't actually buying my time. They're buying my knowledge and my experience. I also realize the amount of money usually at stake when people ask for my advice makes my charges seem like a rounding error. Still, it feels pretty ridiculous to me, really, that anybody's advice can possibly be worth a thousand dollars an hour. I can't imagine what my father would say if he were still alive and found out his son was charging clients that kind of money for, mostly, talking. He would no doubt see it as an out and out scam. Sometimes even I thought it was.

"I'll fill Gerald in on our arrangement, Jack. How soon will you be available?"

"I'm available now. I can devote at least the next few days exclusively to you."

I thought that had a nicely ambiguous ring to it, and I liked it that Pansy smiled after I said it.

"I may need to go back to Hong Kong for a bit next week," I added, "but we ought to have made a good start by that time. Who knows? Maybe we'll even have your problem solved."

"In a few days?"

I spread my hands. "Hey, everybody tells you I'm good, don't they?"

"What do you need to get started?" Pansy laughed. "Some office space?"

"That's not necessary. I can work in the suite. But I want to start by studying the daily casino cash management and currency inventory reports. Can you get them for me going back…say, ninety days?"

"I'll have them delivered to your suite by the end of today."

A few minutes of pleasant conversation followed after that, and Pansy and I both nodded politely through all the detailed talk of casino operations and cash flows. Each of us was trying to hit the socially acceptable level of flirtation without stumbling into wretched excess. That's not nearly as easy as it sounds.

Pansy was walking me to the door when my telephone vibrated in my pocket. I pulled it out and glanced at the screen. It said HENRI'S RESTAURANT, which was when I remembered that I had agreed to talk to Raymond's friend with the immigration problem. Raymond was calling to set up the meeting.

How do I get myself into these things?

AFTER I LEFT PANSY'S office, I found a quiet spot beyond the elevators and called Raymond back.

"This is Henri's, the best loved restaurant in Macau."

"This is Jack Shepherd, the best loved lawyer in Hong Kong."

"No such thing. Nobody loves a lawyer. Not in Hong Kong, not anywhere."

"There's got to be one somewhere. I think it's me."

Raymond didn't laugh. Sometimes I wondered what sort of sense of humor Chinese guys had. Were there Chinese comedians? Had to be, I guess. Could there be a Chinese knockoff of Monty Python out there somewhere? That I would only believe if I saw it with my own eyes.

"Your meeting's at noon," Raymond said.

I glanced at my watch. "You buying us lunch at Henri's?"

"No, not here. Do you know the Ah-Ma Temple?"

Of course I knew the Ah-Ma Temple. Every tourist who had ever visited Macau knew the Ah-Ma Temple. A Taoist complex built on the side of Barra Hill in the fifteenth century, it faced the inner harbor from the southeast corner of the Macau Peninsula. I had walked past it yesterday as I was wandering through the old city, but the mobs of Chinese tourists around the place had made the thought of going inside pretty unattractive. Besides, I had never seen myself as much of a temple kind of guy.

"Get serious, Raymond. You want me to meet this guy at a temple?"

"It's not what I want, it's what he wants."

"Well, it's not what I want. Tell this fellow to come here to the MGM and—"

"Stop!'

I stopped. I didn't ever remember hearing Raymond speak so sharply to anyone before, let alone to me, and now that he had I wasn't sure how to react.

"Look, Jack, I'm sorry, but you've got to do this the way my friend wants to do it. It's important. You have to trust me on that. When you meet him, you'll understand why."

"Wow, I love a mystery."

"Just shut the fuck up, will you? Be at the Ah-Ma Temple at noon. Go in through the main gate between the stone lions and climb the stairs to the Hall of Benevolence."

"The Hall of Benevolence? You're shitting me."

"It's Ming Dynasty. Supposed to be five or six hundred years old. It's the third or maybe the fourth building up the hill."

"You disappoint me, Raymond. You're not sure which building is the Hall of Benevolence? I though you people really knew your temples."

"I'm a Catholic. *Dominus vobiscum*, baby. I know from nothing about all this Taoist mumbo jumbo."

"How will I find this friend of yours when I get there?"

"You won't have to find him. He'll find you."

"You think I should wear a red carnation or something like that?

"Get serious, white boy. You're conspicuous enough around here already. Don't need no red carnation."

"What's this guy's name?"

"Just call him Freddy."

"Freddy?"

"Uh-huh."

"Which I'm certain is his real name. I know a lot of Chinese guys named Freddy."

"Did I say he was Chinese?"

"Well, no, come to think of it, you didn't. But if you play the odds in Macau—"

"Don't worry about it, Jack. Get your butt over to the Ah-Ma Temple at noon, meet the guy, and listen to his story. You can call him Barbra Streisand, for all I care. He won't care either."

"Wait a minute, Raymond, this really does seem a little—"

But I was talking to myself. Raymond had hung up.

I LEFT THE MGM about an hour later and found a taxi right away. Since Macau isn't a very big place, by eleven-thirty I was standing in the little square in front of Barra Hill looking up at the pavilions of the Ah-Ma temple on the rocky hillside. I was early, so I sat down on one of the wooden benches shaded by willow trees that were scattered around the sides of the square. I thought it might not hurt to watch the world for a while before I climbed up to the temple. I didn't know what I was looking for, of course, but I figured looking was a good idea anyway.

The area in front of the temple is called Barra Square, although it really isn't much of a square. It's only a big open space between a wide roadway that runs along the inner harbor and the small hill where the buildings of the temple are wedged into the rock. Bordered on two sides by small Mediterranean-style buildings painted in shades of pink, green, and yellow, the square itself is paved in tiny cream and black mosaic tiles. Right at its center is a five-sided green kiosk selling cheesy souvenirs and packaged ice creams that looks like it was stolen from a Paris Metro station.

The whole area was thronged with Chinese tour groups huddled around guides holding aloft small colored pennants, and the people in each cluster were wearing tags color-coded to match their group's pennant. The whole thing looked as rigidly organized as a national day celebration in North Korea.

After watching the crowds for a while without seeing anything unusual, I walked over to the kiosk and bought a chocolate-covered ice cream bar. When I returned to my bench, I watched them some more while I ate it, but what was I actually looking for? I didn't have a clue. Even if there were surveillance around Raymond's mysterious friend, I wouldn't have spotted it unless everybody involved was wearing a red hat with a rotating beacon on top.

But why would he be under surveillance anyway? Surely the guy wasn't that important. Regardless of what Raymond said, I would still bet he only turned out to be some poor schmo who had gambled away money he had embezzled from a state-owned company in China and was looking for an alternative to going home and getting shot. Who could blame him for that?

After fifteen minutes, the ice cream was gone and so was my patience. I tossed the stick and wrapper into a trash barrel and walked across the square to the temple's elaborate entry gate. It was crowned with dramatically upturned tile ridges and decorated with dozens of colorful ceramic animals I couldn't quite put a name to. I felt like I was entering Disneyland. Which, in a manner of speaking, it turned out I was.

The first pavilion up the steps was the First Palace of the Holy Mountain. Dedicated to Tian Hou, the goddess of seafarers, it is a rectangular granite structure with high gabled walls and an extravagantly upturned roof covered in green glazed tiles. Chinese tourists clogged the doorway, pushing and shoving each other to get inside. It was a good thing the rendezvous hadn't been planned for the First Palace of the Holy Mountain. I would never have been able to fight my way inside through the mob of Chinese seeking divine delivery of fortune and prosperity.

I stood for a moment in front of a round lattice window through which I could see inside the structure. Dozens of giant, conically-shaped coils of red incense hung from the ceiling, each of them burning slowly and giving off tiny tendrils of white smoke that spread the musky fragrance of the incense throughout the temple. The drifting haze gave the whole place a mysterious, otherworldly air, which I suppose was really the whole idea. I rubbed at my eyes with my fingers. Incense made my eyes water. How spiritual was that?

Another thirty yards up the stone staircase, I found the Hall of Benevolence perfectly aligned with the entry gate and the First Palace of the Holy Mountain. Built of faded red granite and white brick with Chinese characters painted on it in yellow, the Hall of Benevolence was much smaller than the other pavilions. Its roof, too, was covered in green glazed tiles and elaborately upturned ridges, but it incorporated into its design a natural recess in the rock of Barra Hill. It looked like a small, if extravagantly decorated, shed built in front of a cave.

There were no crowds of Chinese imploring the deities for riches at the Hall of Benevolence and, blessedly, no drifting clouds of incense. Apparently benevolence had nothing to do with accumulating riches. But then I already knew that.

I stood before the cave with the little shelter in front of it, not sure what to do next. The Hall of Benevolence was very small and a waist-high fence of wooden pickets blocked the only entry. I turned slowly through a full circle. There was no one else near me, and no one who appeared to be waiting for me. After the bedlam below, it was all remarkably peaceful and I rather liked that.

I sat down on a large grey boulder right in front of the Hall of Benevolence and glanced at my watch. Two minutes before noon.

Okay, I was here.

Now what?

9

THE MAN WATCHED WHILE Shepherd ate his ice cream. He was a few yards up a narrow street at the far end of Barra Square, leaning against a maroon Toyota van and pretending to talk on his phone. He moved his lips occasionally to make sure the picture was complete. Just one more Asian talking on a cell phone.

When Shepherd stood up, tossed away his ice cream wrapper, and started toward the temple gate, the man ambled into Barra Square behind him. His eyes quartered the area around Shepherd, looking for other people moving at a similar speed and in a similar direction. He found none. He didn't expect to, but he was a careful man by nature and he was being even more careful under these circumstances than usual.

Shepherd strolled through the temple gate and started up the stone steps. The area was so crowded with Chinese tourists that now the man was able to move up very close to Shepherd without any concern that he would be spotted. One more Asian face in a crowd of hundreds wasn't going to attract the slightest notice from a Caucasian. The man got very close. He was now no more than twenty feet behind and a little to one side of Shepherd. The man studied him as they climbed the stairs.

There was nothing particularly remarkable about Shepherd

physically. Average height, average weight, average age. He looked to be somewhere in his mid-forties and his dark hair was a little long for a lawyer. He was wearing round, rimless sunglasses that didn't look like they belonged to a lawyer either. Dressed as he was in a plain white long-sleeve shirt with the cuffs rolled up over his elbows, khaki pants, and dark brown loafers, he looked less like a lawyer than he did an architect inspecting a project.

The day was hot and the man began to sweat as he climbed the steps. Where was the damn fog when you needed it? He liked Macau well enough, but it was too hot most of the year and the humidity broke his back sometimes. He didn't spend any more time outdoors than he absolutely had to. Nobody did in Macau, except for a few crazy Americans he had seen jogging the streets in their expensive running shoes. If they could afford such nice shoes, couldn't they afford to take a cab wherever they were going? He wiped at his damp forehead and studied Shepherd's face.

His eyes were an unnerving shade of blue and they looked like they could pin you to a wall. His nose was slightly crooked, as if it had been broken, and the rest of his face had the same quality of hard wear. The man hadn't expected Shepherd to seem so beaten up, but he looked tough, too, like an old boot that had been left out in the rain for a long time. He also looked like a man who had given as much as he had gotten. Maybe more.

The man was glad to see that Shepherd hadn't turned out to be a fat guy in a blue suit. He needed an American lawyer, but he didn't need a fat guy in a blue suit. He needed a fighter, a guy who could handle himself in a barroom brawl. Once he committed himself that was what this was going to be: a barroom brawl.

SHEPHERD REACHED THE FIRST Palace of the Holy Mountain and paused to look through the big round latticework window at the Chinese tourists frantically shaking incense sticks and praying for wealth. The man smiled to himself. Every westerner tourist did that. The drifting incense, the flickering candles, the murmured prayers for prosperity. It was everything they had heard about the mysterious east, all in one room.

When Shepherd rubbed at his eyes, the man smiled again. He couldn't stand incense either, and the incense here was particularly unpleasant. It had a musty, old wood smell with something peppery in it. He tried to hold his breath when he walked by without being too obvious about it. If he didn't, he would taste the foul stuff in his mouth for the rest of the day.

Shepherd reached the top of the next set of steps and walked directly to the front of the Hall of Benevolence. He stopped and turned all the way around to see who might be watching him. The man felt Shepherd's eyes slide over him, but they didn't stop. He was anything but surprised at that. He knew that people didn't notice him. Even when they were looking for him, they didn't notice him. He had that kind of face and that kind of body. He was just one more middle-aged Asian guy. A little chubby, losing his hair, not important, not a threat to anyone. It wasn't very flattering but, under the circumstances, it was usually for the best.

Shepherd, on the other hand, did stand out, and not only because he was white. He stood out because he looked like a man who had everything under control. He looked like someone you went to for directions when you were lost. Which, now that the man thought about it, was exactly what he was doing. He was lost, and he needed Shepherd to show him the way home.

The man walked past the Hall of Benevolence without stopping and began to climb the next set of steps. Out of the corner of his eye he saw Shepherd sit down to wait on a big rock at the end of the walkway. Shepherd wasn't going to wait there forever. He had watched Shepherd eat his ice cream, dump the wrapper into a trash barrel, and start into the temple after only a few minutes of checking out his surroundings. Shepherd was not a particularly patient fellow.

The man figured he had about five minutes to decide. After that, Shepherd would get annoyed with waiting for him and leave.

Probably call Raymond before he got to the bottom of the steps and chew him out for wasting his time.

It was now or never, wasn't it?

Now or never…

10

I HAD NEVER REALIZED how much sitting on a rock hurt your butt, and I'd about had enough of it when I spotted the man climbing slowly down the steps from somewhere above the Hall of Benevolence. Since his eyes were locked onto mine, I was anything but surprised when he turned and walked straight toward me. I was clearly about to meet Freddy.

Something about him seemed vaguely familiar. He looked like someone I had seen before, not personally maybe, but perhaps in the newspapers. The idea scratched at me, but I couldn't bring it into focus.

The man was a middle-aged Asian who was round-shouldered and carried more weight than he should for his height. His hair was thinning and what was left of it was cut extremely short. He wore plain, rimless glasses and was dressed in a black, long-sleeved shirt, black chinos, and black loafers. The weight and the glasses made the man appear soft. He made me think of a very large stuffed toy. He looked exactly like the fat kid in elementary school everybody made fun of during recess when the teacher wasn't looking.

Was Freddy Chinese? I couldn't quite decide. The guy certainly wasn't Japanese. Korean? That was a possibility.

It always embarrassed me a bit that I wasn't able to distinguish one Asian nationality from another with any certainty no matter how long I lived in that part of the world. It wasn't that Asians all looked alike. Well, the truth was they do look a little bit alike, but I wouldn't be caught dead uttering that old racist-sounding canard. It was just that I simply couldn't tell them apart. There's a difference there, but it's hard to explain.

The man marched straight up to me and held out his hand. His clothes smelled like a damp wood fire. It was the smell of the clouds of incense drifting around the temple. I probably smelled the same way to him.

"You are Mr. Shepherd, are you not?"

Thank Christ the guy spoke English. I had forgotten to ask Raymond about the language thing. If the guy hadn't spoken English, this would have turned into the shortest conference with a prospective client I had ever had.

I pushed myself off the rock and we shook hands.

"Yes, I'm Jack Shepherd," I said. "Do you really want me to call you Freddy?"

"Yes."

"Okay," I shrugged. "It's your dime."

A puzzled expression slid over Freddy's round face. "My dime? What is a dime?"

"It's…an American expression. Has to do with pay telephones."

"You want me to talk to you on a pay telephone?"

"No, that's not what I meant."

"Then what do pay telephones have to do with this meeting?"

"Nothing."

Freddy seemed to consider that for a moment, but he nodded his head very slowly without saying anything.

"Forget the pay telephone thing," I said, "but let's get something straight right now. I'm only here as a favor to Raymond. I don't normally meet prospective clients like this. Usually they're happy to come to my office."

That wasn't exactly true, I had to admit to myself. Not many of my clients called meetings at temples, that part was true enough, but damn few of them wanted to be seen going in or out of my office either.

"I've got a lot to do," I said, cutting off that particular course of introspection before it went too far. "So let's get to it. Why are we here?"

"I wish to apply for political asylum in America."

"Then you're talking to the wrong guy. I'm only a lawyer. I can give you the name of a Foreign Service officer at the American consulate in Hong Kong. You should be talking to him."

"I do not wish to sound arrogant, but I have something very big to offer in return for asylum. You do not offer something this big to a clerk at a consulate."

I chewed at my lip and studied the guy. He didn't seem like a nutcase, and anyway I doubted Raymond would have sicked an out-and-out screwball on me. My gut told me Freddy was sincere, but...well, it didn't really matter, did it?

"I don't know anything about immigration law," I said. "I don't know anything about political asylum cases. I'm the wrong man for you to talk to."

"You were the right man for Plato Karsarkis."

Christ, was there anyone on the whole planet who didn't know about that?

Plato Karsarkis had for a while been the world's most famous fugitive. He even became a cause for some people, a sort of international version of O.J. Simpson. Karsarkis had hired me to cut a deal for a presidential pardon. He had something to trade, too, something big enough to be worth the deal, and I tried to help him make it.

Things hadn't worked out particularly well. Not for Karsarkis, not for some of the other people who got involved, and certainly not for me. Johnnie Cochran walked O.J. out of the courthouse and Cochran became a hero for a whole lot of people. My association with Plato Karsarkis was less successful. All it got me was sacked from the university where I was teaching.

The outcome may not have been my finest hour, but dealing with Karsarkis forever changed the way I saw the world. I had never trusted governments, but I had always believed there were limits to how far they would go to protect themselves. Now I knew differently. Now I knew there were no limits at all to how far they would go.

"Plato Karsarkis isn't a reference I use very often. Never, actually."

"He needed you because you could take his case right to the White House. That's why I need you, too."

"Even if I could, what do you have that's worth taking to the White House?" I asked.

"If I tell you, I will have given up everything and gotten nothing in return. Would you do such a stupid thing, Mr. Shepherd?"

No, of course I wouldn't.

"YOU'VE GOT TO GIVE me something," I said after the silence stretched almost to the breaking point. "Tell me who you are. Tell me what you have that would make you important enough to be worth someone's attention. You can't ask me to buy a pig in a poke."

"What is—"

"Never mind. Just give me something."

Freddy's eyes rolled around for a moment as if they had suddenly become untethered from his face, and he smiled slightly.

"Within a week," he said, "the Democratic People's Republic of Korea will announce that it attempted to arrest an American who was posing as a journalist but who actually entered the country as a spy. They will tell the world that this person was shot while trying to escape and is now dead. That will not be true, of course, but that will be what they say. This person is very much alive and being held captive in North Korea."

"North Korea?"

Freddy kept smiling.

"Are you Korean?"

He said nothing.

"Are you North Korean?"

He still said nothing.

I knew Macau had connections with what was fancifully known as the Democratic People's Republic of Korea. Several DPRK banks operated in Macau, their only window on the west, and from time to time stories surfaced about them in connection with international arms sales or drug smuggling or one of the other black businesses that North Korea dabbled in to raise hard currency. I had also heard tales that the North Koreans trained their western spies in Macau so they could learn to mix with westerners before they were sent off to the United States or Europe, but I was less certain those stories were true.

Was this guy a North Korean spy who was offering to come over and bring his knowledge of North Korea's arms, currency, and drug smuggling with him? If he was, and if he was trusted enough to be posted here in Macau, he could well be the big fish he seemed to be claiming to be.

"What do you want?" I asked.

"I want to go to Hawaii."

"Doesn't everyone?"

"And when I am safely in Hawaii, I will tell you everything."

"Everything about what?"

Freddy shook his head, but he didn't say anything.

"Look, Freddy, or whoever the hell you really are, that's not the way this works. Nobody can do anything for you unless they understand what you have to offer. Nobody is going to set you up in Hawaii on the come. And telling me some bullshit that North Korea is going to announce anyway at some time in the future isn't going to get it."

"I know that. I just told you to prove I have access to information."

"Yeah, well, but—"

Freddy held up one hand, palm out like a traffic cop.

"Wait until you hear the announcement. If you are satisfied after that I am important enough to be worth your attention, please call me and we will meet again."

He dipped into one trouser pocket and produced a white card about the size of a business card. When he handed it to me, I saw it wasn't a business card at all. Only a plain white rectangle of cardboard with what appeared to be a telephone number written on it in black ink.

"That is a mobile phone that has never been used and cannot be traced to me. But please be discreet. Leave a message saying you will be back in Macau at a certain time. We will meet here again exactly twelve hours after whatever time you give me."

"Is all this cloak and dagger stuff really necessary?"

"Oh yes, Mr. Shepherd. All this and a lot more. I am taking a grave risk talking to you today. I have already put my life in your hands."

"So you can go to Hawaii."

Freddy smiled. "I hear it is very nice there."

"Nice enough to risk your life for?"

Freddy seemed to think about that for a moment. Then he nodded. "Yes, I think it probably is."

He nodded again for good measure, turned away, and walked down the steps to Barra Square. I noticed he never looked back.

11

IT WAS A LITTLE after one when I got back to the MGM. I hadn't eaten anything since breakfast other than an ice cream bar, so I went looking for a sandwich and some coffee.

The area between the MGM's main tower and its casino is a vast vaulted space the hotel calls the *Grande Praça*. I have no clue how to pronounce that and my guess was almost no one else does either.

One end of the *Grande Praça* is said to be modeled on Lisbon's nineteenth century central train station and the other is composed of a vast sandstone staircase rising what looks to be fifty or sixty feet. In between is a tiled area that's supposed to look like a European village square. It's filled with park benches and huge potted trees and lined with shops, sidewalk restaurants, and the false fronts of narrow Mediterranean-styled houses. Above it all soars a curved glass dome supported by graceful white arches.

I walked slowly down one side of the *Grande Praça* and back up the other, stopping to glance at the menus of the restaurants, but everything was far too elaborate to interest me. Surely it was possible to get a sandwich somewhere rather than be required to consume cold lobster flown in from Maine and served with three sauces, so I headed out the south end of the *Grande Praça* and crossed into the casino. The Lion Bar was closed or I might have settled for a beer and some peanuts, and the Chinese cafe in the casino was so jammed with gangs of day-trippers from the mainland that I didn't even consider it.

I kept moving and soon I was all the way across the casino and out the other side so I decided to cross the street to the Wynn Macau to try my luck there. I walked past the Wynn's poker pit, circled a bank of slots, and ran straight into a Starbucks.

Perfect.

IT WASN'T A VERY big Starbucks since it was wedged into a small alcove off the main casino floor. A glass display case filled with baked goods, the coffee-making apparatus, and a cash register were up against the back wall and half a dozen small round tables took up the space between them and the casino floor.

I got myself a large black coffee and a ham and cheese croissant and carried them to the only table that was empty. The rest were filled with other westerners since no Chinese in a casino would even think of wasting time doing anything other than gambling. Certainly not drinking coffee and eating a ham and cheese croissant.

The croissant was surprisingly good and the coffee tasted exactly like it would in Cleveland. I was polishing off the last of both when a man walked up to my table carrying his own cup of coffee.

"Would you mind?"

I glanced up at the sound of the man's American accent and saw him pointing to the empty chair across from me.

"I'm afraid there's no place else to sit," he shrugged apologetically.

"Go ahead."

"Thanks."

While the man pulled out the chair and sat down, I took out my phone and thumbed it on. The contemporary smart phone has become an essential ingredient of modern social intercourse. It is useful for occasionally talking to other people, of course. It is also useful for checking emails, sending SMS messages, or reading the sports pages of the New York Post. But the primary use for the contemporary smart phone is to give us something to do so we don't have to make eye contact with strangers. In an elevator, on the train, or at a restaurant table, staring at your phone is as effective for avoiding other people as putting a bag over your head. And it's a lot more comfortable.

As useful as my telephone might be as an antisocial device, it didn't keep me from taking discreet stock of my companion out of the corner of one eye. He was a big man, well over six feet and heavily built. He had long reddish-blond hair, a pale Nordic complexion, grey eyes, and a prominent nose. There was a boyish quality about his face, but I put his age at late thirties, maybe older.

The man was silent for a minute or two, but then he cleared his throat. "You're Jack Shepherd, aren't you?"

I don't much like being recognized. It happens sometimes, but every time it does I feel awkward. I've had some prominent clients, probably too many, and I understand that has brought me a certain amount of notoriety. Still, being recognized embarrasses me.

"You were Charlie Kitnarok's lawyer."

I nodded without saying anything, hoping my lack of interest in talking about it showed.

"I remember seeing your picture in the newspapers back when Thailand was going through all those troubles. That got a lot of coverage here."

I nodded again and remained silent.

"I'm Harry Pine," the man said, holding out his hand.

I took it out of courtesy. What else was I going to do? We shook.

"I don't mean to bother you," Pine said, "but it's a real pleasure for me running into you like this. Look...can I get you another coffee or something?"

"I've got a meeting soon," I lied automatically. "Thanks anyway."

"But you don't have to leave right this minute, do you?"

Before I could answer, Pine scooted back his chair and stood up.

"Okay, I'm getting us more coffee. You don't want it, leave it. Black, right?"

Pine didn't even wait for me to answer. He headed straight for the counter.

PINE RETURNED WITH TWO paper cups of coffee, put one in front of each of us, and sat back down.

"You in Macau for very long?" he asked.

"I'm not sure."

"You still live in Bangkok?"

It looked to me like I was being drawn into a conversation in spite of myself. It was pretty much the sort of thing that happened all too often for my liking whenever I encountered another American in some exotic place. Why did people automatically adopt a tone of familiarity toward you because you both had been born in the same country? Age, education, occupation…none of that mattered. If you had been born in America, you were supposed to be delighted to meet another American almost anywhere. I wasn't all that often delighted.

"I live in Hong Kong now," I said.

"Is that so? So you come over to Macau a lot?"

"Not really."

"I live here," Pine went on, apparently oblivious to my lack of interest. "I'm in construction contract management. With all the casino and hotel projects going on in Macau, I've got enough work to last me a lifetime."

I nodded some more.

"Yeah, it sounds boring as hell, doesn't it? Spending all day hassling over the details of a construction contract? But I could tell you some stories. I really could. When you deal with construction management in this town you hear all the dirt."

"I can see how you might," I said politely.

"Yeah, right now Steve Wynn's slugging it out with two big Chinese groups over expanding this casino and they're both doing whatever they can to stab him in the back. Everyone's involved. The Chinese government, the local government, the triads. Everyone."

That got my attention.

"The triads?" I asked.

"Oh yeah. No one wants to talk about it, but the triads have their hands in everything here."

"I've always heard the Chinese government has the triads under control."

"Bullshit, pardon my French. China uses the triads and the triads use China. Everybody here uses everybody else. It's the way Macau works." Pine chuckled. "Welcome to Macau. Disneyland with real bullets."

He pulled out his wallet, fished around in it, and extracted a business card. He held it out to me and I accepted it. What else could I do?

Harry T. Pine
Construction Management
Contract Administration Specialist
JMG Limited

At the bottom of the card there was a Macau email address and two local telephone numbers, but no street address.

"Call me the next time you're back here," Pine said. "We can have a couple of beers and I'll give you the real lowdown on what's going on in Macau, not that happy horseshit the government and the casinos try to sell everybody."

I nodded and pocketed the card. "I might do that, but you'll have to excuse me now. I have a meeting."

When I stood, Pine stood as well and we shook hands again.

"This was a real pleasure for me, Mr. Shepherd. I hope you'll call. I know how things really work here and I'd be happy to give you a steer in the right direction with whatever you're doing."

WALKING ACROSS THE CASINO looking for the right exit to get me back to the MGM, I thought about Harry Pine and wondered. He seemed a nice enough fellow, an ordinary Joe doing a job a long way from where he had been born, happy to run into a fellow American in a Chinese city. Still…there was something about the coincidence of Pine suddenly appearing like that at my table in Starbucks. I couldn't shake the creepy feeling that the encounter hadn't been accidental at all.

But if it hadn't been an accidental meeting, what had Pine gotten out of it? We had chatted inconsequentially for a few minutes and Pine had given me a card. He hadn't asked me anything significant and I hadn't told him anything significant. Nothing had happened, so what would the point have been for Pine to engineer the whole thing?

Maybe, I thought, I was becoming too suspicious. Because I lived in a world in which practically everybody had a hidden agenda, it didn't mean that other people lived like that, too. Surely somewhere there were people who were exactly what they seemed to be and who said exactly what they meant.

There had to be, didn't there?

I GOT LOST IN the vast spaces of the Wynn casino and when I finally stepped outside I discovered I was on the side of the building exactly opposite where I wanted to be. So I turned around, went back in, and headed across the casino toward the other side.

Passing a flotilla of blackjack tables crammed with Chinese players I suddenly realized I was looking at Harry Pine's back. He was walking no more than twenty feet in front of me and appeared to be headed in the same direction I was. I lifted my phone by reflex and used it to half cover my face, but I felt foolish the moment I did. If Pine turned around, he would spot me in a second.

Harry Pine didn't turn around. He moved resolutely across the casino, parting the crowds of Chinese gamblers like the Queen Mary through a fleet of dinghies. I stayed back, keeping him in sight, and when he left the casino I followed.

Still holding my phone over the left side of my face, I stopped outside the big brass-trimmed doors and slid into the shadow of one of the huge potted palms that flanked the doorway. A cell phone and the shade of a palm tree. I was a master of concealment, wasn't I?

I watched Pine make straight for a black BMW sedan idling at the curb of the narrow roadway running between the Wynn and the MGM. When he reached it, the front passenger window slowly lowered and Pine bent down to speak to whoever was waiting for him inside the car.

As Pine talked, he rolled his shoulders first to one side and then the other. That gave me a pretty decent view of his profile. On the second shoulder roll, I squeezed off two quick photos with my cell phone. Before Pine could straighten up and spot me, I slipped back through the doorway into the Wynn's casino. I gave it a minute, maybe two, then I went back outside. Both Pine and the black BMW were gone. Had he gotten in and left in the BMW, or had he walked away after delivering whatever message he had for whoever was inside? I had no idea, but now I doubted even more that Harry Pine was just a construction management drone that had joined me in Starbucks entirely by coincidence.

But if he wasn't, who the hell was he? And what did he want with me?

I glanced down at the phone in my hand and opened the camera roll. In the two pictures I had taken, Pine was pretty far away, but I fiddled with them for a bit, cropping and zooming, and before long I found myself looking at two reasonably recognizable pictures of Harry Pine in profile.

I didn't have a clue what I was going to do with them, and I wasn't sure why I had bothered to take them in the first place. But what could it hurt, huh?

12

ON THE WAY BACK up to my suite, an unctuous, slightly chubby middle-aged European man wearing a black suit and a silver necktie intercepted me in the lobby. I instantly pegged him for either an undertaker or a hotel manager, so when he introduced himself as the MGM's resident manager I had no trouble at all believing him.

He told me that while I had been out they had moved me into a new suite at Pansy Ho's personal request, and he insisted on personally escorting me up to it. The new suite was much higher in the tower, quite a bit bigger, and considerably flashier. There was even a bar set up on a sideboard that included a couple of bottles of very respectable malt whiskey. I couldn't help but be impressed by my own obvious importance.

I took a very long, very hot shower to wash off the sweat and grime I had accumulated while climbing around the pavilions of the Ah-Ma Temple. After I toweled off, I wrapped myself in one of the thick bathrobes the hotel had thoughtfully provided and opened my laptop to catch up with my email. I had been working for about an hour when the doorbell rang. It was a bellboy with two thick envelopes, each of which had my name neatly printed on the front. I took the envelopes over to the desk and settled down to see what the Tooth Fairy had brought me.

When I opened the first of the envelopes, I found it contained a stack of printed cash management reports and a single thumb drive. I tore open the other and discovered the currency inventory reports and another thumb drive. I plugged the two drives into a USB port on my laptop one after another and checked their indexes. They were electronic versions of the same reports I had stacked up in front of me in hard copy.

I picked up the pile of cash management reports, swung my feet onto the desk, and started reading.

BY EIGHT O'CLOCK THAT night, I had it figured out.

I poured myself a whiskey from the bar. Then I stretched out on the couch, sipped at it, and let my eyes wander over the stacks of cash management and currency inventory reports I had spread around on the floor. I had been matching them up this way and that, looking for a pattern of unexplained transactions, and I had found one.

Pete's information had been pretty much on the nose. A stream of money from a single source was quite certainly moving through the MGM. I couldn't yet see the stream's origins, of course, but finding them was like tracking the source of a river. First you had to find the river. After that, you rowed upstream until you discovered where it started. At least now I had found the river.

Every second or third day, the MGM cash reports showed a spike of about two hundred thousand dollars above normalized operations. Multiplied by the four casinos that Pete said were involved, that added up roughly to the ten million or so he said was being moved every month.

It was all as regular as clockwork, at least it was once you saw the pattern. One day on and either one or two days off. Normalized operations today, normalized operations plus two hundred thousand dollars tomorrow or the next day. That part had been easy enough to work out, but it didn't really tell me all that much. It was the currency reports that had started me upstream toward the source of the river. At first I hadn't seen it, but then I did.

All of the excess cash flow was accounted for by spikes in only two currencies, and in only two denominations of those two currencies. Although the exact amounts varied slightly from day to day, on average about half the excess cash was in US dollars and half in euros. The US currency was always the $50 bill, and the euro was always the €100 note. Both were green banknotes, although off-hand I couldn't see what the similarity in color had to do with anything. Maybe that part was a coincidence. The rest surely wasn't.

What really mattered was that both the $50 bill and the €100 note were large bills, but not too large. Certainly not so large as to attract excessive attention. If the spikes had been in $100 bills or €500 notes, somebody would probably have picked it up by now, but the $50 bills and €100 notes were a touch under the radar. Exactly where you want to be when you're moving money.

It worked out to about fifteen hundred $50 bills and something under seven hundred €100 notes being moved through the MGM every few days. Now it was obvious that nobody was wheeling a handcart into the MGM stacked with that much currency, so how was it getting into the casino?

I had no doubt about it. MGM was being smurfed. There wasn't any other explanation.

SMURFS ARE CARTOON CHARACTERS, little blue people who live in mushrooms and build villages that eventually become whole societies. There are a huge number of them and they all look nearly the same, but each one is slightly different, too, and they all work together with a sort of harmony seldom seen in real life.

The term 'smurfing' has come to mean breaking a large task into many tiny pieces and having separate people each perform a small part of the overall task. When applied to money laundering, smurfing meant a great many people each moving a little bit of money and thereby rendering each individual transaction small enough to go unnoticed.

In the case of the excess currency turning up at the MGM, on any one day it would take twenty separate transactions of about four thousand dollars each and twenty more transactions of three thousand euros each to bring a total of about two hundred thousand dollars into the casino. There were a lot of different cashiers at the MGM, and casinos are twenty-four hour businesses, so my guess was no more than a dozen separate smurfs coming in and out through the day was all that were needed to pull off those forty or so transactions. Maybe not even that many. Each smurf would exchange a stack of currency for chips at one cashier, spend a few minutes gambling a little, and take the chips to another cashier and cash them in, probably getting Hong Kong dollars, which was the primary currency used in Macau's casinos.

Smurfing worked pretty well for money launderers, but it was a pain in the ass to run. It's difficult to organize all those people. Particularly if you have to keep the whole machine going over a long enough period of time to deal with a lot of money. It takes a lot of manpower to pull it off, and an organization behind that manpower that is tough and scary enough to keep it under control.

And that was what bothered me.

There was only one obvious possibility in Macau for an organization that could control so much manpower without it getting out of hand and handle so much cash without a lot of it sticking to other people's fingers.

The triads.

I didn't care what Pete thought about the amounts involved here being out of the triads' league, there wasn't anybody else in Macau who had the resources to pull off something like this. The MGM was dealing with triad money whether Pete wanted to believe it or not. Had to be.

Poor Pansy. Her enemies were going to beat her to death with this when it got out.

THE NEXT MORNING I was waiting in Brady's office when he came in. I kept the details to a minimum when I told him what I needed, but it was my guess that Brady could read between the lines with the best of them and didn't have much trouble figuring it out.

I said only that an excessive number of $50 bills and €100 notes were coming into the casino, and I asked Brady to arrange to collect security camera pictures of everyone who used more than twenty bills of either denomination to buy casino chips anytime within the next week. I was guessing that a week's worth of pictures would collate into not many more than a dozen different faces, and then I would know for certain that MGM was being smurfed.

What I didn't tell Brady was that nothing about that made much sense, even if it turned out to be true. Why would anyone bother doing what it certainly appeared they were doing at the MGM?

The point of smurfing is to convert dirty cash into clean bank deposits. No matter how compliant a bank might be, the time had long passed when you could wheel a couple of million dollars of currency into a bank and deposit it in an account without the bank asking exactly who you are and you giving them a damn good explanation of where all that currency came from. If this really was a smurfing operation, all that was being accomplished was to convert stacks of $50 bills and €100 notes into stacks of Hong Kong dollars. It was still cash and the smurfs still had to deposit the cash somewhere to get it into the banking system. Why not just deposit the $50 bills and the €100 notes in the first place? Why do all the work of running the money through the casino and still end up holding cash?

There was something else, too.

Why was all the currency that was being laundered solely in $50 bills and €100 notes? That didn't make sense either. If the triads were moving drug, prostitution, and extortion money into the banking system, it wouldn't all come in two neat denominations.

It would be in all sorts of denominations and in all sorts of currencies. And if it originated from the triad's activities in Hong Kong and Macau, a good chunk of it would be in Hong Kong dollars already, not in euros and US dollars.

Whatever the reason, somebody was still doing it. There was no doubt about the appearance of all those extra $50 bills and €100 notes in the cashiers' cages of the MGM casino on a regular schedule. And it sure as hell wasn't being teleported in. It had to be coming in through a smurfing operation. It had to be. But yet…

Something was all fucked up here.

The only thing I could think of to do was to wait until Brady had collected the security camera pictures and see what was on them. Maybe that would solve the mystery. Might turn out to be simple as that.

But probably not.

UNTIL BRADY HAD A week's worth of security camera pictures, there wasn't much more I could do. So when I left Brady's office I went back up to the suite and got my stuff together to go to Hong Kong.

If MGM really was being smurfed, perhaps I could get Pete to find me enough manpower to mount a surveillance operation on some of the smurfs until we figured out who they were working for. If MGM wasn't being smurfed…well, I guess it would be back to the drawing board, wouldn't it? All those $50 bills and €100 notes had to be coming from somewhere. It wasn't a coincidence they were turning up so consistently in such numbers. And if they weren't being smurfed, there was another reason that was happening and I would have to figure out what it was.

I started to toss my cell phone into my briefcase, but on a whim I dialed Pansy's office and asked to speak to her. She was out, so I left a message that I was going back to Hong Kong until Brady had collected some more data I needed and that I would return to Macau in a week or so. I told Pansy's secretary to let her know that she could reach me in Hong Kong if she wanted me. I thought that had a nicely ambiguous ring to it.

TWENTY MINUTES LATER I was at the Macau Ferry Terminal and ten minutes after that I was through the immigration check and sitting in a Super Class seat on the top deck of one of the hourly jetfoils that runs back and forth between Macau and Hong Kong. The cabin was nearly empty. There were no more than half a dozen people scattered around in something like a hundred seats that looked and felt like economy class seats in an old and out-of-date airplane flown by a not very prosperous airline. I closed my eyes and listened to the shouts of the Chinese sailors as they cast off the mooring lines

The jetfoil moved smoothly down the Macau channel, out between the two thin rock jetties marking its edges, and passed under the high bridge called *Ponte de Amizade* that connects the eastern end of the mainland with Taipa. When we cleared the bridge and reached the open ocean, the pilot revved the engines and we rose up on the hydrofoils and skimmed rapidly east over the surface of the South China Sea.

It was a windy morning and the swells in the Pearl River estuary were unusually heavy. The rhythmic porpoising motion of the vessel rising up the faces of the waves and sliding down into the troughs left me with only two alternatives. I could get sick and make a grab for one of the seasick bags the jetfoil company had conveniently placed on each seat, or I could go to sleep.

I decided to go to sleep.

13

I LIVE ALONE IN an apartment in a Hong Kong neighborhood called the Mid-Levels that is roughly halfway up Victoria Peak above the streets of the financial district, streets that are packed day and night with people making money.

It isn't actually my apartment. It belongs to a guy I knew in law school and he's letting me live there for a while. On not much more than a whim, one I have always suspected was almost certainly powered by substantial amounts of alcohol, one day he abruptly resigned from his firm, bought a thirty-eight foot ketch, and sailed out of Hong Kong harbor in the general direction of Bali saying he intended to have some adventures while he was still young enough to enjoy them.

I was in a bad way right then – I had just been fired by the university where I was teaching and Anita, my wife, had decided she would rather live with someone else – so I asked my law school friend if I could use his apartment until he got back. He said sure, and I haven't heard from him in six months.

It's a nice apartment, and I'm happy to be living in it. There's only one real problem. It's not really home. To be completely honest, I'm not even sure I understand what home is supposed to feel like anymore. My life has been in such upheaval the last couple of years that I've become untethered from the whole concept of home. It doesn't seem quite right to say that somehow, but I am.

From time to time a line from Robert Frost drifts through my mind. *Home is the place where, when you have to go there, they have to take you in.* If that really is the definition, I figure I'm pretty much screwed. I'm homeless. Simple as that. It's time for me to buy a shopping cart and be done with it.

What I like most about my borrowed apartment is that the Mid-Levels escalator is just outside the building. Back in the 1990s, in a highly imaginative but ultimately unsuccessful effort to ease Hong Kong's chronic traffic congestion, the city built a half-mile long outdoor escalator running downhill from the Mid-Levels, cutting through the center of SoHo, and ending near the harbor in the financial district everyone calls Central. The thing isn't actually a single long escalator, but rather a ladder of about twenty escalators tied together by glass-roofed walkways and moving belts. In the mornings the whole Rube Goldberg contraption runs downhill and, later in the day, it reverses and runs uphill for the rest of the day.

For me, the Mid-Levels escalator is like an amusement park ride through the mayhem of Hong Kong. Instead of shouldering my way through the dense crowds packed into Hong Kong's steaming streets, I can stand quietly while I am transported slowly downhill into the heart of the city. I love it. I even love smelling Hong Kong as I ride: that peculiar mix of carbon monoxide, sewer gas, rotting food, and stagnant water that is like nowhere else on earth.

I like the Mid-Levels escalator so much that I rented a small office in SoHo about halfway down the hill from my borrowed apartment. It's a stylish neighborhood, but my office is pretty utilitarian. A single, average-sized room on the second floor of an old shophouse above a noodle shop. It doesn't have much to recommend it, except for one thing really. The Mid-Levels escalator runs almost to its front door. I can commute to work by escalator. How cool is that?

WHEN I HEADED DOWNHILL the next morning, the sky was a drab grey, and so was everything else. I got off the escalator at Hollywood Road and went into a Pacific Coffee Company where I got the biggest to-go coffee they would sell me and a couple of Danish pastries, and after that I walked the fifty yards or so to my office. The skies opened as I reached the door. I ducked inside one step ahead of the rain and climbed the two flights of narrow wooden steps to the second floor.

I worked alone just as I lived alone. I had thought about hiring a secretary once. It would have been handy to have someone to do a little filing and bookkeeping every now and then, but I had to admit honestly that it would have been more for the company than anything else. Whatever my motivation, it hadn't happened. Somehow I never got around to it.

My office is in a shophouse as old as anything in Hong Kong is allowed to get. The interior walls are brick with some kind of white glaze over them and they glistened like porcelain even now, generations after the work had been done. On the north side of the room three tall windows look down into Gage Street, a narrow roadway below Hollywood Road that is so overhung with Chinese-language signs dangling from long metal poles that I can barely see it.

Half the buildings on Gage Street are covered in bamboo construction scaffolding, but probably half the buildings in Hong Kong are covered in bamboo construction scaffolding. It's a city where buildings are always being pulled down and rebuilt. A building is hardly finished before it's torn down again and something bigger built in its place. I had no idea how my little shophouse had survived the onslaught, but I was happy it had.

My principle workplace is a long wooden library table I found in a used furniture store. It sits perpendicular to the windows so I won't be too distracted by the chaos outside. The wall behind my table is jammed with five-drawer horizontal filing cabinets that have locking bars welded to their fronts and formidable padlocks dangling from each of their hasps. On the wall to the right, a line of tall bookcases is half-filled with out-of-date legal journals and the items that men accumulate when they are left to their own devices. A green gym bag, a broken coffee maker, a coffee maker that sometimes works, a half dozen ceramic coffee mugs, an unopened bag of potato chips, some magazines, a burl-wood cigar humidor, a couple of ashtrays decorated with beer logos, boxes of matches, and stacks of old copies of The New York Times, The Wall Street Journal, and the Financial Times.

The wall in front of me, the one on which my eyes rest whenever I lift them from whatever I am doing at my big table, has nothing on it except for a single very large oil painting. It is square, about five feet on each side, and doesn't actually depict any form that I can put a name to. It is simply a riot of primary colors splashed over the canvas in a way that seems at a glance to be entirely random, but on closer inspection is as intricately woven as English tweed. It is the only one of Anita's paintings I still have. She took all the others when she left, but she had given me this one for my birthday so it was mine and I had insisted on keeping it. I had brought it with me from Bangkok and hung it in my new office, but almost immediately I realized that really hadn't been such a good idea. Regardless, I had never gotten around to taking it down, and so it was still there.

I COLLECTED THE MAIL that had been pushed through the slot in the door while I was away and dumped it on one end of my worktable without even glancing at it. Nothing important ever came in the mail anymore. I couldn't even remember the last time I had gotten a real letter.

I drank some coffee and read the online edition of the New York Times for a while, then caught up with my email while I ate the two Danish and finished the coffee. After that, I wiped my hands on a napkin and got to work.

For the next hour I wrote case-status reports and looked

through my pending matters to make certain nothing required urgent attention. When I was done with the routine stuff, I turned my attention to Raymond's pal, Freddy. I logged into LexisNexis and poked around a little to see what I could learn about the legal concept of seeking political asylum in the United States. I knew less than nothing about American immigration law, and I hardly had any idea where to begin.

I was far from certain I would ever hear from Freddy again, but if I was going to spend a week or two in Macau running down the source of MGM's unexplained money flows for Pansy Ho, I sure as heck would be eating at Henri's a few times and Raymond was going to ask me what was going on with Freddy. It would be nice to have something halfway intelligent to say to him. Raymond always took good care of me, and a friend was a friend, always.

Besides, what if this guy did turn out to be some big time North Korean spy and I was being presented with a chance to reel him in? The idea of it was entirely too romantic to be believed, but I supposed it was at least possible. Freddy hadn't seemed like a nut case, and he had come with Raymond's endorsement. That had to mean something.

And then there was that stuff Freddy had tossed out about the North Koreans announcing soon that they had shot an American spy. I guess he thought that would scratch my curiosity enough to get my attention, but suppose it actually happened? What would it prove?

Okay, so it did seem unlikely that Freddy could know something like that unless he had connections in North Korea, that is if the whole story wasn't a steaming pile of horse manure. But even if it turned out to be entirely true, that still didn't mean that Freddy was a particularly important guy in North Korea, did it? Maybe he just knew somebody who was important there.

After an hour of reading immigration law and case reports, I was a little wiser, but not much. Apparently the concept of political asylum only applies to people who are physically present on US soil. You can't go down to an American embassy or consulate somewhere and apply for political asylum. You are required to make your claim when you arrive at a port of entry into the United States and then you have one year to file a formal application for asylum. After that, you receive a hearing from an immigration judge and your application is either granted or denied.

There's the catch, right there…

If your application is denied, you are immediately deported. And depending on where you're deported to, the consequences of deportation could be fatal.

I wondered if there was a way to avoid that risk in this case? If Freddy actually turned out to be a good catch, I supposed I could pitch him to the CIA, but my track record with the CIA really wasn't all that good. To tell the truth, it was terrible. I wouldn't be surprised if I was on an enemies list over at Langley, and I had no doubt at all that they had an enemies list over at Langley.

The FBI? The FBI didn't have anything to do with granting political asylum in the United States, of course, but Pete was leaning on me to do this job for Pansy Ho. Perhaps I could hold out on Pete and refuse to tell him anything about what I found unless he did me a favor in return.

I realized, of course, that I was getting way ahead of myself. Okay, I was curious about Freddy. Anybody would have been. But my curiosity had gotten me into trouble too many times before and I had learned to control it.

At least I did most of the time. And I was damn well going to control it this time.

14

THE NEXT MORNING I spotted Pete Logan waiting for me the moment I stepped off the Mid-Levels escalator. He was about fifty yards up Hollywood Road, leaning on the wall in front of my office and playing with his phone.

Fleeing was a possibility, of course, but I hadn't yet had enough coffee to manage a decent flee so I kept walking. When I got to where Pete was waiting for me, I gave him the hardest stare I could manage before breakfast.

"How did you know I was back in Hong Kong?"

Pete smiled.

"And even if you knew I was in Hong Kong, how did you know I was coming to the office this morning?"

"Look, Jack, I'm the fucking FBI," he grinned. "You got no place to hide. We see all and know all."

"And tell all."

"That hurt. That really hurt."

"Tough shit. Coffee?"

"Sure, why not?"

We walked back down to the Pacific Coffee Company together and stood in line behind two drop-dead gorgeous Chinese girls who couldn't have been a day over thirty. They were engaged in an animated discussion about price options trends on the Hong Kong commodity exchange.

"I don't know what's wrong with young people today," Pete said.

When we both had firm grips on large take-away cups of black coffee, Pete stopped and took another long look at the two women, now sitting at a table and bending earnestly toward each other as they continued their conversation. He sighed and shook his head.

"How do you talk to women like that, Jack?"

Pete sighed heavily again, and we started walking back to my office.

"SO WHAT'S GOING ON?" Pete asked as soon as we were upstairs.

"I thought the FBI saw all and knew all."

"Well…sometimes the picture is a little foggier than we'd really like. You want to clear it up for me?"

So I drank my coffee and told Pete about the MGM's cash management reports and the river of $50 bills and €100 notes flowing through their casino.

"It's got to be some kind of smurfing deal," I finished, "but I won't know for sure until I see a few days' worth of security pictures. If it is, that puts the triads squarely in the frame, regardless of what you say."

"It's not the triads."

"Get serious, Pete. Who else could organize a big-time smurfing operation in Macau? The girl scouts?"

"It's not the triads."

"And this you know exactly how?"

"I just know."

"What is it you're not telling me here, Pete?"

"All kinds of shit, but none of it has anything to do with this."

"It sounds to me like you already know who's behind this."

Pete shook his head. "I don't."

"At least you suspect somebody."

"Other than the triads, and you, it could be anybody."

"No, it couldn't be anybody. It would have to be somebody with manpower and organization on the ground in Macau. I spell that—"

"It's not the triads."

"Horseshit."

We both drank a little coffee and thought about all that for a while. I finished thinking first.

"You said some other casinos were involved," I reminded him. "Is the same thing happening at them?"

Pete reached around, shoved his hand down the back of his collar, and scratched at his neck. "I don't know for sure that it's exactly the same thing. If the smurfing business pans out, you better talk to some other people, too."

"Like who?"

"Let me have a word with Steve Wynn, maybe Sheldon Adelson, too. See if I can get you into their places."

"So you and Steve and Shelly are real pals, are you, Pete? I didn't know that."

"There's a lot you don't know about me, pal. You should keep that in mind."

"Yeah, but here's what I'm wondering. How much of that other stuff do I really want to know?"

Pete mimed a laugh and abruptly jumped to his feet.

"Got to go. Heads to break. Asses to kick. When are you heading back to Macau?"

"Probably next week."

Pete got about halfway to the door before he stopped and turned around.

"One big thing bothers me about your theory. Why would anyone be smurfing money into a casino and back out again? And why would it be just two denominations of two currencies? I never heard of anything like that before."

"Neither have I."

Pete thought about that and eventually he nodded slightly.

"Okay," he said. "Let me talk to some guys."

He made his thumb and index finger into a little gun and pointed it at my chest.

"I'll be around," he said.

And then he was gone.

LATER THAT AFTERNOON MY office phone rang. I didn't get many calls on the office phone. Most of my clients communicated with me by email, and most of my friends called my cell. I figured it had to be Pete.

It wasn't. It was Pansy Ho.

"Is this the man I'm supposed to call about the tacos?"

"Yes, ma'am, it is indeed."

"I'm in Hong Kong. How about tonight?"

"Ah...maybe I should warn you. The place I was talking about isn't very fancy. In fact, it's kind of a dump. They don't even take reservations."

Pansy chuckled. The sound of it was low and throaty and warm, and I liked it a lot.

"Somehow I've never had any trouble getting a table at any restaurant I wanted to go to. I guess I'm just lucky that way."

Now it was my turn to chuckle, but I doubted I sounded nearly as good as Pansy when I did it.

"Tell me where to meet you," she said.

"I'm afraid the place is in Lan Kwai Fong."

Lan Kwai Fong is a trendy district on Hong Kong Island about a quarter of a mile up D'Aguilar Street from Central. A narrow, L-shaped lane closed to vehicle traffic forms a rectangle with a sharp turn in D'Aguilar Street, and the rectangle and most of the area around it is filled with trendy, expensive bars and restaurants. Decades ago, Lan Kwai Fong was called Marriage Arranger Lane for the large number of female marriage arrangers who worked in the area organizing marriages for traditional Chinese families. Today, some might say that Lan Kwai Fong is exactly the opposite, more like a marriage un-arranger lane.

Throughout Hong Kong, the area is known for two things. Loud, cool bars and mobs of foreigners – most of whom are equally loud but not nearly as cool – drinking energetically and prowling for women. It's only a certain sort of local who would be caught dead surrounded by big, frequently drunken foreign louts giving the eye to any local woman who happens into view. I had no idea if Pansy Ho was one of those locals or not.

"Are you still game?" I asked.

"Does the Pope…well, you know how that goes."

I laughed. "Eight o'clock?"

"Eight o'clock."

"It's called Brickhouse," I said. And I told her how to find it, which wasn't easy.

"Got it. See you there at eight."

Well, how about that? I thought when she had hung up. *I'm having tacos with Pansy Ho tonight. Maybe I ought to shave…*

ALL COOL RESTAURANTS ARE difficult to find, which is probably why Brickhouse is at the end of a dark, narrow alleyway off D'Aguilar Street. The place doesn't even have a sign. You have to tell people to walk down the alley to a street stand that sells counterfeit handbags, back up a couple of paces, and look behind the stand. That's the only way to find it and that was the way I explained it to Pansy Ho.

Brickhouse is all bare brick walls and exposed ceilings and concrete floors. It has tables that could have been stolen from a homeless shelter and rough wood benches and little red stools. It's hip and funky, and of course it knows that all too well.

I got there a little after seven-thirty since I couldn't imagine anything worse than making Pansy Ho hang around on her own in a place like Brickhouse waiting for me to show up. I ordered a

Carta Blanca, got some tostada chips and a tub of guacamole to stave off hunger, and settled in to wait. I wondered exactly how late Pansy would be…

She was five minutes early. An unheard of thing, in my experience, for almost any woman. Particularly in Asia.

Pansy was wearing jeans, a man's white dress shirt with the sleeves rolled up, and brown loafers. She had on very little makeup and wore no jewelry at all. I thought she looked absolutely terrific.

As she walked toward the table she waved at a waiter and pointed to my Carta Blanca and another bottle arrived at almost the same moment she did. I pushed the chips and guacamole toward her and smiled as she dug in.

We chatted easily for a while about one thing and another. The cave-like design of the place made it so loud that to be heard we had to bend toward each other and put our heads close together. I didn't mind a bit. Eventually we opened our menus and ordered. Three platters of tacos – rib eye, pork, and chicken – some beans, some Mexican sweetcorn, a watermelon salad. And two more beers.

PANSY DIDN'T ASK ME what I had found out so far about the money moving over MGM's tables, and I was glad she didn't. I wasn't going to lie to her if she did ask, but I didn't want to tell her what I suspected quite yet either. It would worry her, and maybe I was wrong.

But when we finished eating, the table had been cleared, and another round of beers delivered, she did ask.

So I reluctantly told her about the possibility that MGM was being smurfed with large quantities of $50 bills and €100 notes.

"It's only a theory at this point," I added quickly when I was done. "I'm not certain of anything yet."

"But that might be happening?"

I nodded.

Pansy thought about that for a minute, took a pull on her Carta

Blanca, and said, "That wouldn't look very good for me, would it?"

"Even if it's true, it's not necessarily the triads who are responsible."

"Who else could it be?"

I didn't have a good answer for that so I didn't say anything.

"What am I going to do, Jack?"

I didn't have a good answer for that either.

The change of subject had put a damper on the evening, and now the noise in the place was starting to feel more irritating than charming, so I pointed toward the door and raised my eyebrows in a question. Pansy nodded.

I pulled out some bills and dropped them on the table, and we headed out into the night.

WE TURNED DOWNHILL ON D'Aguilar Street and walked together for a few minutes without talking. It was Pansy who finally broke the silence.

"I need you to fix this for me, Jack."

"I don't know for sure yet what needs to be fixed."

"If the triads are responsible—"

"I don't know that they are."

"If they are, you need to fix it for me."

I couldn't imagine what Pansy meant by that. Fix it? Fix it how? Go tell the triads to stop being bad boys? Cover it up so that no one found out? The possibilities were endless and all of them seemed to me to be pretty unappealing. So I settled for a reply that committed me to very little.

"I'll do what I can."

I had no doubt at all Pansy understood I had slipped the question without giving her a direct answer, but she let me and she only nodded. I was grateful for that. It had been a nice evening. I didn't want to spoil it.

Pansy produced a cell phone from her bag and pushed at a speed dial. She spoke a few words in rapid Cantonese and hung up. I thought I caught her mention D'Aguilar Street somewhere in there, but I wasn't certain.

Suddenly a black Mercedes with dark windows was at the curb right in front of us and a big, swarthy Chinese in a too-tight blue suit was standing outside holding open the rear door. The car had appeared so quickly that it might have risen up right through the pavement,

Pansy stopped walking.

"You've got to fix this for me, Jack."

Not knowing what else to do, I just nodded.

"Thanks for dinner. It was fun. Next time it's my treat."

Pansy leaned over, kissed me on the cheek, and slid into the car. The big Chinese slammed the door and jumped into the front passenger seat, and I stood there and watched the big car power away west on Queen's Road.

Next time, huh? Well, how about that?

15

IT RAINED IN HONG KONG for the next three days straight. Generally I like the rain, particularly when I am in a big city, watching it cleanse the streets and rinse the buildings. The idea of a city being purified by the rain is an awful cliché, but it became a cliché because there is so much truth in it. Still, this rain was a bit too much of a good thing. It was steady and drenching. It filled the streets and overflowed onto the sidewalks.

I avoided going anywhere except to make a quick run down the Mid-Levels escalator to the office each day. It wasn't that I was afraid of getting wet, but rather that I had no intention of tangling with crowds of Chinese wielding umbrellas. Even on the best of days, walking in Hong Kong is the next thing to hand-to-hand combat. Arm all those frenzied Chinese pedestrians with open umbrellas and it becomes nothing short of medieval warfare.

I spent my days loafing around the office tidying up the cases I had going. I also reread the MGM cash reports and currency inventories looking for anything I might have missed the first time through. I found nothing. In spite of my optimism that something would come to me that could explain the extra money flowing through the casino other than it being smurfed by the triads, not a single penetrating insight put in an appearance.

I wanted to help Pansy if I could. And not because she was an attractive woman worth several billion dollars who appeared to like me.

Or maybe that was it.

BY THE THIRD DAY the rain slowed to an on-and-off drizzle. I had a bad case of cabin fever from being penned up in the office and was thinking about going out somewhere interesting for lunch. Before I could decide where to go, someone knocked at the office door.

The sound was so alien to me that at first I didn't even know what it was. Almost no one ever came to the office. And I certainly wasn't expecting anyone then. Still half convinced there had to be some other explanation for the knocking sound, I walked over and opened the door.

A small Chinese woman was standing there. She was no more than five feet tall and looked to be not more than thirty, but I had long since given up trying to guess the age of any Asian woman. This one could be anything between twenty-five and fifty-five. She wore heavy black glasses with wide, rectangular lenses that gave her face a quizzical air, and she was dressed in a plain grey jacket and matching trousers.

"Are you Mr. Jack Shepherd?"

When I nodded, she thrust a business card at me and I accepted it with two hands in the gesture of courtesy expected in Asia when somebody hands you a business card.

I glanced down at the little white card printed in some elaborate typeface.

> Cynthia Cheung
> Assistant Business Editor
> South China Morning Post

A reporter?

Uh-oh, I thought, *this can't be good...*

"MAY I TALK TO you for a moment, Mr. Shepherd?"

"Look, Miss Cheung, I really—"

"Call me Cindy. I won't keep you for long, I promise."

Before I could say anything else, the woman walked past me into the office and seated herself in one of the two guest chairs in front of my library table. They were battered captain's chairs that I had found in yet another used furniture shop, and their uncushioned wooden seats were profoundly uncomfortable. Which was exactly how I thought the guest chairs in any office where I was working ought to be.

I closed the door and sat down behind the table. Cindy looked harmless enough, but that didn't make me feel any better.

This *really* couldn't be good…

IT WASN'T.

"I understand you are investigating money laundering at the MGM Macau, Mr. Shepherd."

I tried for a chuckle, but the noise that came out sounded more like I was being strangled. Which, more or less, I was.

"I can't imagine where you heard that, Cindy."

"I have a very reliable source."

Yes, you fucking well do, I thought.

But of course that wasn't what I said.

"I'm a lawyer, Cindy. I don't investigate anything. I advise clients."

"Are you advising the MGM Macau about money laundering at their casino?"

I cleared my throat and shifted my weight in the chair and I immediately regretted doing it. I had made it obvious to the woman that she was making me uncomfortable. Which, of course, meant that she had me dead to rights.

"You're putting me in a difficult position, Cindy. You must already know that a lawyer can't talk about his clients at all, let alone tell anyone exactly what he's doing for them. But if I say that to you, you're going to take it as a confirmation that you're right, even if you're completely wrong."

A pretty good piece of double-talk if I do say so myself.

"We are running a story tomorrow saying that the MGM Macau and some other casinos have recently experienced unusual spikes in their gambling revenue. It also says that the MGM suspects they have a significant money laundering problem and that they have hired you to determine the source of the unidentified funds. Would you like to comment?"

"No."

"You do understand we are running the story regardless of whether you comment or not?"

"You may well be, Cindy, but that doesn't change the fact that I won't talk about my clients."

"That sounds to me like a confirmation that the MGM Macau is your client."

It does indeed, I thought, *even to me.*

"It is well known that you represented Plato Karsarkis when he was a fugitive from the United States," the woman continued. "Will you talk about him?"

"If it's so well known, I don't see why you need me to talk about him."

"I'm only trying to get some personal material, Mr. Shepherd. Something I can use to give my story a little color. Can you tell me something about your background?"

"Cindy, if you really are going to run that story, you're on your own. You're not going to get any help from me."

I smiled and kept my voice low and even. That was something all good lawyers learned to do. To appear totally unconcerned while the building burned down around you. To keep smiling and to keep murmuring all the while, *Fire? What fire? I don't see any fire.*

"This isn't getting us anywhere, is it?" Cindy said with the kind of smile that suggested she hadn't really expected it to.

"Doesn't bother me," I shrugged. "I'm not trying to go anywhere."

A little silence fell after that and I used it to think as fast as I could.

There was a leak somewhere and that scared me. I did not want to be publicly fingered as a guy hired by MGM to investigate money laundering at their casino. If the triads were responsible for whatever was going on there and I was identified as the guy who was supposed to prove it...well, I didn't even want to think about that. The last guy who tried to investigate the triads in Macau had his car blown up.

So, okay, let's start with who could possibly have leaked it. Who knew about what I was doing in Macau? The MGM people knew, of course. Pansy and Gerald Brady and probably a few others. And the FBI knew. Pete and whoever he was working with. Was there anyone else? Whoever was muling the money into the MGM knew what they were doing, of course, but I didn't think they knew anyone was onto them or that I was involved. And even if they did know, they would hardly announce it to a newspaper reporter about. Who else might know? Try as I might, I couldn't think of anyone.

I was going around in circles. Surely neither MGM nor the FBI could be the source of the Cindy's information since it would hardly be in either of their best interests for all of this to become public, and I couldn't think of anyone else who knew what I was doing.

"Has it occurred to you, Cindy, that by running a story like that you're putting me in danger?"

"How am I putting you in danger?"

"Whether your story is true or not, if you cause people out there to think I'm trying to prove they're guilty of money laundering—"

"You think the triads are behind this, don't you?"

Gotcha! I could almost hear her screaming.

I was digging myself in deeper and deeper by continuing to chat politely with this woman. She wasn't going to tell me her source – I wasn't even going to bother to ask – and she was running that story regardless of what I said.

"Would it make any difference if I told you that your story is wrong?" I asked, mostly for form.

"Of course. I would include your denial in it."

"But you would run it anyway."

"Yes. I trust my source."

I sighed. Screwed was screwed, wasn't it?

So I stood up and offered her my hand.

"Okay, Cindy. It's been real."

She didn't reply. She just stood and shook my hand and smiled the sort of smile that said the conversation had gone exactly the way she had thought it would. Then she turned and left the office.

Well, fuck a goddamned duck, I sat there thinking when she was gone. *I'm toast.*

"CALM DOWN, JACK," PETE Logan kept saying when I finally got him on the telephone. "Just calm down."

"This *is* calm!"

"Well, man, I got to say you really don't sound calm to me."

"I don't? Then, fuck you, Pete. It's not your name that's going to be in the South China Morning Post tomorrow. This is calm for knowing that every triad gangster in Hong Kong and Macau is going to learn over their morning coffee that I'm being paid to nail their skinny butts."

"In my experience, Jack, most triad gangsters don't drink coffee, so it seems to me you've really got nothing at all to worry about."

"Very fucking funny. Go ahead, joke about it. There's a leak somewhere, Pete, and all the shit that's squirting out is going to land on my head, not on yours."

"The leak isn't here, Jack."

"How can you be so sure?"

"Because I'm the only guy here who knows what you're doing."

"And it wasn't you?"

"And it wasn't me."

I thought about that for a moment but it got me nowhere.

"But why would anyone at MGM leak it?" I asked Pete. "They certainly wouldn't want something like this to get out."

"Beats me."

Something suddenly occurred to me. "You said you were going to talk to Wynn and Adelson. Maybe one of them put the word out to mess with Pansy."

"That might make sense," Pete said, "except for one thing."

"What's that?"

"I haven't talked to either one of them yet."

"So you're saying that nobody but the two of us and the MGM people know about the money spike at the MGM?"

"Nobody I'm aware of."

"And that nobody but the two of us and the MGM people know anything about me being hired to find out about it?"

"That's what I'm saying."

"So you didn't tell anybody?"

"I didn't tell anybody."

"Well…shit."

That almost certainly meant somebody at MGM had been Cindy's source, but…why? Did somebody on the inside there have it in for Pansy? Was that what the leak was all about? Company politics? Strange…

My mind suddenly leaped to another strange occurrence in Macau.

"Have you ever heard of a guy named Harry Pine?" I asked Pete.

"Harry Pine?" Pete either thought about it, or made a show of thinking about it. "No, I don't think so. Why do you ask?"

"He's a guy who introduced himself to me in Macau for no particular reason. It seemed to me there was something a little off about him."

"Did you tell him why you were there?"

"I'm not even going to bother to answer that, Pete."

"Well…if you didn't, I don't see how he has anything to do with your problem."

"My problem? My problem? Well, fuck you very much, Pete. Maybe I'll catch the next plane for Monte Carlo and it can be your problem."

"Don't be so touchy, Jack. You know what I meant."

"Yeah, I know exactly what you meant. Tomorrow a whole army of violent gangsters is going to be told I'm trying to put them in the frame for a big-time money laundering scheme, and you're going to be sitting in some Bangkok go-go bar watching the girls and having a good chuckle about it. I could always call Cindy and tell her about your involvement here and we can both go out together. Put a sort of a Butch and Sundance finish to this whole fiasco? What do you think?"

"Who's Cindy?"

"The South China Morning Post reporter who has the story."

"You screwing her?"

"Pete, I only met her a half hour ago."

"Doesn't rule it out."

"This conversation is falling apart."

"Good-bye, Jack. Let me know when you come up with something useful."

"I'll call you from the hospital," I said, "assuming I make it that far."

I HAD TWO MORE calls to make.

My first was to Pansy. She needed to prepare herself before somebody told her about that story in the SCMP or, worse, she stumbled over it herself. It wasn't going to go down well with her. Her worst fear was that the money laundering MGM was experiencing would have triad links, and that the mud would stick to her even though she had nothing to do with it.

Now the whole story was going public, and before we knew what the real source of the activity was or even if it really was a money laundering operation. Pansy was going to get a bucket of mud right in the face and I doubted she would ever be able to wash it off, no matter what we eventually found out.

I called her office rather than her cell phone because I didn't want to dump all this on her at an awkward moment. It was going to go down hard enough and I didn't want her to have to deal with it at an awkward time. I had seen too many men answering cell phones while peeing into a urinal to be comfortable delivering difficult news over one. I wasn't actually concerned that Pansy would answer her phone while sitting on the toilet, of course, but the principle there was still pretty much the same.

I wanted Pansy's full attention when I broke the news to her and I wanted it at a time when she wasn't distracted by other things. So I called her office and left a message that it was urgent and she should call me back when she was able to talk. That was about as much hint as I could give her that this wasn't going to be a fun phone call without saying something like, *Yo, baby, you are about to become the triad's babe of the day on the front page of the South China Morning Post.*

Pansy called back in less than ten minutes and I told her about Cindy Cheung and the story that the SCMP was running tomorrow without trying to soften the blow. She took it better than I thought she would. She made some listening noises while I talked, but when I finished she said nothing at all.

When the silence had stretched out to the point of embarrassment, she suddenly spoke up.

"Do you ever wonder if it's all worth it, Jack?"

"I'm not sure what you mean, Pansy."

I knew exactly what she meant, of course, but I didn't think admitting it right away was the thing to do. I really didn't want Pansy to feel as lousy as she obviously did so I tried to end the conversation on a comforting and cheery note. That's what I tried to do, but I felt like what I actually did was murmur a lot of stupid platitudes and make an ass out of myself.

MY SECOND CALL WAS to a guy named Archie Ward.

Archie isn't an easy guy to get in touch with. He may be the guy who knows everything that's happening almost anywhere in Asia, but he isn't a guy who answers his phone. Actually, I'm not even sure he has a phone. Well, of course, he has a phone, but I don't have the number and I doubt many other people do either.

You don't call Archie. The only way to reach him is to sprinkle some messages around Hong Kong and hope that eventually he calls you back.

I hadn't talked to Archie in a while, but I still had a number for what he once told me was his direct line at the main office of the Hongkong and Shanghai Bank, where he claimed half-heartedly to work. The woman who answered told me that Archie Ward no longer worked there, which is exactly what Archie had told me the last time we had spoken, but of course I wasn't sure that Archie had ever actually worked there so his not working there anymore seemed to be a mixed message at best. Brushing aside the woman's categorical insistence that she couldn't help me, I left my name and my office number and asked her to have Archie call.

I had a couple of other Hong Kong numbers for Archie, too, so I called those, too. One was a mobile that didn't ring and had apparently been abandoned, but at the other number a woman's voice answered with a simple, "Yes?"

I smiled at the sound of the woman's Australian accent, obvious even in that single word, and told her I was calling for Archie. Before she could protest her ignorance that any such person existed, I gave her my name and number, told her that Archie knew me, and said I needed to talk to him urgently. The woman told me she didn't have any idea what I was talking about, of course, and I thanked her and hung up.

After that, all I could do was wait.

16

ARCHIE WARD IS A redheaded, pathologically profane Aussie I met a couple of years back when the Hongkong and Shanghai Bank hired me to review some transactions that had an unmistakably ripe odor to them. Large amounts of money were moving back and forth between the bank's main office in Hong Kong and some of its branches in Europe. The coordinated way the transfers were occurring caused them to suspect that the bank might be unwittingly facilitating some pretty questionable transactions, but they couldn't figure out what kind of questionable transactions they were.

Archie was my contact at HSBC. He had been introduced to me as a security consultant for the bank and while we were making small talk he threw out the name of a Washington lawyer I had known for quite a long time. I didn't think that was accidental so I called the fellow to ask who the hell Archie really was. What he gave Archie was the sort of roundabout endorsement that was the traditional indication that Archie had an official connection of some kind with the intelligence business, but naturally he was vague as to who that connection was with.

The whole thing felt a little screwy, but I liked Archie, and I had no doubt that he was one of the good guys, so I had given him a hand without asking too many questions. When I eventually traced the transfers to a Greek born arms dealer who operated out of a ritzy beach resort about an hour north of Sydney, it occurred to me that the connection between the source of the transfers and my new pal's colorful Aussie accent might be something less than a complete coincidence.

It was pretty obvious to me that Archie wasn't really employed by HSBC at all. My guess was that Archie actually worked for ASIS, the Australian Secret Intelligence Service, and that HSBC was providing cover for an ASIS investigation. Regardless, following accepted etiquette in such matters, I pretended not to have figured that out and, for his part, Archie pretended not to know that I had.

Archie called me fairly often after that with questions about corporate finance matters I had always been happy to answer for him. We hadn't become friends exactly, but something pretty close to it. I had come to trust Archie and I was pretty sure that Archie liked and respected me, too. Once or twice I asked Archie for bits of information and advice, but I was careful not to test our friendship unduly. Archie was a big player of some kind up on the government level. I was only a guy trying to make a living.

The last time I had talked to Archie was back when the Asian Bank of Commerce was coming apart and threatening to pull me down with it for all sorts of reasons I would just as soon forget about right now. Archie had nudged me in the direction I needed to go to understand exactly what I was up against there. He pretty much saved my butt, to tell the truth. Without his help I would have floundered around until I sunk, and I'm not absolutely certain I would have come up again.

Back then, Archie told me he had gone independent. He left exactly what that meant a little murky, of course, but I had a pretty good idea. Asia was filled with freelancing spooks who told you they were now in something they usually called the information business. Most of these guys had spent their lives as government employees but, when they saw how many of their contemporaries who had left public service to freelance and were making a pile, they made a grab for their own brass ring. Some of them were ex-CIA, some had once been Mi6, but there were also a bunch of Russians, Frenchmen, Australians, and New Zealanders out there. I even met a guy once who had told me with a perfectly straight face that he had been deputy chief of Icelandic Intelligence. Maybe he had been. That certainly wouldn't be the strangest resume I had encountered among the kind of guys I had met in Asia, not by a long shot.

A military man who left the military and became a soldier for hire used to be called a mercenary. Now he was called a security contractor. Pretty much the same thing, of course, without the smell. I wasn't sure what you called an intelligence officer who left government and went independent. Archie could probably tell me that. I'd have to remember to ask him.

ABOUT AN HOUR LATER my phone rang.

"This a clean line, mate?"

"Hello to you, too, Archie. It's been quite—"

"I asked you if this phone is clean."

"I'm not exactly calling you about the Iranian nuclear program."

"You're saying you don't have any idea if it's clean or not."

"Well..ah, I honestly never thought about it. The calls I make on it aren't really—"

"One hour. The lobby of the Langham Hotel in Tsim Sha Tsui."

"Should I carry—"

I heard the click of Archie disconnecting.

"— a folded newspaper?" I finished, but I was talking to myself.

I guess that's what you call a spy who goes independent.

Paranoid.

ARCHIE MATERIALIZED BEHIND ME as soon as I walked into the Langham's rather grand lobby. He put a hand lightly on my shoulder and spoke in a voice that didn't carry much further than my left ear.

"Christ, as I live and breathe. It's Jack Shepherd in the flesh. You're looking well, mate."

"You, too, Archie."

"Had lunch yet?"

I shook my head and Archie pointed toward a pair of glass doors to the left of the reception desk.

I followed him across the marble floored lobby, remaining silent in deference to his apparent disinterest in public conversation. We went down some steps and through another door, and a minute or two later we were seated in a back booth in the Langham's Main Street Deli. Archie was facing the door, of course, with the wall behind him. I didn't know if there was something up or if he was only doing it out of habit. I didn't ask. I figured he would tell me if he wanted to.

"BEST CORNED BEEF SANDWICH in Asia, mate. Makes me old fella twitch thinking about it."

Archie was something of a professional Australian, at least he was when he wanted to be. Most of the time he used his accent and a barrage of picturesque Australian expressions to camouflage himself in plain sight as just another colorful Aussie larrikin. He looked the part, too. Average height, lean and weathered with a bad haircut, he had a long, thin face that looked like a dropped pie. He was wearing a blue dress shirt with the sleeves rolled up, neatly pressed jeans, and a gold Rolex that probably didn't cost any more than your average Mercedes.

At a glance, Archie would probably strike most people as an easy-going, working-class guy, one of those fellows having a beer and a laugh down at the pub after a hard day's work in some dead-end job. He could have been a jackaroo on horseback or a rigger on the Sydney Harbour Bridge. He could have been, but he wasn't.

I had heard some stories about Archie, and I believed every one of them. When the Aussie accent was peeled away and the harmless prankster pose was back in storage, what you had left was a hard guy who knew his way around the back alleys of Asia. He knew where the bodies were buried, which made sense because he had buried a lot of them.

"You've obviously been doing okay," I said, inclining my head toward his watch.

"Fair dinkum, matey."

"Filling your empty hours then?"

"I reckon. I've been as busy as a cat burying shit. How's yourself?"

"Gettin' by. Practicing law in my own special way."

Archie nodded and offered a sleepy-looking smile. "Heard you lost a client recently."

If anybody other than Archie had said that, I would have assumed they were referring to Plato Karsarkis because of all the publicity that case had gotten. But I had no doubt at all that Archie was talking about Charlie Kitnarok, the former prime minister of Thailand who, for my sins, I had tried to help with some of his financial dealings and darn near got sucked into a civil war in the bargain. My involvement with Charlie hadn't been publicly mentioned anywhere as far as I knew. Which was exactly why Archie would know all about it.

"I've still got one or two clients left," I said. "You enjoying yourself these days?"

"Bloody oath! Finally making a quid, too. All me mates thought I'd gone troppo when I quit, but—"

"You're going to have to translate that one for me, Archie."

He grinned again. "Means catching a bit of tropical fever from being in Asia too long. Like the heat has gotten to me."

"More likely the women."

"Got no idea what you're talking about," Archie grinned. "No idea at all."

"Look, Archie, let me tell you about—"

"Reckon we ought to order first, mate. I'm so hungry I could eat the arse out of a low flyin' duck."

Archie waved for a waiter and ordered a corned beef on rye with Russian dressing, coleslaw, and potato salad. I had a pastrami on rye with mustard. We both ordered cream sodas. We could have been having lunch in Brooklyn, but we weren't. We were in the basement of one of Hong Kong's finest hotels and we were the only two guys in the room who weren't Chinese. I guess this was what people meant when they talked about internationalization.

WE MADE SMALL TALK until the food came, then we made more small talk while we ate. We were waltzing around so much I started worrying that one of us would fall asleep before we got to the point of the lunch. So, when Archie popped the last crust of rye bread into his mouth, I told him why I had called.

"I need your help, Archie."

"Figured you hadn't called to say you missed me."

I told him about being summoned to Macau by MGM and about their suspicions that large amounts of money were being laundered through their casino. I told him about Pansy Ho's fear that it would turn out to be triad money and how much a revelation like that would damage her. I told him about my guess that MGM was being smurfed and the probability that made whatever was happening a triad deal. I even told him about my initial reluctance to take the job and Pete Logan's role in getting me to do it. I told Archie everything, because eventually Archie would find out everything anyway and I wanted him on my side. Lying to him, or leaving out something important, would come back to bite me in the ass with a guy like Archie.

"Why would the FBI be interested in the triads laundering money through a casino in Macau?" he asked.

"Beats me."

Archie didn't seem particularly surprised at that and he didn't comment. He picked at what was left of his potato salad, drank the rest of his cream soda, and waited for me to tell him the rest. So I told him about Cindy Cheung coming to my office this morning and about the story The South China Morning Post was going to run tomorrow fingering me as the guy investigating triad money laundering in Macau.

"So here's the deal," I finished. "I need somebody to watch my back."

"Bloody oath, I reckon you do."

"I don't know anything about Macau. I don't know who's screwing who or who's stealing what. And now I'm going to have the triads on my ass before I've even started. How about I put you on the payroll?"

"Well fuck me dead, mate! You mean there's money in this for me?"

"I told Pansy I might have to bring in some help and she gave me carte blanche. Tell me what your usual fee for a little consulting would be and I'll add it to my bill. She's scared to death, Archie. Money isn't a problem."

"Before we go any further maybe you ought to tell me exactly what kind of consulting you have in mind."

"I just want you to be available to answer my questions about how things really work in Macau. Make a few introductions for me. Let me run whatever I find out by you before I talk to anyone else about it. Like that. No dramas. No heavy lifting."

Archie nodded, thinking about it.

"There is one other thing," I added.

Archie gave me a crooked 'I-knew-there-was-a-catch' grin.

"I'll need the number of a telephone you actually answer. I don't want to go through this song and dance of leaving messages around town every damn time I need to talk to you."

"Oh, Jacko, that could be a problem. I only give women my real phone number."

"Yeah? For what you're probably going to charge me, Archie, you ought to be willing to throw in their phone numbers, too."

FIFTEEN MINUTES LATER I was stepping onto an MTR train at the Tsim Sha Tsui station that would take me back under the harbor to the station beneath Central. From there I could walk over to the Mid-Levels escalator and ride it up to my office in Soho. In my pocket, I had my cell phone and in it was a number that Archie swore he actually answered, at least most of the time. I still didn't have any telephone numbers for Archie's girlfriends. I figured that was the real treasure, but he wouldn't give them up.

Pansy Ho called while I was walking up Des Voeux Road to the bottom of the Mid-Levels escalator. She was all business.

"Gerald has brought me the security photographs you asked him to collect."

"Was I right about the smurfing?" I asked.

"Yes. No question about it. But, Jack, I think there's something a little bit odd going on here."

"Odd? How?"

"You need to see the pictures yourself. I might be wrong. When can you get here?"

"Tomorrow?"

"Tomorrow's fine. The suite is waiting for you. Call me when you're in the hotel."

I TOOK A SHORT CUT through the Chong Hing Bank Building and turned north on Queen's Road.

The smurfing of MGM was no longer a theory, and tomorrow I would have to head back to Macau and try to figure out who exactly was responsible for it. I had no idea what Pansy meant when she said there was something odd about the security photographs, but I didn't see what difference it made. If MGM was being smurfed, who else could be running an operation like that in Macau other than the triads? So all I had to do now was identify at least some of the people who had been photographed smurfing money into the casino, connect those people to the triads, and hand everything over to Pete. After that, it would be a law enforcement matter and I was out of it, right?

There were two problems with that, of course.

First, Pansy was going to take an awful hit in spite of having no connection with whatever was going on. The mere mention of the triads and her name in the same sentence would be fatal for her. She was carrying too much baggage from her father to shrug it off.

I wanted to help Pansy, even protect her if it was possible, but I didn't see what I could do. If the triads were involved, and it was becoming clearer day by day that they were, Pansy was finished. It was a simple as that.

But there was something else, too, something that was even worse from my personal point of view.

According to that South China Morning Post reporter who showed up in my office, tomorrow morning the SCMP was running a story that would blow my cover. They were going to tell every triad gangster in Macau that Jack Shepherd was on their tail and looking to nail them for large scale money laundering.

Not good for me.

Not good at all.

Nothing left to do but save the little bastards some trouble and wear a t-shirt with a big bullseye right on the front.

17

THE NEXT MORNING I took the Mid-Levels escalator down to the office exactly like I always did. I was stalling a little, I admit. I had promised Pansy I would go back to Macau today, but I wanted to put my feet up, drink some coffee, and think about everything a bit more before I got on that ferry. I figured I ought at least to have some kind of a sensible plan in mind before I got to Macau and served myself up to the triads. Surely there was something smart I could do here. There was always something smart I could do here. I just had to work out what it was.

I stopped at the Pacific Coffee Company for my usual black coffee and Danish, and this morning I bought a copy of The South China Morning Post to go with them. I seldom read the SCMP, and I really wasn't at all anxious to read it today, but I had to find out what was in Cindy Cheung's story sooner or later. And sooner was better.

When I got to the office I drank half the coffee while I ate my Danish and checked my email. After I was suitably caffeinated and well on my way to a sugar high, I decided I was at last amped up enough face Cindy's story. I tilted back in my chair, swung my feet up onto my library table, and unfolded the paper.

Nothing on the first page. Nothing on the second or third pages either. *Thank God,* I told myself, at least the story was buried in the back somewhere.

I drank some more coffee and kept turning pages.

When I found nothing at all in the first section, I unfolded the business section and went through it page by page. Nothing there either.

Was it possible the SCMP hadn't run the story?

I checked the date on the front of the paper just to be certain I hadn't picked up an old one by mistake. No, I had this morning's paper all right. I laid it flat on my table and slowly turned through every page again, checking both the heads and the bylines. No stories by Cindy Cheung, no mention of Macau, no mention of money laundering, and – best of all from my point of view – no mention of Jack Shepherd.

I had dodged a bullet.

But how had I dodged a bullet?

I didn't want to look the proverbial gift horse in the mouth, but I didn't really believe in gift horses. Cindy had the story dead to rights, and allegations of large-scale triad money laundering at the MGM in Macau should have been big news locally, if for no other reason because of its impact on the price of casino stocks. Yet The South China Morning Post hadn't run Cindy's story.

Why not? What were they up to?

Was it possible they held it today because they had something even bigger and better coming?

Perhaps this wasn't such good news after all…

I THOUGHT ABOUT ALL that while I answered some emails and drank the rest of my coffee, but I didn't come up with any answers. If the SCMP did have something bigger, I didn't have a clue what it was. When I finished with the email I closed my laptop and, having nothing better to do, reached over and scooped up the pile of mail I had dumped unexamined on my worktable when I had returned to the office several days ago. It all looked like junk, of course. Even bills seemed to come mostly online these days. Still, flipping through the envelopes and one by one sailing them unopened into the garbage can was in its own way a curiously exhilarating experience. About halfway through the pile, however, I stopped flipping envelopes into the trash, sat up abruptly, and swung my feet to the floor.

The plain white envelope was addressed to me in blue ink in what appeared to be a feminine hand. It bore no return address, but the stamps were from the UK and it felt lumpy, as if it contained something other than a letter. Did I know any women in the UK who might be sending me something? No one came readily to mind, and who wrote personal letters these days anyway?

I slid my finger under the flap and tore the envelope open. Inside was a single piece of stationery wrapped around another envelope, this one small and ivory-colored, the kind of envelope in which people sent party invitations or thank-you notes. Written on the second envelope was a single word: *Jack*.

I recognized the handwriting immediately. I was in no doubt at all.

I laid the small envelope on the table and unfolded the sheet of paper that had been folded around it. It was fine, expensive stationery that had the texture of money. Across the top was printed SALLY KITNAROK.

My stint as a lawyer for Sally's famous husband Charlie had not been my finest hour, but Sally and I had remained friends through it all. And now that I thought about it, someone had told me a few months ago that Sally had moved back to London.

The note was short. I read it slowly and with a degree of trepidation. I could not imagine it contained anything I would be happy to hear.

It didn't.

Jack, I don't know if I am doing the right thing here, but I bumped into Anita quite by accident yesterday. She asked me if I could tell her how to reach you. I didn't feel I should do that, but I told her I could get a message to you. She sat right down and wrote something and sealed it in the envelope I have enclosed. I hope by sending it to you I am not reopening wounds and causing you pain for no reason. I just didn't know what else to do. Fondly, Sally

I GOT UP AND walked over to the windows and stood there for a long time staring out into Gage Street.

The rain was hammering down again, spraying the walls of the buildings along the narrow road. The gutters were little rivers rushing downhill to the harbor, and the umbrellas wielded by pedestrians covered both sidewalks like black toadstools wobbling on a riverbank. I watched the fat globs of rain run slowly down the windows, form into narrow rivulets, and drip over the sills onto the umbrellas below. Sometimes rain in the city looks cleansing. Sometimes it seems to scrub the city of all its accumulated grief and sweep it clean of sorrow. Sometimes it feels as if it is announcing a new day.

This wasn't that kind of rain. This rain looked grey and tired, as if it could barely be bothered to fall. I knew exactly how it felt.

ALL OF A SUDDEN I was ready to go to Macau. To be completely honest, I would have gone most anywhere right then. Getting myself into motion seemed a good thing to do and Macau was as good a destination as anywhere.

I dumped my laptop and charger into my briefcase and thought about what else I might need while I was away. Nothing immediately came to mind. It was not so many years ago that preparation for a business trip was a tedious process for a lawyer. You had to gather up piles of case files and locate all your notes and diaries and address books so that you would be prepared to cope with whatever issues might arise while you were traveling. No more. Now all that information is stored away on your laptop, and probably for good measure on your tablet and your phone, too. Nobody carries around paper anymore, just like nobody writes letters anymore.

Or almost nobody.

I picked up the little ivory envelope with Anita's handwriting on it and I dropped it into my briefcase without opening it.

My eyes flicked over The South China Morning Post lying on my table and I thought again of the story that wasn't in it. Whatever the reason they hadn't run Miss Cheung's story today, they surely would run it tomorrow or the day after. It was too good a story for the SCMP to pass up. And when they did run it, every triad soldier in Macau would be on the lookout for me.

That caused me to think of something else it might be handy to take to Macau.

I went to last filing cabinet on the back wall and opened the heavy padlock holding the security bar. The bar thunked against the floor as I pushed it down and freed the cabinet's drawers. I opened the bottom one.

Hong Kong has some of the most restrictive gun laws in the world. With very few exceptions, private citizens simply aren't allowed to own guns and the possession of firearms is restricted to law enforcement agencies, the military, and some private security firms. Any private citizen who is found with a firearm pulls a long stretch in prison. No excuses, no argument.

I lifted the case out of the filing cabinet and pushed the bottom drawer closed with my foot. The case looked like a briefcase, but was slightly smaller and slightly squarer and made of highly polished aluminum that glinted even in the dull light of my office. I put it on my library table, snapped open the catches, and raised the lid. I stood for a moment looking down at the Ruger LC9 9mm held in place with foam inserts. Three pockets cut into the inserts held two boxes of hollow points, an Osprey sound suppressor, and a black nylon belly holster.

The Ruger is an ugly little handgun, barely six inches long. Its blued-steel frame is chunky and square. Aesthetics aside, the Ruger is a weapon with a couple of decided advantages. It's small enough for easy concealment, and it has a laser sight built into its trigger guard. The little red dot that it projects onto a target gave even a lousy shooter like me a fighting chance to hit whatever he's aiming at.

This particularly Ruger was properly licensed to Charlie Kitnarok, my former client. It might be impossible for private citizens to own guns in Hong Kong, but this was Asia. The impossible is always possible, if you know the right people and have the right amount of money. Charlie easily qualified on both counts. He had carried the Ruger occasionally when he was in Hong Kong, mostly in the winter when he wore jackets that concealed it. I couldn't think of any good reason for him to carry it. Charlie had never been in any danger in Hong Kong, at least not that I heard about. I figured he just liked the idea of knowing he was armed when nobody else was.

The thing was, Charlie hadn't been in Hong Kong in a year and wouldn't be coming back again. He had left his gun with me, his lawyer, for safekeeping. So here it was, sitting on my desk now all perfectly legal and proper. But if I closed up the case and took the Ruger with me to Macau, that would be the end of legal and proper. I wasn't licensed to carry it, Charlie was. And wherever Charlie was hanging out these days, it wasn't anywhere near Macau.

There was no security check on the ferry between Hong Kong and Macau, and I had never even seen a customs agent when I entered Macau. I could take the Ruger with me if I really wanted to and nobody would ever be the wiser, probably. Still, was it worth even a tiny risk to have it?

Back when I lived in Washington, DC, I had a friend who was a DEA agent and he had taken me out to the DEA range a few times and given me some tips on handling a handgun. Something he said then came back to me as I stood in my office in Hong Kong, looking down at Charlie's Ruger nestled in that little aluminum case.

Better to have a gun and not need one, than to need a gun and not have one.

I closed the case, snapped the locks, and shoved it down into my briefcase next to my laptop.

I LEFT THE OFFICE about midday. I had booked a seat on the three o'clock jetfoil for Macau and I needed to go back to the apartment and pack some things first. As I squished my way up the wet sidewalk along Hollywood Road toward the Mid-Levels escalator, there were a lot of things I should have been worrying about. The SCMP story that wasn't there, the MGM smurfing operation, and the security pictures that were waiting for me in Macau were three of those things. But none of them were on my mind at that moment. All I could think about was that ivory-colored envelope with Anita's handwriting on it I had tucked into my briefcase.

It had stopped raining, and that disappointed me. When I left the office I had thought I would be walking home in the rain, which seemed to me to be a romantic gesture entirely appropriate to the circumstances. Now I was being deprived of even that.

I had not seen or spoken to Anita since the night she left our apartment in Bangkok. What did we have to talk about? Anita had found somebody she liked better, she had left me, and we had gotten divorced. She broke my fucking heart. That pretty much covered everything.

But now this.

Old bones. Bones buried so deeply I had been certain no one would ever find them again, not even me. But now, here they were. Rising up out of the past right at my feet.

Nothing is ever really over, is it? The clock ticks and nothing changes. Whether you remember the past or not, it remembers you.

William Faulkner said that this way: *The past isn't dead. It isn't even past.*

I rubbed at my eyes and walked on.

18

THE HYDROFOIL WALLOWED AT its dock as the gangway was cranked away and the boarding door down on the lower deck slammed shut. The engines started and I heard the shouts of the Chinese sailors casting off the mooring lines.

The Super Class seats up on the second deck were mostly empty as they usually were. The Chinese went to Macau to gamble. Wasting good gambling money buying a more comfortable seat in order to get there wasn't all that popular.

I was sitting by a window and had the pair of seats in the second row entirely to myself. For that matter, there was no one else at all sitting within sight of me and I was looking forward to catching a nap on the way to Macau. I reclined my seat and closed my eyes. I heard footsteps coming up the stairs from the lower deck and felt rather than heard someone walking forward up the aisle behind me. Whoever it was stopped at the seat right next to me and sat down. Naturally I turned my head and opened my eyes to see what kind of a jerk would choose that seat to sit in when almost the whole damn cabin was completely empty.

Archie Ward smiled at me and gave me a little nod.

"I don't suppose," I said, "I should look on this as a remarkable coincidence."

Archie said nothing. But he smiled some more.

"How in the world did you know I was on this jetfoil?" I asked.

"Did we have lunch yesterday?"

"We did."

"And did you hire me to watch your back in Macau?"

"I did."

"And did you do that because your old mate Archie has ways and means of knowing things that transcend the abilities of mere mortals?"

"I see your point."

"I thought you would."

The cabin attendant was a young-looking woman with short dark hair wearing a blue jacket and matching blue slacks. She looked like she could have been Indonesian, but was almost certainly Chinese. Without a word, she released our tray tables from the seats in front of us and slapped down two plastic-topped boxes that appeared to contain some facsimile of sandwiches. After a moment she returned with a tray with some clear plastic bottles of water and a few red cans of Coca-Cola on it and thrust it toward us. Archie took a Coke while I chose water.

"Thank you," I said.

The woman regarded me curiously for a moment, examining me the way you might examine a dog that had suddenly spoken up to wish you a nice day, and moved away without a word.

"Service with a smile," Archie said as he popped the top on his Coke and took a long pull. "I wonder if it's true that Hong Kong is the friendliest city on earth?"

"I don't think so."

Archie belched slightly and wiped his mouth with the back of his hand. "Me neither."

WE SAT IN SILENCE as the engines rumbled to life and the screws churned the greasy waters of the harbour. The jetfoil gradually edged away from the dock while I watched the towers of

Kowloon through the window. Today the pilot chose to cross the harbour and go north of Lantau Island rather than take the more usual route to the south. Maybe it was the weather. I eyed the swells building in the brown water and wondered how rough the crossing was going to be.

On the other side of the Yau Ma Tei Typhoon Shelter we slipped by Stonecutter's Island and passed under the Tsing Ma Bridge that connected Kowloon to Lantau Island and the Hong Kong International Airport. When we turned west toward Macau and the pilot pushed the engines to full power, our jetfoil rose gracefully above the sea on its hydrofoils and I felt our speed increase as we skimmed over the surface above the chop. Maybe it wasn't going to be so rough after all.

"WHY ARE YOU HERE, Archie?'

"Thought I might be of some help to you, mate. Figured you'd be happy as Larry to see me."

"The SCMP didn't run that story this morning."

"I know."

"You don't happen to know why they didn't run it, do you?"

Archie made a face and scratched at his ear, but he didn't say anything.

"So how'd you do it?" I asked. "You going to tell me what you promised them to get them to hold the story?"

"I promised them a better story, of course. That's what you always promise an editor to get them to kill something."

"And what's the better story?"

"Well crikey, mate, do I have to do everything? I figured you'd come up with something."

"They're going to be pissed with you when you don't come through, Archie."

"Not likely. I told them you had a better story that you'd give them if they killed this one and that I was making the call as a favor to you since their publisher knew me personally." Archie turned his head and cut me a huge wink. "So you better come up with something, Jacko, or those ratbags are going to be up you like a rat up a drainpipe."

Archie yawned and bent forward to examine the little plastic box the cabin attendant had put in front on him. He removed the lid and poked with one finger at the spongy piece of white bread, underneath which I could see the edge of a single leaf of limp lettuce.

"I'm hungry," he said, "but not that hungry."

Archie waved at the cabin attendant and when she shuffled over he made little pushing gestures at the box on his tray table. She scooped it up and looked at me. I nodded and she collected mine, too.

"Get me another of these, will you, sweetheart?" Archie asked wiggling his empty Coke can at her. She didn't acknowledge hearing him, but a couple of minutes later she brought him another can of Coke. When she put it on his tray table, she even smiled. Sort of. Then she walked away without bothering to ask if I wanted another bottle of water.

"You old charmer you," I said.

"Treat 'em mean, keep 'em keen."

"You going to tell me why you're really here, Archie?"

"Would you believe a fortune teller told me to take a long sea voyage?"

I didn't say anything. I just waited. Archie sighed and popped the tab on his fresh can of Coke.

"When you told me about Pansy, I wasn't entirely honest with you about something. Probably I should have been."

I waited some more. When it became clear I wasn't going to say anything else until he did, Archie started talking again.

"I've known Stanley Ho for a long time," he said. "I like Stan. He's pretty much at the end of his life now. I don't want to see any mud stick to him."

"What are you talking about?"

"If this money laundering operation you're trying to nail down has anything to do with the triads, it will come back on Stan like it'll come back on Pansy. He's an old man. He deserves better now."

"Does Stanley Ho have anything to do with the triads?"

Archie cut his eyes quickly at me then away again, but he didn't say anything.

"If this is triad money, Archie, it is. I'm being paid to find out where it came from. I got nothing to do with the comeback or who gets hurt. That's not on me."

"You don't want Pansy hurt, do you?"

"No, I don't. And it would be unfair for her to have triads hung around her neck only because they're laundering money through the MGM. Assuming she has nothing to do with it, which I'm certain she doesn't. But I don't know how to protect her. People will say what they will. I can't stop them."

"It would be just as unfair for it to be hung on Stan if he has nothing to do with it either."

"Maybe. But I don't see what you can do about that either. Facts are facts. If it's the triads doing this, it is. What other people make out of it is way beyond our control."

Archie nodded slowly. He tilted up the can and finished the Coke. Then he tossed the empty can in the seat across the aisle and folded away his tray table.

"I'll do what I can to help you," he said after a moment. "And I'll do what I can to help Pansy, too, but I want to be honest with you here, Jack. Above all else, I'm going to be looking out for Stan. Like I said, I want him to go out a winner. You understand?"

"Yes, I understand."

"I thought you would."

With that, Archie tilted his seat back and closed his eyes. I did the same thing, and it was not very long before the steady drone of the jetfoil's big engines took full control of my consciousness and lulled me into a brief and fitful sleep.

19

WHEN I GOT TO the MGM late in the afternoon, the suite was waiting for me like Pansy had said it would be. I thought the security photos I asked for might be waiting for me, too, but they weren't.

I had suggested to Archie that he stay at the MGM as well, but he told me he had already made other arrangements. He didn't volunteer exactly what those arrangements were, and I didn't think I ought to ask. I figured he would tell me if he wanted to. So we shook hands at the ferry terminal and agreed to talk the next day.

I unpacked, which didn't take long. The few clothes I had brought with me went into the closet and the top drawer of the chest, my laptop went onto the desk, and the case holding the Ruger went into the room safe. I didn't really want a maid to stumble over it and blow the whistle on me.

After I was done with my housekeeping I called Pansy's office to check in, but her secretary said she was away and wouldn't be back until tomorrow. I left a message that I was in the hotel and ready to go to work, then I headed out in search of a drink. It was nearly six o'clock, and I thought I damned well deserved one. Maybe two.

I LEFT THE MGM by the main entrance on *Avenida Dr. Sun Yat-Sen* and turned east toward what I remembered was a strip of local bars famed for their enthusiastic Filipino bands and equally enthusiastic Filipina waitresses. But it was early, way early by Macau standards, so all that enthusiasm was in short supply.

The first bar I came to was a narrow shophouse with rough plank floors. It was open across the front, and battered wooden chairs that had an unobstructed view of the passing parade surrounded most of the wooden tables. Of course, that meant the passing parade would also have an unobstructed view of me, so I kept walking.

The second place was called the Moonwalker Bar and appeared considerably more promising. The main room was softly lit and had a high-ceilinged industrial appearance to it. At the back was a bar with half a dozen stools that faced an immense display of liquor bottles backlit in soft white that rose all the way to the ceiling. A pair of middle-aged westerner men deep in conversation occupied two of the stools. The rest of the place was empty.

Perfect.

I picked a table off where I could see the television set suspended from the ceiling on which the BBC news service played silently. A tall Chinese girl who didn't seem to be a day over sixteen came over with a menu, but I waved it away and asked for a gin martini with a twist. Ordering a martini almost anywhere outside the continental United States was always a gamble against strong odds, but Macau was the land of gambling so what the hell? No guts no glory, right?

While I waited for my drink I sat, tried to keep my mind as empty as possible, and counted the bottles tiered up behind the bar. That turned out to be a happily vacant and slightly soporific way to pass the time. Like counting sheep, but with a little more kick.

Around the time I ran out of liquor bottles to count, the tall Chinese girl returned with my martini. I lifted the tall v-shaped glass and examined it with suspicion. It looked authentic enough, which was at least a step in the right direction, so I took a tentative sip. To my surprise, it was really pretty good. Not as good as it would have been in New York, of course, but pretty darn good for China, I had to admit.

I spotted an abandoned newspaper on a nearby table and laid claim to it out of sheer desperation for something to do while I drank my martini. It turned out to be that day's Wall Street Journal Asia. I would have preferred the New York Post, but that was a little too much to hope for in a bar in Macau.

I folded the Journal open on the tabletop and while I sipped at my martini I read two stories about the most recent meeting of the United States Federal Reserve Open Market Committee without having the slightest idea what either one of them said. The martini really wasn't bad and the truth was I was paying more attention to it than I was to the Asian Wall Street Journal, but I folded it over to the front page and started skimming the main news stories anyway.

The headline was at the bottom on the right.

NORTH KOREANS SAY AMERICAN SPY
SHOT WHILE TRYING TO ESCAPE

I blinked when I saw it. For a moment I even wondered if I was imagining it, but I looked away and looked back and the headline was still there.

I lifted the paper and read slowly through the story, but there wasn't really much more information in it than the headline had already conveyed. The North Koreans had made an announcement that morning that they had discovered an American in the country as a journalist who was actually a spy, but when they attempted an arrest the suspected spy tried to escape and had been shot. That was it. There was nothing about who the accused spy was, even whether it was a man or a woman, and no mention of what news organization this supposed spy claimed to work for.

Freddy – or whoever he really was – had told me a week ago I would read in the newspapers about an American spy being shot in North Korea. Now I was sitting in a bar in Macau where I had just unfolded a newspaper and here was the exact story he had told me a week ago I was going to read.

Was it only a coincidence? That was a little hard to believe, no matter how much I might want to think so. The details of the story were all perfect. They suggested foreknowledge, not coincidence. Freddy knew about the announcement before it was made. Simple as that.

Okay, so Freddy did have some connection with North Korea, but that didn't necessarily prove that he was a North Korean intelligence officer, did it? Still, it proved something, I had no doubt about that. Now all I had to do was work out exactly what it was…

I FINISHED MY MARTINI, dropped enough money on the table to cover my bill, and walked back to the MGM with the Wall Street Journal Asia tucked under my arm. Up in the suite I opened my laptop and checked the major news sites: CNN, BBC, Fox, The New York Times, and The Washington Post. Everybody had the story. I even checked the South China Morning Post and the story was there, too. Had I missed it when I searched through the SCMP this morning for the story fingering me as digging into a money laundering operation at the MGM? No, of course I hadn't. I would have spotted it in a moment. The story must not have hit the wires until after the edition of the SCMP I had read was closed.

All the major news sources had the same story, but none of them had any more details than had been in the Journal. Which is to say, no details at all.

So now what? Was I going to call Freddy like he had asked me to and get sucked into whatever was going on with him? Or was I just going to do the job Pansy had hired me to do and spend my idle hours ducking triad soldiers pissed at me for outing their money laundering operation?

I fished around in my briefcase until I found the white card on which Freddy had written the number to what he said was a clean cell phone. It was nestled right next to the little ivory envelope with Anita's handwriting on it. I took out both the card and the envelope and laid them beside each other on the desk.

Picking up the white card, I walked back over to the sofa and sat holding it and looking at the number for a long time. I told myself I was trying to decide whether I was going to get involved with Freddy, but I wasn't really. I knew perfectly well that my curiosity was in full control of my good sense and I was helpless to do anything else.

I dialed the number on the card from my cell phone. When a robotic voice answered and announced I was connected to voice mail, I left this message: "Hello, my friend. Just letting you know I'll be back in Macau at eleven o'clock tonight. Perhaps we can catch up while I'm here. Call me. Bye."

If I had correctly understood what Freddy told me, he would interpret that to mean we would meet in front of the Hall of Benevolence at the Ah-Ma Temple at eleven o'clock tomorrow morning. And if I hadn't correctly understood what Freddy told me, I wouldn't meet anybody when I went back to the Ah-Ma Temple tomorrow at eleven o'clock. I could live with either outcome.

AFTER I HUNG UP I sat on the sofa for a while doing absolutely nothing, thinking absolutely nothing. Eventually I took a Montecristo out of my briefcase, cut it, lit it with a wooden match, and stood in front of the window looking out at the sky and smoking quietly. I tried my best to keep on thinking nothing, but it didn't work. Sooner or later I was going to have to decide sometime what to do with that damned envelope with Anita's handwriting on it. It wasn't going to disappear.

It had occurred to me that the envelope looked a little like a wedding invitation, but I didn't really think it was. It was too small and, besides, Anita might be many things but she was not a cruel person. Sending me a wedding invitation would serve no purpose other than to inflict pain, and surely Anita knew that.

I walked over, picked up the envelope and propped it against the big crystal ashtray on the coffee table. I sat down, leaned back against the thick cushions, and idly flipped a box of cigar matches around in my left hand while I drew on my cigar.

What could be in the envelope? A bill for something? No, of course not. Anita's key to our old apartment in Bangkok? Now I was getting silly. A note asking me to contact her? That really seemed the only reasonable possibility, didn't it?

I thought for a while about where Anita might be living, and who she might be living there with. Back when we were married Anita and I had lived in one of Bangkok's tonier apartment buildings. I had been teaching at Chulalongkorn University and Anita had been painting. Her large and colorful canvases had made her modestly famous in some European art circles. *Surely she was still painting,* I thought, but of course I didn't really know.

Sally had said she bumped into Anita in London, but that didn't mean Anita was living in London, did it? A lot of people visited London. Anita had been born there, which made it likely she might be visiting there.

I was going around in circles, of course, and I wanted to stop. I wanted to stop thinking about Anita altogether, but as long as that damned envelope was sitting there staring at me I was powerless to do it. Was I going to open it and read what was inside, or wasn't I?

And all at once I saw exactly what I was going to do. As with so many other big decisions in life, I didn't know when I had decided. I only realized that I had already decided.

I continued to smoke my Montecristo and think about it for a while. There would be no going back, of course. So I wanted to be sure. I wanted to be absolutely sure.

I smoked the Montecristo right down to the butt and gave

myself as much time as possible to reconsider, but eventually it was finished. I bent forward, gently tapped the cigar out against the bottom of the ashtray, and dropped what was left of it inside.

I was sure. I was absolutely sure.

I slid open the box of wooden matches I had been turning around in my hand and I lit one. I held the ivory envelope between my thumb and forefinger and moved one corner back and forth through the flame until the paper caught. I shook out the match, but I continued to hold the burning envelope until the heat became too much for my hand. Finally I dropped it into the ashtray and flipped the spent match in on top of it. I sat very still and watched until nothing was left of the envelope except curly wisps of black ash scattered over the remains of my cigar. And I kept watching until the flame had burned itself completely out.

After a while I stood up and walked over to the window. The neon of the casino signs were burning hot in the soft grey light of the early evening and they infused Macau with a shimmering radiance I hadn't really noticed before. The hard, unpleasant edges of a tough town had been blurred into blemish-free beauty. Suddenly Macau was like an aging movie star with great makeup, better lighting, and a Vaseline-smeared lens.

It didn't look half bad to me…

20

IT WAS A LITTLE before eleven the next morning when Shepherd got out of a cab in Barra Square. Freddy was sitting behind the wheel of a dirty brown Toyota parked in a little cul de sac at the bottom of Rua da Barra. The car was so nondescript as to be functionally invisible and, exactly as Freddy had intended, Shepherd didn't pay the slightest attention to him.

Freddy had a clear view of most of the square and he watched as Shepherd walked toward the temple gate. He wasn't an expert in surveillance, but he knew a little bit about it, and he was reasonably certain Shepherd wasn't being followed. The movement of people around him all appeared random. No one seemed to speed up or slow down in response to Shepherd's pace.

He gave it a few minutes so he could be sure, but when nothing changed he got out of the Toyota and walked slowly through the square, following more or less the same path Shepherd had followed.

When Freddy reached the temple gate he stopped suddenly, spun around, and started walking quickly back to the car as if he had forgotten something. He wasn't absolutely sure, but he thought he saw sudden movement out of the corner of his eye so he stopped again and looked around very slowly like a man trying to decide what to do. Which was exactly what he was.

Had that movement been someone who had him under surveillance? He thought it might have been possible that Shepherd might have watchers, but he was pretty certain that he was in the clear. Had he been careless and missed something?

When he got back to the Toyota, Freddy slid behind the wheel again and carefully scanned Barra Square, but he saw no one who looked out of place or who seemed to be paying the slightest attention to him. He had probably been mistaken about the sudden movement. But still...

He watched a while longer and thought about whether he should walk away to be on the safe side. If he took much longer to make up his mind, he knew he wouldn't have anything to decide because Shepherd would get impatient and leave. He read the man as somewhat abrupt and frequently cranky. Those weren't really bad characteristics in a protector, but Shepherd was still a long way from becoming his protector, wasn't he?

He had to make up his mind right now.

Go, or walk away?

This might well be the best chance he would ever have. And he didn't like the idea of blowing it out of nothing more than paranoia. He had grown up with paranoia. Paranoia was part of his soul. He thought he had to learn to control it, not let it control him. He supposed it was time to find out if he really had.

He took another careful look at Barra Square. When he still saw nothing unusual, he shook his head, got back out of the Toyota again, and walked toward the temple.

SHEPHERD WAS SITTING ON the same rock in front of the Hall of Benevolence where he had been sitting the first time they met. Apparently a man of habit. Or perhaps there wasn't anywhere else to sit. That was possible, too, he supposed.

"You're late," Shepherd snapped as soon as he saw Freddy coming up the steps. "It's hot out here."

It was hot. Shepherd was right about that. Freddy tried to shape his face into an appropriately apologetic expression. That's how westerners saw Asians, wasn't it? Mild mannered and deferential? He didn't do those things very well. Was that how he would have to behave all the time when he was in Hawaii? If it was, God help him.

"I am very sorry," Freddy murmured in what he thought was the correct tone of voice. "I was only being careful."

"Careful about what?"

"I thought there might be some possibility you were being followed."

Shepherd looked surprised at that, but at least it seemed to shut him up.

Freddy stood close enough to Shepherd not to have to speak loudly and turned his body slightly to the side so he could watch the steps behind them while they talked.

"You saw the story in the newspapers?" he asked.

"I saw it."

"So now you believe that I have knowledge worth trading for political asylum?"

"Now I believe that you know someone in North Korea, or maybe you know someone who knows someone in North Korea. That's all that newspaper story tells me. That's all I believe now."

Freddy had not expected Shepherd to be so hard to persuade. He had expected Shepherd to be more interested, more enthusiastic. He had very little experience dealing with Americans, almost none really. Were they all this skeptical of everything?

"I want to go to Hawaii. I want you to get me political asylum in Hawaii."

Freddy instantly regretted both what he said and the way he said it. He sounded petulant, like a kid addressing a parent who was denying him a treat. He had to be careful about that. He didn't want Shepherd to feel he had control of the situation.

Shepherd smiled, but he didn't say anything.

"What else can I tell you," Freddy asked, trying for a recovery, "to convince you to help me get political asylum in America? "

"You could start with who you are."

Freddy hesitated. Yes, he could tell Shepherd who he was. He had no doubt at all that would get Shepherd's full and undivided attention. But he wasn't ready to do that yet. He wasn't sure yet that he entirely trusted Shepherd. And besides, that was his last card. If he showed it now, he would have nothing left. He had learned that from his father, at least. Always have one card to play that nobody expects. That is how you stay on top of people. You keep them guessing.

"I am sorry, but I cannot do that yet."

"Then, pal," Shepherd said as he slid off the rock into a standing position and offered his hand, "it's been nice knowing you. I wish you all the best."

Out beyond Shepherd's outstretched hand, Freddy noticed the two men coming up the steps from below. They caught his eye because they both wore cheap looking grey suits with white shirts and ties that glinted like polyester. No one wore a suit in Macau, at least no one visiting the Ah-Ma Temple at high noon.

Both men had on very dark glasses that hid part of their faces and it took a moment to register with Freddy that they were Koreans.

But the moment it did, he knew he was in trouble.

THE TWO MEN STOPPED about thirty feet away and moved slightly apart. They took their time about it, and their movements were slow and measured. For a moment he had the crazy thought that these two guys were about to break into a coordinated dance routine. Sort of a Korean version of the Blues Brothers. But then Freddy saw both men reach under their jackets almost simultaneously, he saw the butts of the handguns coming into view, and he stopped kidding himself.

Shepherd obviously noticed the alarm on Freddy's face and

began to turn his head to see what had caused it. For a moment Freddy felt almost like a disinterested observer. Would Shepherd get his head around before the men started shooting at them, or would the gunfire come as a complete surprise to him?

To Freddy's surprise, Shepherd began to react before his head was more than halfway through its turn. Both arms drove straight out, palms open and extended, and he shoved Freddy toward the big rock on which he had been sitting. Freddy stumbled and fell, but fortunately rolled a few feet down the hillside behind the rock. Shepherd dived down right on top of him. At the same moment Shepherd landed, two shots ricocheted off the rock right where they had been standing.

Freddy realized almost at once that he hadn't actually heard the shots, only the ricochets. The men were using silencers. They weren't there to scare somebody. They were there to kill somebody.

The hillside where he and Shepherd lay was steep and rocky, and there was no place to hide. About fifty feet directly below them was the back wall of The First Palace of the Holy Mountain. Freddy knew that right below it was the entry gate and Barra Square.

Even while he was still lying there on the ground thinking that they might be safe if they could get that far, Shepherd was already moving. He rose into a half crouch and gave Freddy another shove. Freddy began to slide on the loose dirt, bounced off a rock, rolled over more times than he could count, and finally bumped into the back wall of The First Palace of the Holy Mountain.

Freddy lifted his head and shook the dirt out of his eyes. The two men were about a hundred feet above him now, aiming their guns down, and he scrambled around the corner as more shots zinged off the wall of the temple. He looked around and saw that somehow Shepherd had gotten there before him.

"What the fuck is going on?" Shepherd bellowed.

Freddy didn't know what to say so he shook his head and said nothing.

Shepherd looked exasperated, but he grabbed Freddy by the arm, turned him downhill, and snapped, "Stay with me!"

Thirty feet more and they stumbled out from behind The First Palace of the Holy Mountain right into the middle of a huge mass of Chinese tourists. They were grouped obediently around a pretty young girl wearing a red uniform and holding a red pennant over her head. Freddy had never thought he would be glad to see a huge mass of Chinese tourists anywhere, but right here and right now they seemed to him to have been sent by whatever god it was that ruled over the Ah-Ma Temple.

Shepherd was already pushing his way through the crowd and Freddy fell in right behind him. The Chinese muttered in irritation at the rude westerner and his chubby companion who were suddenly in their midst, and Freddy risked a quick glance over his shoulder to see if the two shooters were coming down the steps to intercept them. He couldn't see anything. The mob of Chinese jammed the walkway so completely that he couldn't see anything past them. If the two men were coming after them, at least it would take them a while to get through.

"For Christ's sake, keep up!" Shepherd snapped, glancing back over his shoulder.

A moment later they were down the steps, through the gate, and out into Barra Square. Shepherd turned left and plunged through the crowds, but Freddy turned right. He ran past the kiosk in the middle of the square and made straight for where he had left the Toyota.

His hand shook as he shoved the key into the ignition. He said a little prayer as he turned it and it must have been answered because the old car started immediately. His eyes were on the square as he lurched away from the curb and he barely missed an old man riding a battered motorbike. But he couldn't see either of the two men coming after him.

Thirty feet and a hard left, fifty feet more and a hard right, and he was in the *Rua do Almirante Sergio*, losing himself in the heavy traffic moving north along the harbor toward the Chinese border.

Freddy knew he couldn't go home, but he almost never stayed there anyway. He usually slept in some hotel. He liked to move around, and Macau was the perfect place to do that. It had a lot of hotels and most of them were very big.

It would take them a while to find him even if they came looking, but he wasn't sure they would. He was thinking the men were there to disrupt his meeting with Shepherd, and they had done that. Hunting him down now might not serve any purpose, and it could cause whoever was behind it all sorts of problems.

No, the more Freddy thought about it the surer he became that he was safe, at least for a while. He wondered what had happened to Shepherd? If he was safe, too?

He hoped so. He didn't want any more on his conscience than there already was.

21

"WHO THE FUCK IS he, Raymond?"

The lunch rush was on at Henri's, the place was packed, and everyone there stopped eating and stared. A dirty, disheveled American nose to nose with Raymond and screaming into his face was something they didn't see every day. At least, not as far as I knew...

Raymond made little shushing gestures with his open hands and tried to back away, but I wasn't having any of it.

"I said, who the fuck is he?"

It had taken me less than fifteen minutes to jog to Henri's from the Ah-Ma Temple, but it was uphill and down and I had been looking over my shoulder most of the way so I was breathing pretty hard when I got there. I had no idea what had happened to Freddy. I lost track of him somewhere in Barra Square. Had the gunmen gotten him? I hoped not, but...

"One more chance, Raymond, and then I'm going to lose it!"

Raymond's face showed pure amazement. "You mean for you *this* isn't losing it?"

I tried not to laugh and spoil my outrage, but I couldn't help it. Raymond jumped in quickly before I had time to work up a fresh mad on.

"Come back to the office," he said, "and you can explain to me what you're talking about."

Raymond swept me in front of him through a door into the kitchen, then through another door next to the walk-in freezer. Behind it was a small office, and I let myself be nudged inside. A passing waiter had four bottles of Macau Beer on his tray and Raymond grabbed two of them, followed me into the office, and kicked the door shut behind him. I sucked down half of my beer in one pull while Raymond settled into a chair behind the desk.

"Now what is this all about?" he asked.

I collapsed on a beaten up wooden chair in front of the desk and took another pull on my beer.

And I told him.

"SO THAT'S WHY YOU look like shit," Raymond said.

"Rolling down a hill trying to get away from two triad shooters is a dirty business."

"How do you know the shooters were triad?"

"You have some other kind of gangsters in Macau, Raymond? Who do you think they were, the UCLA trap shooting team?" I held up both hands, palms out like a traffic cop. "And please don't tell me this happens all the time here. I've already heard that one. These guys weren't plinking for the fun of it. They were there to kill somebody."

"Perhaps you misinterpreted what happened."

"If that's the kind of shit I'm going to get from you, pal, you better find me another beer real quick."

"Well, isn't it possible—"

"Horse shit, Raymond. These two triad goons were shooting at us. And they sure as hell intended to kill at least one of us."

"Okay, let's assume for a moment that's true. How do you know they were after Freddy? You could have been the target."

I had thought long and hard about that possibility the whole time I was jogging toward Henri's and looking back over my shoulder half expecting to see these guys coming after me on motorcycles. When you've had to duck bullets twice in the same week, it certainly does raise the possibility that you're wearing a target on your chest.

It raised that possibility, but I didn't think it was true.

I honestly couldn't think of a single reason anyone would want to take the risk of shooting me, certainly not in public. The story about me being hired by MGM to track down the source of the money flowing through their casino hadn't become public knowledge yet, and I wasn't involved in anything else in Macau that was even slightly controversial.

Besides, if someone did want me dead, they didn't have to engage in theatrics like spraying the outside of the Wynn with gunfire or staging a shoot out in the middle of the Ah-Ma Temple. I was visible and accessible and didn't have any security. There were a hundred times every day when anyone could walk up behind me or knock on my door and make me quietly dead.

No, I might have been uncomfortably close to the business end of some bullets recently, but it didn't make any sense to conclude they were meant for me. I didn't know who the target outside the Wynn might have been, if there was a target at all, but I didn't have the slightest doubt who the target was today. It was Freddy.

"Who the fuck is he, Raymond?"

Raymond looked so uncomfortable that I almost felt sorry for him.

"I can't tell you, Jack. I'm sorry, but I can't. I gave him my word that I wouldn't."

I stopped feeling sorry for him.

"That's bullshit."

"Confucius say, 'There are things a man will do and things he will not'."

"Oh crap. Don't try to pull that Asia wisdom horseshit on me, pal. Confucius didn't say any such thing."

Raymond shrugged and fell silent.

"You got me into this, Raymond. You set me up, whether you intended to or not."

"Jack, I never thought for a minute—"

I rose up out of the chair, leaned across Raymond's desk, and planted one open hand on each side of him. "You fucking owe me a straight answer, pal, and I'm going to get it out of you one way or another."

"You don't have to threaten me, Jack."

"It looks to me like I do."

Raymond sighed and leaned as far away from me as he could without actually moving his chair back. "Sit down," he said after a moment. "Just sit down."

I sat back down, folded my arms, and waited.

"You're probably not going to like it when I tell you."

"You haven't told me yet, and already I don't like it."

Raymond nodded and went back to studying that spot above my head.

"Okay, here it is," he finally said. "He's Kim Jong-Nam."

AT FIRST I DIDN'T know what to say, and then I did.

"You're shitting me, man."

Raymond shook his head, but he didn't say anything else.

"You mean Freddy is the dictator who runs North Korea?" I asked.

"No, Jack, that's Kim Jong-Un. This is Kim Jong-Nam. He's the older brother."

It took me a minute to process that. Actually, it took a lot longer than a minute and Raymond started talking again before I could say anything.

"Kim Il-Sung was called the Great Leader. He ran Korea from the end of World War Two until he died in 1994. Then his son, Kim Jong-Il, took over and ran Korea until he died too in 2011. They called him the Dear Leader. After that, his youngest son Kim Jong-Un took over. He's a kid, only about thirty."

"What do they call him? The Little Leader?"

Raymond didn't laugh. "He's called the Great Successor."

"Snappy."

"Kim Jong-Nam is the oldest son. He would have been his father's successor but they had a falling out when he tried to enter Japan on a false passport in about 2001."

"Why did he do that?"

"He wanted to go to Disneyland."

I had said it before a moment earlier, but it still seemed the only thing to say.

"You're shitting me."

"I shit you not, brother. The Japanese busted Freddy trying to sneak into the country to go to Disneyland. After that, his father pretty much banished him. The next son in line was Kim Jong-Chul, but his father thought he was too effeminate and the succession passed to Kim Jong-Un, who was the youngest."

"Let me get this absolutely clear, Raymond. Are you telling me the older brother of the guy who runs North Korea is living right here in Macau?"

"That's exactly what I'm telling you. He's lived here quietly for years. For what it's worth, he has two wives, at least two mistresses, and several children. One wife lives here with some of the children and a mistress lives here, too. I think the other wife and mistress live in Beijing."

"And now he's trying to defect to the United States?"

Raymond nodded. "He wants to live in Hawaii."

"Don't we all."

"Look, Jack, Freddy doesn't have anything to do with what's going on in North Korea. He was just a kid who wanted to go to Disneyland. Now he's just a chubby middle-aged guy who wants to live a quiet life. He's like that fat kid we all went to school with. Nice enough, a little shy, and a bit self-conscious. He's an ordinary, simple guy."

"He's the brother of the guy who threatened a nuclear attack on the United States."

Yeah, well," Raymond shrugged, "we can't choose our relatives."

I SAT THERE IN silence, trying to get my mind around what Raymond was telling me.

"Do you think Freddy got away from those guys?" he eventually asked when he got tired of waiting for me to say something.

"I don't know. I never saw him after we got down to the square. It was too crowded and he headed off in a different direction."

"The North Koreans must have been trying to keep Freddy from defecting."

"Does he know something they don't want him telling us?"

"He hasn't been in North Korea in ten years so I don't know what it would be. He didn't even go back for his father's funeral. He was afraid they wouldn't let him out again."

"It doesn't matter. Having the older brother of King Jong-Un defect to the US and move to Hawaii would be a huge embarrassment for them. That's probably a good enough reason to kill him right there, regardless of what he might actually know."

Raymond thought about that for a moment. "Okay, Jack, so what are you going to do?"

"What am I going to do? I'm going to go back to my comfortable hotel suite and take a long, hot shower. What do you think I'm going to do?"

"You got to find Freddy, Jack. He's just an ordinary guy who must be scared out of his wits now."

"When you're the older brother of a guy who goes around screaming about launching a nuclear first strike on the United States, I think that probably goes with the territory."

"Freddy's my friend, Jack. I promised him you'd help him and now his own people are trying to kill him."

"You had no business promising him anything."

"Whether I did or didn't, you can't walk away now and leave him caught in the middle like this."

"What do you expect me to do, Raymond?"

"Find him. Find Freddy and help him get to Hawaii."

"And how do you think I'm going to do that? I'm not the fucking CIA. I'm just a guy."

"Yeah, but you're a guy who knows people. You fix things. Fix this."

"Raymond, think about what you're saying. You asking me to hunt down the older brother of Kim Jong-Un before the North Koreans get to him, rescue him from the North Korean secret police or whatever these guys with guns are, then sneak him out of Macau and smuggle him into Hawaii, where he can apply for political amnesty."

"Yes."

"Are you out of your fucking mind?"

"You want another beer, Jack?"

"No, I don't want another beer! How did I ever let you talk me into getting involved in this?"

"Doesn't matter. You are involved. You started talking to Freddy and somehow the North Koreans found out so now they're trying to kill him. You got him into this, and now you've got to get him out of it."

"I got him into this? *I got him into this?*"

Raymond shrugged. "You know you can't walk away, Jack."

"I can't, huh? Watch me!"

But I didn't move, of course. I didn't even stand up. Raymond had me and he knew it.

There was no way I was going to walk away from something this outlandish. Outlandish was what I did, and I would never come across anything more outlandish than the older brother of Kim Jong-Un asking me to help him defect to the United States. Raymond was right. This was just too good to miss out on.

AFTER I FIGURED A decent enough interval had passed to demonstrate how well and truly pissed off at Raymond I actually was, I cleared my throat.

"Do you know how to reach him?" I asked.

"I have a phone number."

I fished around in my pants pockets until I came up with the white card Freddy had given me and I slapped it on the desk in front of Raymond.

"Is this the number?"

Raymond's eyes flicked down, but he didn't move his head.

"No," he said.

I pointed to the cell phone lying on Raymond's desk. "Call the number you have."

Raymond picked up his phone, thumbed quickly through the directory, and pushed the call button. He listened for a few seconds, then he took the phone away from his ear and said…

"Voicemail."

I pointed to the white card.

"Try that number."

Raymond glanced at the card and punched out the number on his phone.

A pause.

"Voicemail again."

I was hardly surprised.

"Do you know where Freddy lives?" I asked.

"He has a house on Coloane, but I don't think he actually lives there."

"What does that mean?"

"The way I hear it, one of his wives lives there with some of his children."

"So where does Freddy live?"

"He moves around. Stays in hotels mostly. He uses one for a while and then moves on to another. You can't blame him for being a little paranoid."

"Assuming he got away, he had to go somewhere. Where do you think he might be now?"

Raymond shook his head and I gave him a hard stare.

"No, really," Raymond protested. "I have absolutely no idea. But I'll make some calls. It's a small town. People talk."

"You make those calls. And if I were you, I'd make them quick. Whoever sent those shooters is probably making the same calls."

"He's a good guy, Jack. I want to help him if I possibly can. I want you to help him."

"I can't believe you got me into this. Didn't you think, man? Didn't it ever occur to you that this could all blow up like this?"

Raymond grinned and threw up his hands.

"Hey, Jack, shit happens, huh?" he said. "You really don't want another beer?"

22

AFTER HE FLED THE temple, Freddy drove north for a while. He felt safe in the Toyota. It was wonderful camouflage. He would have liked to keep driving until he was somewhere else altogether, but that was a luxury that Macau couldn't offer him. Even in the heaviest traffic, the border crossing into China was no more than twenty minutes north of the big casinos, and that was it. No other roads that went anywhere at all. Nothing on every other side of the place but water. Macau was too small for him sometimes.

The house Freddy owned was on the south coast of Coloane all the way across Macau in the opposite direction from the Chinese border. Eighteen largely identical houses were arrayed in a tidy crescent around a cove across from the Westin Resort. He had bought the first three houses along the crescent several years ago, and these days his second wife and their children lived in the one closest to the sea. The other two houses were empty. His security people had lived in the second one for a while, but he did not have security people anymore.

The houses were all three stories high and built of white tile and concrete that had been turned grey and dirty by decades of exposure to salt air. There was a sort of fortress quality to them since heavy black wrought iron gates guarded all the entrances, and the windows were small and narrow. With the gates and high walls and roof decks instead of outdoor spaces, living in one of them was about as isolated as you could be in a teeming anthill like Macau.

His wife thought the houses were lonely looking, and he supposed they were. Particularly the way they sat around the empty cove with the windswept brown waters of the South China Sea in front and a low hill behind. But he didn't mind. He could manage lonely as long as he had privacy.

Actually, none of that really mattered now, Freddy knew. He certainly couldn't go back there now.

There was privacy in isolation, but there was also privacy in crowds as long as they were suitably anonymous crowds, and there was no crowd as anonymous as people staying in a hotel in a gambling town like Macau. So he spent most of his time in hotels now. He liked hotels. He liked their disposable nature in particular. You lived in them, you walked away whenever you felt like it, and you came back and found everything exactly the way it had been before. Few things in life required less personal commitment than staying in a hotel.

ABOUT A MILE SOUTH of the border Freddy passed Mong Ha Hill Park and on a whim he stopped and walked into the park. He followed a path at random as it wound up the low hill, and when he came upon a bench that faced out over the inner harbor he sat down. He liked the winter in Macau. It was never particularly cold and the light fogs that generally cloaked the city brought a softness to Macau that he thought suited it. Freddy could almost feel the tension draining out of his body and after about a half hour he began methodically to think through what had happened and where that left him now.

Was someone trying to kill him? And if so, who was it?

Well, he knew the answer to the second question at least. If someone was trying to kill him, the source of the malice could only be in one place: his nearly forgotten homeland of North Korea.

The first part of the question was harder. Would his brother really issue an order to kill him? He had heard that his brother had two of his old girlfriends shot for some transgression or another, real or imagined, but blood was blood. You didn't kill your own family. At least you didn't if they were no threat to you, and how could he be a threat to Kim Jong-Un by living here in Macau and minding his own business?

Of course, if his brother knew he was seeking political asylum in the United States that would be something else again. That could well make him enough of a threat to turn him into a target. But his brother didn't know. He couldn't. Freddy had told nobody but Raymond and Shepherd, and he didn't see how they could have told anyone who knew his brother. That didn't make sense.

Suddenly he had a thought. Was it possible the gunmen had been targeting Shepherd? He hadn't really considered that. Would that be ironic? The brother of the leader of North Korea contacts a lawyer to seek political asylum in the United States and two Korean gunmen attempt to kill the lawyer for some reason. It seemed terribly unlikely, but he supposed it was at least possible. Perhaps he should call Raymond and ask him what he thought.

And when Raymond's name came to mind, so did another idea.

He needed to go to ground for a while and sitting on this bench wasn't going to get it done. Perhaps he ought to ask Raymond to get a suite for him in some hotel where he had never stayed before and to book it in Raymond's name so that it couldn't be traced back to him. Freddy was sure he would do that for him if he asked.

Raymond was a real friend and, as nearly as Freddy could tell, he didn't want anything in return for his friendship. Freddy could tell that other people he knew, and who knew who he was, did want something. They assumed he was powerful or rich or probably both. He was neither, of course, not really, but they didn't know that. When they found out, he was pretty sure that he wouldn't have many friends left. But he was also pretty sure that

Raymond would be one of them.

Now where should he ask Raymond to book him a suite?

Someplace quiet that wasn't part of a huge casino complex would be best, but most of the hotels that didn't have casinos weren't particularly nice and he wasn't going to stay in a dump. Perhaps the Grand Lapa. That was an idea. It had been called the Mandarin Oriental Macau until they built a bigger, fancier Mandarin Oriental over near the MGM, but the old place had to still be a pretty good hotel. It did have a small casino, but he had never been in it and no one there knew him. Best of all, the Grand Lapa was near the ferry terminal where the helicopter shuttle to Hong Kong operated. If worst came to worst, he could be on a helicopter in ten minutes and in Hong Kong in twenty-five.

The more Freddy thought about it, the better the idea sounded, but he was having second thoughts about getting Raymond involved. He would ask Raymond not to tell Shepherd or anyone else where he was, of course, but how could he be certain that Raymond would respect his confidence? He trusted Raymond, he really did, but it was always possible that Raymond had loyalties to Shepherd that were even greater than the loyalties Raymond had to him. Raymond might feel he had to tell Shepherd where he was, in spite of promising not to.

Why did he need Raymond anyway? He had a couple of fake passports in the little suitcase he always carried in the back of the Toyota that would work for the hotel, even if using them to leave Macau might be risky. They were good, but not that good. Surely the Grand Lapa would have a room available and he could be at there in half an hour. He could check himself in with one of his false passports, take a shower, and order up room service. That ought to buy him at least a couple of days in the clear to think things through and come up with a long range plan. Yes, the more he thought about, the more that sounded like just the ticket.

Freddy took out his phone to call the Grand Lapa and was surprised to see that it was after three o'clock. Was it really possible that he had been sitting there all that time without seeing another soul? That was something he loved about Macau, the yin and yang of it. The city was all noise and crowds and upheaval, and yet here he had sat under a thick clump of banana trees since noon watching wisps of fog curling over the harbor without encountering another living human.

It had been a good day not to encounter another living human being. Not until he figured out what was going on, and what he was going to do next.

23

"YOU LOOK LIKE YOU'VE had a rough morning, my friend."

I was crossing the lobby of the MGM on the way to the elevators when I heard the voice behind me. I was dirty and disheveled from sliding down the hillside at the Ah-Ma Temple and still a little slack-jawed from Raymond's confession that Freddy was really Kim Jong-Nam. I didn't much feel like a chat with anyone.

I turned around and I recognized the guy walking toward me, but I couldn't immediately place him. He was wearing jeans and a black polo shirt and looked like half the westerners I had ever seen in Asia. He could have been anybody.

"I'll bet you've forgotten me already, Jack." The guy held out his hand. "I'm Harry Pine. Remember? I bumped into you at Starbucks over in the Wynn?"

We shook hands and then I remembered. This was that strange guy who had plopped himself down at the table with me in Starbucks and claimed to recognize me from somewhere. I had a feeling back then something was off about the guy, and finding him hanging around the lobby of the MGM now of all times reminded me of that.

"What happened to you, Jack? Fall off a hill somewhere?"

My pants were a little dirty and my shirt was a little wrinkled and my hair was probably mussed, but fell down a hill? That was an odd thing to say to someone who was a little rumpled and sweaty. Unless, of course, Pine already knew exactly why I was rumpled and dirty, although I didn't really see how he could.

"What are you doing here?" I asked.

"I told you before. I live here."

"You live here at the MGM Hotel?"

"No, of course not. I mean I live in Macau. I had lunch over at the Wynn and I was walking through the MGM to get a cab back to my office."

"You couldn't get a cab at the Wynn?"

"I probably could, but it's easier here. Why the third degree, man? I saw you walking across the lobby and thought I'd say hello. Maybe I shouldn't have bothered."

No, he also said I looked like I fell down a hill, which was so close to the truth that it was hard to shrug it off as nothing more than a coincidence. Still, how could he know?

I was probably being paranoid and I knew it. Almost certainly Pine was nothing but who he seemed to be: an ordinary joe who thought every fellow American he met in Macau wanted to be his pal for life just because they had been born in the same country. Who else could he be?

"Sorry," I said, "it's been a lousy day, but I shouldn't be taking it out on you."

"What happened?"

There was no way on earth I was going to tell a stranger the truth so I shrugged and said, "I fell down. It was a little embarrassing."

"I'll bet," Pine chuckled, "and at this time of day you've got to take full responsibility. You can't even pin the blame on a couple of extra martinis, can you?"

I dutifully shook my head and chuckled right back, but there wasn't any actual humor in it.

"Anyway," Pine said, "at least now you're back at your hotel so that'll be the end of your embarrassment."

"Why do you think that?"

"Well..." Pine looked confused, "because now you can shower and change and nobody will know you fell down someplace."

"I meant how do you know I'm staying here at the MGM?"

"You told me when we were having coffee together at Starbucks."

There were two problems with that.

First, Pine and I were not having coffee together at Starbucks. I was grabbing a quick sandwich for lunch when Pine barged in, introduced himself, and sat down at my table.

And second...

"I didn't tell you I was staying at the MGM."

"You must have, Jack. Otherwise, how would I know?"

How would Pine know, indeed? And more to the point, why would he care?

IT DIDN'T TAKE ME very long after that to get rid of Pine. I mumbled something insincere about how good it was to see him again, walked on to the elevators, and went straight upstairs. The guy gave me a creepy feeling, but what could he possibly be up to?

When I let myself into the suite, I immediately saw the red light blinking on the telephone. There was a message from Pansy. She was back in her office and wanted me to come down as soon as I could. After taking a quick shower, I thought about shaving but decided that would be overdoing it, so I settled for combing my hair and putting on fresh jeans and a clean shirt. A quick glance in the mirror told me I looked pretty good so I went downstairs and to Pansy's office. She looked a lot better.

PANSY WAS WEARING A blue blazer over a pink shirt and she had a blue man's necktie threaded through the collar and loosely knotted around her neck. On some women that outfit would have looked a little butch. On Pansy it looked terrific.

"There's been nothing in the South China Morning Post about

any investigation of money laundering anywhere, let alone here," she said.

No small talk. No messing around. Straight to the point. I liked that.

"Do you know why they didn't run the story?" she asked before I could say anything.

I hesitated. I didn't really want to lie to Pansy, but I didn't much want to bring Archie into the discussion either. At least not without telling him I was going to. He wasn't the sort of guy who liked to be mentioned in dispatches.

Pansy must have caught my hesitation, but she completely misinterpreted it.

"It was your doing, wasn't it, Jack? You got them to kill that story."

"I can't take the credit for that."

"Of course you can. The paper would never have dropped that story without somebody leaning on them. It was too good. And who else knew? Who else could have shut them down?"

"Well, it wasn't—"

"Don't be so modest, Jack. Thank you. I'm more grateful than I can ever tell you."

I didn't know exactly what to say to Pansy. She was right about one thing: the SCMP would have run the story if somebody hadn't put the screws to them not to. That was obvious. And since I didn't want to tell her about Archie, that didn't leave anyone else but me to have done it. I was uncomfortable taking credit for something I hadn't done, but I was still trying to figure out how to get out of it when Pansy changed the subject.

"I've looked at the security photos that you asked Gerald to collect," she said. "I don't really know what to make of them."

She picked up a fat manila envelope from one side of her desk and handed it to me. "That's everyone over a five day period who presented a substantial amount of either $50 bills or €100 notes to any of our cashiers."

"You said on the telephone that there was something odd about these pictures. What is it?"

"First tell me what you see."

I pulled the flap of the envelope open and slid out a thick stack of photographs. I flipped through them quickly, but nothing in particular caught my eye. There were a lot of photos that appeared to be of the same people dressed differently, but that would be the way, wouldn't it? There would be a finite number of smurfs involved and they would each make multiple runs. Nothing odd about that. What was I missing that Pansy had seen?

I went back and examined the pictures individually for a few moments. None of them were very good photographs since they had all been printed from surveillance video. Each picture was slightly distorted at the edges from the effects of the camera's wide-angle lens, and the color was washed-out and unnatural.

The first picture was of a woman. She appeared to be in her thirties and was plainly dressed and unremarkable. She had an Asian face, but I couldn't guess what nationality she was from the photo. She could have been from almost anywhere.

The rest of the photos were similar. About two-thirds of the people in the photographs were women and one-third were men. Each person looked to be in their twenties or thirties and appeared generically Asian. The mode of dress changed often from one photograph to another, but only the most rudimentary kind of disguises had been employed. The women changed their hair from up to down, and either wore glasses or removed them. The men sometimes wore hats and sometimes didn't. It was enough variety not to attract the notice of any of the cashiers even if they were reasonably attentive, but in the photos the subterfuge looked pretty amateurish.

I got up from the chair and starting dealing the photos out onto Pansy's carpet, arranging them in rows with the photos placed tightly side by side. When I finished, I stood with my back to the wall and tried to take in the entire collection with a single glance.

Pansy had not said a word the entire time I was laying out the photographs, but now she walked around from behind her desk and stood next to me.

"I don't know what I'm looking at," I finally said after a few minutes of examining the photographs in silence.

"I know what you're not looking at, Jack."

I shifted my eyes to Pansy and waited.

"You're not looking at the kind of people you see on the floor of my casino," she said.

"What do you mean?"

"I'll bet you a million dollars that none of those people are Chinese."

I didn't have the million with which to call Pansy's bet, but if I had, I wouldn't have done it.

It was partly a matter of facial features, partly build and size, partly clothing, and partly body language, but I didn't think people in those pictures were either mainland or local Chinese. And mainland and local Chinese made up almost all of the gamblers in Macau.

"This isn't a triad operation then," I said.

"Not unless the triads are hiring outside help these days," Pansy said, "and I don't think they are."

We both went back to studying the pictures in silence. Finally, I spoke up and broke it.

"So who are they, Pansy?"

"No idea."

"They look a little Chinese, don't they? Some of them at least? Could they be Singaporeans?"

"Sure," Pansy nodded. "They could be from Singapore. They could also be from New Jersey. I'm only telling you these people aren't locals, and they aren't mainlanders either."

She was right about that. I had no doubt now at all.

But if the smurfs weren't Chinese, then who the hell were they?

24

I LEFT PANSY'S OFFICE and took all the security photographs up to my suite to play with them for a while. I hoped that spending some time shuffling them around into various combinations might cause something brilliant to come to me. So I did, but it didn't.

I was looking at two big problems that were completely unrelated. But try as I might, I could only think of one possible solution, and it was the same for both.

These were my problems: how to find out who those people smurfing money through the MGM casino were, and where to find Freddy or Kim Jong-Nam or whatever the hell I was supposed to call him now.

And this was my solution to both: call Archie Ward.

ARCHIE DIDN'T ANSWER HIS phone, of course, which wasn't a big surprise to me, but nobody else answered either. Not even a robot voice asking me to leave a message. The number Archie gave me rang and rang and nothing at all happened, which was a little bit disconcerting in this day when every known form of media provided you with multiple ways to leave messages for everyone. All I could do now was assume Archie's phone had registered my call and that he would call me back.

So I hung up and waited. It seemed to me I was always doing that: waiting for somebody to call me back. I didn't really believe in heaven and hell, but if I had I would have imagined hell as sitting in a chair and waiting all eternity for somebody to call me back. I had no idea what heaven might be, but I resolved to give that matter some serious thought first chance I got.

I spent the next hour stacking and unstacking the security photos and sorting them into different combinations. Finally I went slowly through each of the piles of photos, keeping my mind as empty as I could and trying to let the photos tell me whatever they wanted to. After a half hour of that mumbo jumbo I gave up and admitted the truth to myself. They didn't want to tell me shit.

The whole process was so fruitless and tedious that I was more than ready to abandon it when Archie finally called back.

"I THOUGHT WE HAD a deal, Archie. You were supposed to give me the number of the phone you actually answer."

"Did anyone else answer when you called the number I gave you?"

"No."

"So there you go. This is the phone number I answer."

"But you didn't answer."

"Well…now you're getting into technicalities, mate. Fucking lawyers. It's always a bunch of technicalities with you guys, isn't it?"

I didn't say anything right away so Archie started talking again.

"You asked me for the number of the phone that I answer, didn't you?"

"Yes."

"That's what I gave you. If anyone answers the number I gave you, it's me."

"This isn't getting us anywhere."

"I was hoping you'd see that."

Sometimes I thought Archie did this sort of thing for fun, and sometimes I thought he did it to polish up his reputation for being a deeply irritating prick. But he also had a reputation for being uniquely well informed and incredibly well connected all over Asia, so I put up with nonsense like this. Sometimes I wondered how many people did.

"I've got some pictures I need to show you," I said.

"Of what?"

"They're the security camera pictures of the people who brought large numbers of $50 and €100 bills to the MGM cashiers during the last week."

"Okay," Archie said. "You want to do it right now?"

"Yeah, right now. Where are you?"

Archie gave me an address. I didn't recognize it, but I wrote it down.

"Is this where you're staying?" I asked.

I didn't get any answer. Archie had already hung up.

WHEN THE CAB STOPPED and I got out, my first thought was that the driver had misunderstood my no doubt fractured pronunciation of the Portuguese street name and taken me to the wrong place. We were somewhere in the far north of Macau close to the Chinese border in a narrow alleyway paved in worn cobblestones. It was a little after sunset and the filigreed iron lampposts spaced every fifty feet or so lit the whole area with a dim, slightly amber glow. Two story, Mediterranean looking buildings lined both sides of the alleyway. Their pitted and cracked concrete facades were colored in faded pastels and most of the windows that I could see were covered with heavy, mostly black or dark green shutters. There wasn't a living soul in sight.

Gesturing for the driver to wait, I tucked the envelope with the photos under my arm, pulled out my phone, and dialed Archie's number. I heard Archie's phone ringing behind a door no more than ten feet further up the street so I walked up to the door and opened it without knocking.

Archie sat in an old-fashioned black and white barber chair

covered in a sheet. His face had a thick layer of lather on it and an elderly man wearing a tan smock was shaving him with a straight razor. Archie's telephone lay on a narrow shelf under a large mirror and it continued to ring without anyone appearing to give a damn.

"Hang up that fucking phone, mate. The noise is driving me around the twist."

"You could answer it."

"Why?" Archie sounded genuinely puzzled. "You're standing right here."

He had a point.

I PAID OFF MY cab, went back inside, and sat in another barber chair toward the back of the room with the envelope on my lap.

"You want a shave?" Archie lifted his thumb toward the old man with a wrinkled and wizened face who was methodically swiping a straight razor through the thick layer of white foam on his face. It sounded like somebody was sandpapering a table.

"No, I don't want a shave."

"Suit yourself." I thought I could see Archie shrug underneath the sheet tied around his neck.

"I have something important to talk to you about, and this doesn't really seem to me to be the place or time to do it."

"Don't worry about Carlos. He doesn't speak a word of English. You can say whatever you want."

I thought about that for a moment and finally tossed out my own shrug. Pulling the thick stack of photographs out of the envelope, I held them out. Archie snaked one arm from under the sheet and took them. Carlos paid no attention at all and kept on methodically shaving Archie's face.

I said nothing as Archie slowly worked his way through the stack of photographs. He looked at each one for a beat, shuffled it to the bottom of the stack, and looked at the next one. When he had seen them all, he held the stack out to me and I took it back.

"Okay, what's your question?" Archie asked.

"Are this people mainland Chinese?"

"No."

"Local Chinese?"

"No."

"You think the triads are bringing in outside help these days?"

"No."

"It's not the triads smurfing the MGM, is it?"

"Doesn't look like it."

"So here's my question: who the hell is it?"

In the silence that followed, I listened to the straight razor scratching against Archie's whiskers under the lather.

"Can I have those photos back?" Archie asked after a minute or two had passed that way. "I want to show them to somebody."

"Who?"

Archie said nothing.

"Okay, never mind," I said. I slipped the photos back in the envelope and handed it to Archie. "Sure. Keep the photos. Keep the envelope, too. Get me some kind of clue who the hell these people are and they're yours forever."

Carlos stopped shaving Archie and stropped his razor back and forth a few times on a long leather strap hanging from the side of the barber chair. He moved around the chair and went to work on the other side of Archie's face.

"Anything else?" Archie asked me.

"Do you have any way of locating a guy who's gone to ground here in Macau?" I asked. "Someone who doesn't really want to be found?"

"Could be. You talking about one of the people in the photos?"

"No, this is a completely different deal."

Archie waited for me to explain, but I didn't. After a while, he got impatient. "I already told you that Carlos doesn't speak—"

"I don't give a shit, Archie. I'll tell you this one when you're done and we're out of here."

Archie grunted, but he didn't say anything.

TEN MINUTES LATER WE were walking away from the barbershop and up the cobblestone alleyway in what I thought was more or less the direction of the casino district. Archie swung the envelope with the photos rhythmically from one hand as we walked and it made a swishing sound every time it brushed against his pants leg.

I cleared my throat and told Archie about Raymond asking me to meet Freddy and about Freddy pitching me to represent him to seek political asylum in the United States. Archie didn't react, at least not that I could see. He kept trudging steadily along, occasionally patting the envelope of security camera photographs against his thigh.

So I told him about the gunmen who attacked us when I met Freddy at the Ah-Ma Temple and Freddy taking off for parts unknown after we had escaped down the hillside into Barre Square. Archie listened and nodded.

Finally I told him that Raymond had admitted to me, under a certain amount of duress, that Freddy was really Kim Jong-Nam and the older brother of North Korea's Little Leader.

"Huh," Archie said. "No shit."

His tone of voice held about as much interest as if I had just announced that today was my cat's birthday. But I don't have a cat, so I might be wrong about that.

"You don't sound very surprised," I said. "Did you already know Kim Jong-Nam was living here in Macau?"

"Sure. Didn't you?"

"Up until recently, I wouldn't have cared much if he was living in Cleveland."

"But I didn't know that KJN wanted to defect," he said. "I'm buggered if I'd heard about that."

"He wants to live in Hawaii."

"Crikey! If little brother finds out about that, KJN has about as much chance of getting out of Macau alive as he does of pushing shit uphill with a rubber fork. No wonder he's done a runner."

"If he's still in Macau, can you find him?"

In the dim half light I couldn't quite read the expression on Archie's face, but it looked a bit like a smile.

"Reckon I could if I wanted to."

"Then I want you to want to."

WE EMERGED FROM THE cobblestone alleyway into what could have been a small residential square in the heart of Lisbon. A green and white tiled fountain that looked like a giant birdbath dribbled sheets of water into a tiny pool in the center, and four story Mediterranean style buildings with heavy wooden shutters and iron balconies lined all four sides. Here and there trees poked up through the paving stones and under most of them were benches made of green wooden slats and black wrought iron legs.

"What does this guy look like?" Archie asked.

I described Freddy as well as I could.

Archie pointed to a bench on the far side of the square. "Take a load off over there for a few minutes, mate. I'll make a couple of calls. See what I can do."

Archie paced around the fountain punching out numbers on his cell phone, talking a bit, and then punching out more numbers. It was less than ten minutes before he broke off from his circling of the fountain, punched the phone off, and pocketed it. He walked toward me with a big smile on his face.

"We're apples, mate!" Archie said when he got back to where I was waiting. "Cost some bickies, it did, but I got the drum."

"What the hell does all that mean?"

"Means it cost you a few dollars, but I know where he is."

"Where?"

"He's at the Grand Lapa. Checked in under another name, but it's KJN. No doubt about it."

"How do you know?"

"Bloody hell, mate, you know better than to ask me shit like that."

"You mean you paid somebody off, and—"

Archie tossed out a crooked grin.

"This is Macau, mate. What else did you expect?"

THERE WAS NO TRAFFIC in the quiet little square, so there were no taxis around either, but I could see a busy road in the distance that held out the promise of available transportation. I led Archie toward it at a brisk pace.

"What's your hurry?" he asked.

"I want to get to Freddy before anything happens to him or he decides something is about to happen and he disappears again."

"Why do you think something's going to happen to him?"

"If you found him in ten minutes, the bad guys can find him, too."

"For Christ's sake, slow down. Two minutes one way or the other isn't going to make any difference."

"What's the matter, old man? Can't keep up?"

"Nah, it's this new shave I got. Don't want to ruin it."

I laughed, but I slowed down a bit anyway. Archie was right. A couple of minutes one way or the other wasn't going to matter.

We walked on at a more measured pace toward the roadway where I could now clearly see the occasional passing taxi.

"You going to help this guy?" Archie asked.

The truth was that I wasn't sure yet, so I didn't answer Archie's question.

The first thing I had to do was find Freddy. There would be plenty of time after that to decide what to do.

25

THE GRAND LAPA PUT him in a suite on the top floor that looked down over the Macau Sands. As soon as he was upstairs, Freddy took a shower and ordered a club sandwich from room service. It had been a long, rotten day and he was dirty and hungry and tired.

The bag he kept in the back of the Toyota with his emergency supplies had a few extra clothes in it for those nights he didn't make it back to wherever he might be sleeping right then. Fishing around in it, he came up with a fresh black polo shirt and a pair of black cotton pants. He wore black a lot. Someone once told him black made people look thinner and, since he really didn't care that much what color he was wearing anyway, he wore mostly black, on the off chance it really did make him look thinner.

The shower made him feel good and the club sandwich and the two beers made him feel even better. He pushed the room service trolley into a corner, picked up what was left of his second beer, and walked over the big floor-to-ceiling windows that formed one wall of the suite's living room.

While he sipped at the beer he watched the garish display of neon that danced silently back and forth over the Macau Sands. Sometimes he wondered why casinos bothered with light displays and dancing fountains and outrageous architecture. Did they really attract more gamblers with their cheesy displays? Perhaps they did in America where gambling was mostly about having fun, but that had nothing to do with why the Chinese gambled in Macau. The Chinese gambled to make money. No other reason. It was another form of work that, like all work, had the purpose of increasing one's wealth. Fun had nothing to do with it.

The Sands had been the first of the foreign casinos to open in Macau, but now it was looking a little old and tired. There were rumors that it was going to be torn down and something vastly larger and more elaborate built in its place, but Freddy wasn't so sure about that. There were rumors in Macau that almost everything was going to be torn down and something vastly larger and more elaborate built in its place. Generally the rumors were true, but not always. He hoped the rumors about the Sands weren't true. The building had aged a little now, that was true, and the Venetian and the Wynn and the MGM were much more lavish, but he liked the Sands anyway. It seemed…well, real. He hoped it survived.

FREDDY FINISHED HIS BEER thinking about survival. First, the survival of the Sands, and then, inevitably, his own survival. He might be safe and dry in the Grand Lapa tonight, but he couldn't stay here forever. What was he going to do?

Macau was a lousy place to hide out. It was small and didn't offer many places to lay low, of course, but there was an even worse problem than that. When you weren't Chinese, you felt anonymous in Macau, a cork drifting in a disinterested sea of indifferent people. But the truth was you were anything other than anonymous. Everywhere you went, somebody saw you, and everybody who saw you knew people they could tell. The place was a maze of local networks and ethnic connections no outsider would ever see, or understand.

How many hotels were there in Macau? Maybe fifty? Probably

seventy-five, if you included the whorehouses. Anyone who was looking for him wouldn't find his name on a registration list anywhere, of course, but that wouldn't stop them for long. All they had to do was tap into one of the local networks and put his description out there. How many people could have checked into a hotel in Macau today? A couple thousand at most? And how many of them were single men staying alone? A couple of hundred? And how many of them matched his general description? Two or three? If the bastards wanted him, they would be at his door in twenty-four hours, perhaps less.

Freddy knew the obvious answer was to get out of Macau, but that wasn't easy either. The airport was small, and trying to slip out inconspicuously that way was out of the question. Otherwise, once you ruled out flying, from Macau you could go to China or you could go to Hong Kong. That was pretty much it. The Hong Kong International Airport would be a much better bet since it was huge and sprawling and from there he could find a flight to almost anyplace on earth. The problem was he wasn't sure his passport was good enough to get him into another country. It might get him onto an airplane, but eventually he was going to have to walk up to an immigration counter somewhere and he didn't think the odds of making it past one were all that great. He hadn't even been able to get into Japan to go to Disneyland, and that was more than ten years ago. Who knew how many more ways there were these days of detecting phony passports?

No, neither hiding out in Macau nor running to another country would work. He needed someone with the right connections to talk to the right people for him, someone to smooth the way for him to get to a safe place.

The solution was obvious enough. He needed Jack Shepherd to get him asylum in the United States.

FREDDY WENT INTO THE bedroom where he had dumped his stuff. He dug out up the throwaway phone on which Shepherd had called him and checked the number the call had come from. It had a Macau dialing code that almost certainly meant it wasn't Shepherd's personal cell phone. Regardless, it was all he had so he punched CALL BACK and listened for a moment. When the operator at the MGM answered, he quickly hung up, but almost immediately he began wondering why he had.

Obviously Shepherd was staying at the MGM. What was wrong with calling him there? Had he gotten so paranoid that he really believed all the lines at a huge resort like the MGM Macau could be monitored? Besides, there was nothing to connect the cell phone on which he was making the call to him. Even if somehow somebody were watching the calls coming into Shepherd's room, his number would mean nothing to anyone. Better yet, he could call from his room phone, couldn't he? What would be more innocuous than a call coming into the MGM telephone system from out of the Grand Lapa telephone system? Somebody at one big hotel calling somebody at another big hotel. Had to happen a thousand times a day.

Picking up the room phone he dialed the MGM again and asked for Jack Shepherd. When he did, he pitched his voice lower than usual and tried to put on a British accent. He felt completely ridiculous doing it, but he did it anyway. There was a brief pause and he heard the phone ringing in Shepherd's room. It rang steadily for about a minute before a voice mail announcement began to play. As he listened to the instructions for leaving a message he decided all over again that might not be a very good idea after all, so after the announcement was done he hung up.

Shepherd wasn't there. He could either leave a message or keep calling until he answered. And leaving a message that said where he was or how to reach him was probably idiotic.

FREDDY SAT THERE FOR a minute holding the room phone trying to decide what to do now. He couldn't think of anything so he decided to go to bed. It had been a bad enough day already. No point in making it even worse by working himself up into a lather trying to solve all his problems at once. Maybe Shepherd would answer his phone tomorrow morning. Maybe, at the very least, everything would look different in the light of a new day.

Before Freddy put down the phone he pushed the speed dial button for room service and told them to pick up the cart on which his dinner had been delivered, which is why he wasn't particularly startled when there was a knock on the door of his suite a few minutes later.

26

WHEN THEY GOT INTO the taxi, Archie asked the driver to take them to the Sands.

"I thought you told me Freddy was at the Grand Lapa," I said.

Archie cut his eyes toward the back of the driver's head and shook his head slightly.

"My mistake," I muttered and turned to look out the window.

We rode in silence along *Avenida do Coronel Mesquita* in the general direction of the harbor and circled around the north side of Guia Hill, the highest point in Macau, which isn't really very high.

The Portuguese built a fortress on Guia Hill in the 1600's to defend their hold on their little colony, and in the 1800's they had also built the first western-style lighthouse on the China coast up there. The fortress is now a largely ignored tourist attraction, but the lighthouse still sends out its beam every night exactly as it has for a hundred and fifty years.

As I watched the light etch lazy circles into the thin winter fog lying over the city, I thought about the generations of sailors on the South China Sea who had seen that light in the last century and a half and looked upon it as a signal light beckoning them toward safety. I wanted very much to feel the same way right then myself, but these days safety was a far more complicated concept than it had been for some eighteenth century sailors. I allowed myself a moment of pure envy, and the feeling passed.

On the other side of Guia Hill we turned south on *Estrada do Reservadrio* and the Macau Ferry Terminal was right in front of us. The ferry terminal had been Macau's sole connection with the outside world until the airport opened in 1995. It was still its most important connection. Every few minutes a giant hydrofoil slipped its moorings and set out on a rapid passage to some part of Hong Kong or up the Pearl River Delta to Shenzhen and Guangzhou. There was even a regular helicopter service from the roof of the ferry building that ran back and forth to Hong Kong every half hour. Someone once told me that the one way fare for the fifteen minute flight was more than $500. That sounded crazy to me when a first class ticket for the one hour trip on the hydrofoil was about $40, but I suppose Chinese high rollers who push $10,000 or $100,000 onto the baccarat table every time the cards are dealt don't really care what it costs to get to Macau as long as it gets them there fast and gives them more time at the tables.

I looked up at the roof as we passed and saw a blue and white helicopter with its rotor blades idling lazily. It sat in a pool of white light so blinding that the landing pad looked as if were suspended weightlessly in the blackness of the night sky. I cranked down the window and listened to the noise of the blades. Archie looked at me strangely, but he said nothing.

That was probably a good thing. I didn't really want to admit to Archie I was thinking that all I would have to do was tell the taxi driver to stop, climb up to the roof of the ferry building, get into that helicopter. Then I could fly away from Macau and leave behind the MGM and the triads and the bales of laundered money and Freddy and whoever was trying to kill him. Just like that, I could be done with them all.

But of course I didn't tell the taxi driver to stop. I just rolled the window back up and sat quietly as the taxi continued on to the Sands.

AT THE MAIN ENTRANCE to the Sands, Archie paid off the driver and we stood together in silence watching him drive away. After the taillights disappeared into the traffic on *Avenida da Amizade*, I turned to Archie and asked what seemed to me to be the obvious question.

"Why are we are the Sands instead of the Grand Lapa?"

"What did you expect to do, Jacko? Walk into the lobby of the Grand Lapa, ask for Freddy's room number, then go up and tap politely on his door?"

"You didn't answer my question."

"We have no idea what we're walking into. Don't you think we ought to do a reconnaissance before we blunder in there?"

"How about reconnaissance by fire?"

"What's that?"

"We shoot at him. If he shoots back, we know he's there."

"Very funny."

Archie may have said that was very funny, but I noticed he didn't laugh. Too bad. I thought it really *was* funny.

"ARE WE AT LEAST somewhere close to the Grand Lapa?" I asked.

Archie pointed at a white building right next door to the Sands. It was about eighteen stories high and looked as if it had been built in the sixties. I tilted my head back and saw on the top a gold neon sign that said THE GRAND LAPA.

Between the Sands and the Grand Lapa there was a sort of lonely looking plaza with a few concrete benches scattered around in it. It was shadowy and empty in the darkness, and tentacles of fog twisted through its grey half light like smoke from unseen fires. We walked to the nearest bench, sat down, and looked up at the lights that were on in about half the rooms of the Grand Lapa.

"You sure he's there?" I asked.

"I know a guy who has access to most of the hotel reservations systems in Macau."

"You hacked the Grand Lapa's computer system?"

Archie gave me a long look. I shrugged and gestured for him to continue.

"Between noon and six today only nine single males traveling alone checked into Macau hotels. We talked to the front desk managers in each of the hotels involved and the single male who checked into the Grand Lapa more or less matches the description you gave me of Freddy. The others don't." Archie shrugged again. "That's as close to sure as I can get you."

"What name is he registered under?"

"Does it matter?"

"I guess not. As long as you have the room number."

"1801." Archie lifted his arm and pointed. "It's on the top floor. Left hand corner of the building."

I looked where he was pointing. The lights in that room were on.

"How do you think we ought to do this?" I asked.

"It seems to me there are two distinct possibilities here. Either he'll be happy as hell to see you since you could be his protector from whoever is after him. Or he thinks you set him up in the first place and will put a bullet in you the moment you knock at his door."

"I don't think he's armed."

"Look, Jack, you don't know a damned thing about this guy except that he's the older brother of the kid who runs North Korea and periodically threatens to blow up a couple of million people. Maybe he has a private security team. Maybe he's surrounded by a squad of crack North Korean commandos."

"He was alone both times I met him."

"How do you know?"

"I looked. I didn't see anything that looked like a security detail."

"Was he under surveillance?"

"I don't think so."

"If he wasn't under surveillance, where did the two shooters come from?"

It was a good question and I didn't have a good answer, so I said nothing.

"How did you come to the conclusion he wasn't under surveillance? I'll bet you sat somewhere looking around for a few minutes like we're doing now and then you walked right up to him, didn't you?"

Archie knew me too well.

He stood up and brushed off the seat of his trousers with one hand. "We'll try to do a little better than that this time."

THIRTY MINUTES LATER WE had walked all four sides of the building without seeing anything unusual. We went into the hotel through the main entrance that faced a circular driveway off *Avenida da Amizade* and Archie led me across the quiet lobby and up the stairs to the mezzanine where we took seats in an uncrowded bar with a view straight down to the entrance of the hotel. Archie dumped the envelope with the security photos into the seat of an empty chair and ordered a double Johnny Walker on the rocks. I ordered a Coke. Archie shook his head in disgust.

"What now?" I asked after the drinks had come and the waiter had disappeared again.

"We watch the lobby," Archie said and slumped back into his chair with his whiskey glass balanced on his stomach.

"For what?"

"We'll know if we see it."

We watched for nearly an hour and I didn't see anything that looked unusual to me. Occasionally people wandered in and out of the lobby, but mostly it was pretty quiet. There were several couples who were checking in with their luggage and a few who were checking in without it, a group of four women headed out for a night on the town, a lone male who looked like he had much the same thing in mind, and a couple of hookers who were obviously on duty. None of them looked to me like part of a North Korean hit team.

After a while Archie ordered a second double Johnny Walker, but I passed on a second Coke. You can only drink so much before it affects your judgment.

When the waiter left, I looked at Archie's drink as pointedly as I could. "If we have to shoot somebody, I guess it's going to be up to me to handle that now."

"Nope," Archie shook his head. "I've got the gun, and I'm keeping it."

"You're carrying a gun?"

"I've always got a gun, mate. Never know when something unhappy might come up."

FIFTEEN MINUTES LATER, ARCHIE finished his whiskey, tapped the empty glass smartly against the table, and pushed himself to his feet.

"Time to rock and roll, Jacko."

"What are we going to do?"

"I don't see any signs of either surveillance or security, so we'll go with your original plan."

"My original plan? I never had a plan."

"Sure you did. You were just going to take an elevator upstairs and knock on his door."

That wasn't exactly what I'd said, but I didn't bother arguing with Archie. I only reminded him of what he had told me before. "I thought you were afraid he'd shoot me if I did that."

"I am," Archie grinned, "but as long as he doesn't shoot me I figure we'll be okay."

He winked at me, scooped up the envelope with the security photos in it, and walked out of the bar. I dropped some money on the table and, not having any better idea what to do, followed.

27

FREDDY WAS EXPECTING SOMEONE to pick up his dinner trolley so he opened the door without bothering to look through the viewer. He was surprised to find a middle-aged western male standing there rather than a room service waiter. The man was big, well over six feet tall and stoutly built, and he was wearing a black t-shirt and jeans. Freddy's first impulse was to slam the door and double lock it, but he would have felt so stupid doing that so he didn't.

"You have the wrong room."

"No, man, this is where I'm supposed to be."

The fellow had a half smile on his face and spoke softly in what sounded like an American accent. He seemed friendly enough and Freddy began to relax even if he still couldn't understand what the man was doing here. Perhaps it had something to do with whoever had been in the suite before he checked in.

"Can I come in?" the man asked.

Before Freddy could say anything, the man stepped forward, gently moved Freddy aside with one hand, and walked into the suite.

Now Freddy was more pissed off than scared. His voice rose. "I said you have the wrong room."

The man seated himself on a green and white upholstered chair, crossed his legs, and pointed to the matching couch. "Sit down, Freddy. You did tell Shepherd to call you Freddy, didn't you?"

Freddy's mouth dropped open as surprise turned to shock.

"Come on, sit down," the man repeated. His voice was still soft and pleasant and he pointed toward the couch again. "I'm not here to hurt you."

Freddy was so stunned he couldn't think, so he walked over to the couch and sat down exactly as he had been told to. The man was sitting there in that chair, leaning back, legs crossed, smiling at Freddy like an old friend who had unexpectedly dropped in for a cup of tea.

Freddy's mind raced. He was desperately trying to remember if he knew this man from somewhere, but he was drawing a complete blank. The man had long reddish-blond hair, a pale Nordic complexion, grey eyes, and a prominent nose. There was a boyish quality about his face, but he was at least in his mid-forties, maybe older. Freddy was sure he had never met him before. Pretty sure, at least.

And even if he had met him somewhere, what difference did it make? Not remembering the man wasn't the problem at the moment. The problem was that he somehow knew Freddy had talked to Shepherd. Nobody knew Freddy had talked to Shepherd. Nobody except Raymond, and Shepherd himself, of course. Could Shepherd have sent this guy? Or Raymond? No, that didn't make any sense...

Freddy remembered the two guys with guns who had interrupted his meeting with Shepherd at the Ah-Ma temple and finally admitted to himself that somebody other than Raymond and Shepherd did know. And that was when he began to smell the fear coming off his body in waves. If his brother had somehow found out that he was trying to get political asylum in the United States...well, he wasn't certain exactly what his brother would do, but it wouldn't be pretty. Would his brother go so far as to issue orders to have him killed?

Surely not. They were brothers, for God's sake. Assuming that mattered anymore…

And obviously this man hadn't been sent by his brother to kill him. If he had, why was he sitting there smiling like an old friend? That didn't make any sense.

But there was something else that made even less sense. How had this man known where to find Freddy? Freddy himself hadn't known he was going to the Grand Lapa until a few hours ago, and he had only been in this particular room for a couple of hours. Did that mean his brother had had him under surveillance? *Oh God*, Freddy thought to himself, if he had been under surveillance for very long, they knew absolutely everything.

FREDDY KEPT WATCHING THE man, waiting for him to say something that might give him some clue how he knew about Shepherd and why he was here now, but the man said nothing. The silence stretched out to the point it made Freddy want to scream.

"Who are you?" he finally asked, mostly to break the goddamned silence. He wasn't all that sure he actually wanted to know who this man was.

"My name is Harry Pine. Well, it isn't really, but your name isn't Freddy either, is it?"

His brother had sent this man. He had no doubt now. He didn't know for sure how his brother had found out what he was doing, but what difference did that make now? His brother knew. That was what mattered. And he was never going to let Freddy go to the United States. Something like that would be far too embarrassing for him. It was that simple.

Freddy eyed the door to the hallway. Maybe he should make a break for it right now. Pine wouldn't pull out a gun and shoot him here on the top floor of the Grand Lapa Hotel, would he?

Freddy was a little afraid he was being too obvious about checking out a route to the door, but Pine didn't appear to notice.

Could he get off the couch and out the door before Pine caught up with him? And if he could, how far was it to a stairwell? He sure as hell wasn't going to press the elevator button and stand around waiting for an elevator to show up. Pine looked athletic, and Freddy really didn't fancy his chances of outrunning him, but what else was he going to do? Even if he only had one chance in ten to make it, he had to try. Sitting here on this couch he had exactly no chances in ten.

"You look jumpy, Freddy. You shouldn't be. Everything is going to be fine."

Freddy nodded, but he said nothing. He was too busy imagining himself vaulting over the end of the couch, sprinting half a dozen steps to the door, and plunging out into the hallway. Maybe he should start screaming the moment he opened the door. What could it hurt? Perhaps he would even attract enough attention to get the guy to run.

"I only want to talk to you, Freddy."

Freddy nodded again and tried to steady his breathing. Over the arm of the couch, six quick steps to the door, outside, and down the hall. How hard could that be?

"You do know who I really am and why I'm here, don't you, Freddy?"

Another nod. A deep breath.

"Your brother asked me to talk to you."

Another deep breath.

"He's not happy about you meeting with Shepherd."

Fuck it, Freddy thought. *Go!*

The vault over the arm of the couch was harder than he expected. His thigh caught on something and he fell into a table. A lamp and an ashtray thumped onto the carpet. At least he fell in the direction of the door.

Righting himself, he pumped his legs as fast as he could, but out of the corner of his eye he was dimly aware that Harry Pine hadn't moved from his chair. He hadn't even uncrossed his legs.

Freddy didn't understand that. It didn't make much sense that Pine wouldn't even bother chasing him, but he wasn't going to stick around a while and ask him why he wasn't.

Freddy's hand hit the handle and he jerked the door open. He plunged through it and out into the hallway.

That was when he found out why Pine hadn't bothered to get out of his chair.

THE TWO MEN WAITING outside dragged Freddy back into the suite and dumped him on the couch more or less exactly where he had been sitting before.

"You're being an asshole, Freddy." Pine shook his head. "Don't be an asshole."

Freddy nodded. That was exactly what he felt like. A complete asshole. "You sent those two guys to the Ah-Ma temple. You tried to kill me when I met Shepherd there."

"They were only supposed to scare you. Or at least scare Shepherd. Who they scared didn't really matter. The point was to stop your meetings and put an end to this silly idea you have of seeking asylum in the United States." Pine sighed heavily, uncrossed his legs, and crossed them back the other way. "If I had wanted you dead, Freddy, you'd be dead. My guys don't miss, except on purpose."

Freddy was slowly settling into a state of resignation. He had made his bed and now he was lying in it. His dream of going to America was over and he was in the hands of his brother. All that mattered now was what his brother intended to do with him. Nothing he could say would make any difference.

"Why do you want to go over to the Americans, Freddy?"

"You should know. You're an American, aren't you?"

"Oh man, I really hate people thinking I'm an American. It's the damned accent, isn't it?" Pine grinned. "I'm Canadian. At least I think I am. I've been so many things that I have a little trouble now remembering what I was when I started out. Hell, maybe I am an American. Who knows?"

Freddy started to say something about loyalty to the land of one's birth, but it occurred to him that was a pretty silly thing to be coming out of his mouth so he said nothing.

"So have you figured out who I really am now, Freddy?"

Freddy shrugged.

"Come on, man. Pay attention. I told you I was a Canadian. I work for the Democratic People's Republic of Korea. Don't tell me you've never heard—"

"You're the guy they call the Canadian?" Freddy interrupted.

"You thought the Canadian was like the boogeyman, didn't you? Just a made-up story used to frighten the children."

Pine grinned and shook his head.

"Nope, I'm real. And, unfortunately for you, right now I'm sitting here in this hotel suite where you thought nobody knew you were."

There had been stories around for years that the DPRK had extensive operations in Macau, that Macau was effectively the center of all of the DPRK's international undertakings. And the sexiest of those rumors was that the DPRK's operations in Macau were actually run by a foreigner everybody called the Canadian.

Freddy believed the first part of the story since he did know some of the things the DPRK was doing in Macau, even if he had nothing to do with them, but he thought the part about some mysterious figure called the Canadian running everything was only a fairy tale the DPRK put around to make them seem more organized and international than they actually were. Could it really be true?

"I do a lot of things for your motherland here in Macau, Freddy. I run some commercial enterprises, I handle banking operations, I sell a few bombs and rockets here and there. I even supervise preparation of the men and women the DPRK sends here to be prepared for insertion into the US and Europe as active intelligence agents. But right now you shouldn't be thinking about any of that. One of the other things I do is keep an eye on you, friend. That's what you really should be thinking about."

"You've been following me?"

"Don't be silly. I don't do shit like that. At least not personally." Pine gestured at the two goons who had dragged Freddy back into the suite when he made his absurd break for freedom. "That's why I've got guys like this working for me."

Now that Freddy looked at the men more carefully, he realized they did look a bit Korean, only not that much. They looked somehow generically Asian, like the gunmen who had come after him at the Ah-Ma temple. That did seem weird, now that he thought about it.

"We've got a doctor here who touches our people up a little," Pine explained, since he could easily see what Freddy was thinking. "A nip here and a tuck there, and in the US or Europe they can pass for anything from a Chinese to a Thai. No point in going around letting their faces advertise who they really are, is there?"

Freddy wished he had thought of that, he really did. If he had, he might be on some beach in Hawaii right now.

PINE LOOKED AROUND THE hotel suite for a moment like a man contemplating the possibility of buying it, but eventually he shifted his attention back to Freddy.

"What did you offer the Americans in return for that house in Hawaii?"

Freddy looked at the floor.

"You don't really have anything to give them, do you? You could probably tell them about a couple of our Macau front companies, but that's about it, isn't it? Of course, they don't know that. You were running a little con on the Yanks, weren't you, Freddy? I got to admit I admire you for having the balls to do that. I really do."

Freddy kept his face empty and stayed silent.

"But of course you understand it would still be a problem for your brother if you really did go over to the Americans. Jesus, can you imagine how silly that would make him look?"

"Get to the point. What happens now?"

"Ah well, that's the real question, isn't it?"

Pine got to his feet and Freddy lifted his hands and flinched away from him.

"Jesus, Freddy, relax, would you? You're going to turn me into a nervous wreck."

Pine walked over to the window and stared out at the Sands for a moment. The garish neon forms leapt and danced over the building in a sad parody of fun and good cheer while inside the casino relentlessly drained the pockets of rich and poor alike.

"Here's my problem, Freddy. I got orders today to kill you."

Turning away from the window, Pine saw that Freddy's face had gone slack and he had sunk back into the couch. He looked like a blow up doll after somebody had let the air out.

"Take it easy, man. I'm not going to do that. At least not right now."

Freddy looked up. His expression said that he expected a trick of some kind. He was dealing with the DPRK. Everything was some kind of a trick, even if they had sometimes forgotten how the trick worked.

"The order came through channels and I can't be absolutely sure where it originated. If somebody high up is figuring I have too much influence and wants to cut my throat, they could have sent me an order to kill the brother of the big guy without the big guy knowing about it. Then, when he finds out…well, you could imagine what would happen to me. On the other hand, if the order to kill you did come from the big guy and I don't kill you, that would go even worse for me. You do see my problem here, don't you?"

Pine looked at Freddy and raised his eyebrows as if he actually expected Freddy to voice his opinion on the dilemma he was facing. Freddy tried to remain still, but his head, almost as if it were operating independently of Freddy's conscious thoughts, nodded anyway.

"Yeah," Pine nodded back, "that's what I thought. So here's what I've decided to do…"

Pine returned to the chair where he had been sitting and resumed his previous posture. Leaning back, legs crossed, slight smile.

"You're going to go with these two gentlemen to a place we've prepared for you. We're going to keep you there until I can confirm who wants you killed and who doesn't. If the Little Leader gives you a thumbs down, I promise we'll get it over with as painlessly as we can. If he gives you a thumbs up, we'll turn you loose and you're on your own. Sound fair?"

Freddy nodded again. He hated himself for doing it, but he did it anyway.

"Oh, one more thing. I know you won't give them any trouble when you're leaving the hotel, will you?"

Freddy shook his head.

"Good. I didn't think you would. Still, to be on the safe side, we're going to give you a little shot to relax you. Nothing heavy duty. It will look like my friends here are helping out a buddy who had a little too much to drink."

Pine pointed his forefinger at one of the goons, who quickly stepped forward and produced a packaged hypodermic needle from his coat pocket. He opened the package, popped the cap off the needle, and went into the familiar ritual of turning the barrel of the hypodermic upright and tapping against it to force out any air bubbles.

Freddy thought about resisting. How did he know what they were really shooting him up with? Perhaps this was how they intended to kill him and they were trying to keep him calm. The more he thought about it, the more he supposed it didn't matter. Pine had been right about one thing. If his brother wanted him dead, he was going to be killed. Here, later, sometime. Whenever they wanted really. In the end, what could he do about it?

Freddy pushed up his left sleeve and stoically stared straight ahead. If he was going to be dead, maybe this was even the best way for it to happen.

It only took a minute before whatever was in the hypodermic to hit him. At first he felt dizzy. Then he simply fell into a black hole. The last thing he remembered was hearing the sound of Harry Pine's voice from somewhere very far away.

"I need a fucking drink," Pine was saying.

28

HARRY PINE WAS ALONE. I ran straight into him walking into the mezzanine bar just as I was leaving it to follow Archie to the elevators and then upstairs to the room where Freddy was presumably registered. Pine looked like a man in serious need of a drink.

What the hell was he doing here anyway? Was he following me around Macau for some reason? No, that didn't make any sense. Why would some guy who reads construction contracts for a living want to follow me?

Still, it was an odd coincidence all the same that Pine kept turning up wherever I went. If coincidence was what it really was. I wouldn't have been particularly happy to see Pine anywhere or any time, but right here and right now it was absolutely the last thing I wanted.

“““Well, I'll be damned,” he said. “We're going to have to stop meeting like this, Jack. People will talk.”

“Sorry, Harry,” I muttered. “I'm with somebody. Can't talk.”

“Hey, man, what's your hurry? Who is she anyway?”

I kept walking.

“Slow down,” Pine called out. “Let me buy you a drink.”

I didn't slow down, didn't even look back. I only lifted my right hand and wiggled it in a sort of wave that Pine could see over my shoulder. As far as I was concerned, he could interpret that wave any damn way he wanted.

All the way to the elevators, I could feel Pine's eyes on my back. And somehow I couldn't shake the feeling that he was smiling at me.

ARCHIE AND I RODE up to the eighteenth floor without speaking. When the doors opened, I saw that 1801 was all the way down at the end of the hallway. I figured that gave us a good forty-five seconds to come up with a clever plan. Maybe a whole minute. Unless of course Archie already had a clever plan he hadn't gotten around to telling me about yet.

"What are we going to do?" I asked as we started down the corridor.

"Knock on the door. See if anyone answers."

So much for Archie having a clever plan.

ARCHIE KNOCKED ON THE door, just like he said he was going to. In fact, he knocked twice, hard, but no one answered. Either the room was empty, or Freddy didn't want to see anybody.

"Now what?" I asked, ever helpful.

Archie pulled out his wallet and extracted a silver card that looked to be made of heavy plastic. It was about the same size as a credit card, and that's what I would have thought it was if I hadn't noticed that it had nothing printed on either side.

Archie slipped the silver card into the slot on the top of the electronic lock, a little light on the side turned green, and the door to room 1801 clicked open.

"You have a key to Freddy's room?"

"I have a key to every room," Archie said.

"To every room in the Grand Lapa?"

"To every room in every hotel in Macau."

"I'm not sure I want to know about that."

"Good choice."

Archie stepped to one side of the doorway. He slid a Glock 19 out of a holster nestled into the small of his back and racked the slide to chamber a round. The Glock is an ugly little gun, chunky and square and about as sexy as a plastic trash can, but very reliable.

"Don't shoot him," I said.

"Not unless he shoots me first."

"I don't think Freddy's a shooter."

"For your sake, you better hope not. Because if he shoots me, I'm shooting you next."

Archie gestured me away from the doorway, laid the palm of his left hand flat against the inside edge of the door, and gave it a little push.

ROOMS WITHOUT HUMAN BEINGS in them feel empty. The air itself is unmarked. You sense immediately it isn't air that has been breathed and exhaled again. Freddy was gone, if he had ever been there in the first place.

"It's empty," I said.

Archie glanced at me, but he didn't say anything. He stepped into the room and immediately moved to one side of the door. I started to follow him, but Archie put out his hand and stopped me. With the barrel of the Glock he gestured off across the suite, and I took in the turned over table, the lamp, and the ashtray lying on the plain baize carpet. They didn't necessarily mean anything, I told myself, but of course I knew they did. People didn't knock over a table and simply walk out of a hotel suite; not, that is, if they are doing the walking out entirely on their own.

"I don't see anything else out of place," I said. "If somebody was here and there was a struggle, there wasn't much to it."

Archie didn't reply. He stepped quickly across to the bedroom, did a head bob into it and out again, and followed the muzzle of the Glock through the doorway. A moment later he came back out and holstered his gun.

"Bedroom, bathroom, and closet are all clear," Archie said. "A few clothes hung up, a few more on the bathroom floor along with some dirty towels, one small bag on the luggage rack. Nothing else appears to have been disturbed."

"You think he was here, don't you?"

"Somebody was here."

I walked into the bedroom and quickly scanned the room. Then I went into the bathroom and looked down at the wadded up shirt and trousers lying on the tile. A glance was all it took.

"Those are the clothes Freddy was wearing at the temple," I told Archie when I went back out to the living room. "He was here all right."

Archie squatted down where the mahogany table lay on its side. I noticed his knees didn't even crack when he did it. Bastard.

The green ceramic lamp, its cream shade pushed lopsided across the light bulb, lay next to the table, and a glass ashtray was upside down directly between them. Archie examined the area around the turned-over table carefully, but I really couldn't imagine what he was looking for. It didn't seem to me that there was very much to see.

After a moment Archie stood up and began walking slowly toward the couch. His eyes were on the carpet and he turned his head slightly side to side while he walked as if he expected to encounter a land mine. Right next to the couch he stopped and went down on one knee. He rubbed his open hand gently over the carpet and picked up something between his thumb and forefinger, although from where I was I couldn't see what he had found. He walked back to me and held out his hand, palm up. In it lay a tiny red plastic cap. It looked like the top of a very small tube of toothpaste.

"I give up," I said. "What is it?"

"I suppose it could be a lot of things, but my guess is it's the cap off a hypodermic needle."

"You think somebody shot Freddy up with some kind of tranquilizer and dragged him out of here, which explains why there wasn't much of a struggle."

"Could be. But even if that's what did happen and it actually was KJN, that still leaves a pretty big question."

"Hit me with it."

"How did somebody just walk in here and stick a hypodermic needle in his arm?"

"Maybe it was somebody he knew."

Archie shrugged. "And maybe it was somebody who stuck a big fucking gun in his face."

AFTER THAT WE WENT through the whole suite carefully, checking inside and even under every drawer and cabinet, but we found nothing of any interest. We left after about twenty minutes, closing the door quietly behind us, and we didn't speak again until we were in the elevator.

"What do you think?" I asked as soon as the doors closed.

Archie didn't say anything. He just shrugged.

When the elevator stopped at the lobby we walked out the hotel's main doors and turned west along the *Avenida da Amizade*.

"You're sure those were Freddy's clothes?" Archie asked.

"Yes. And you think somebody drugged him and grabbed him?"

"Yeah, probably."

"You going to help me find him again?"

"Let's go somewhere and have another drink," Archie said.

"I don't want another drink."

"Well, I do, so tough shit."

WE WALKED UP *Avenida da Amizade* until we got to the Wynn Macau, went through the east entrance, and into a place called Bar Cristal that is right off the lobby of the Encore Tower. I hate Bar Cristal. There are mirrors everywhere and the place glitters with so much cut glass it would give Liberace a headache. Drinking there is like drinking inside a chandelier.

Archie ordered another Johnny Walker, although I noticed it was only a single this time, and I had another Coke. Archie gave me a look, but he didn't say anything about my choice of libation. In fact, he didn't say anything at all until the waitress had returned with our drinks, set them out, and departed again. Then he cleared his throat…

"What have you got yourself into here, Jacko?"

"A friend asked me to talk to Freddy. That's all I did. We're not pals and he's not my client."

"Yet you were concerned enough about him that you started looking for him when he disappeared."

"Yes."

"And now you want me to help you get him back from whoever grabbed him."

"Yes."

"You have any idea who that might be?"

"I think we can both guess."

"Probably."

"Look, Archie, Freddy is—"

"His name's not Freddy. It's Kim Jong-Nam."

"I prefer Freddy. It sounds a lot friendlier, don't you think?"

"What makes you think this guy's friendly?"

"He's a big teddy bear, Archie."

"So, I hear, was Herman Goering."

"He's not Herman Goering. He's just a fat kid who wants to live in Hawaii."

We sat in silence for a while after that fiddling with our drinks. I could tell Archie had something he wanted to ask me so I sat and waited for him to get to it. Eventually he did.

"What's the connection between KJN and this money laundering gig you're doing for Pansy Ho?" Archie asked.

"None at all."

"You sure?"

"Of course I'm sure. I only met Freddy because a friend of mine asked me to talk to him."

"And you only met Pansy Ho because a friend of yours asked you to talk to her."

"Different friend."

"And absolutely no connection between them?"

I thought about that for a minute. The FBI in the person of Pete Logan had asked me to get to the bottom of Pansy Ho's money laundering problem, and a Macau restaurant proprietor named Raymond had asked me to meet with his friend Freddy. I didn't know for sure whether they had ever met, but I doubted it. Was Archie getting at something specific, or just asking questions?

"No," I told Archie, "there's no connection."

"Well, that's funny."

"I don't see you laughing."

"Funny peculiar, mate, not funny ha-ha."

Archie had dumped the envelope with all the security pictures of the MGM smurfs onto the table when we sat down. It felt like it had been about a week since I had given it to him, but it had only been a few hours ago back in the barbershop. Archie had glanced through the pictures and put them back in the envelope, and he had been carrying them around with him ever since. Now he reached out and pushed the envelope across the table to me, and I looked at him with a puzzled expression.

"I thought you wanted to keep the pictures for a while and show them to some other people."

"I don't need to show them to anybody else anymore."

"Why not?"

"Because I get it now."

"Get what, for Christ's sake?"

The lights of Bar Cristal flickered over Archie's face. He looked like a man standing under a spinning disco ball. But there was no dance floor and no disco, just a tiny bar table where two tired middle-aged guys were having a conversation that all of a sudden didn't make any sense to me at all.

Until Archie told me what he had seen in the security photos.

And then everything made even less sense.

ARCHIE REACHED OUT WITH his forefinger and tapped it slowly on the envelope that held the photos from the MGM. "You don't know who any of these people are, do you?"

I shook my head.

"Neither do I," he said, "but I can tell you at least one thing about them for sure."

"I'm all ears."

"They Koreans. Every single one of your money laundering smurfs is a Korean."

I grabbed the envelope, pulled out the stack of photos, and hastily thumbed through them.

"Koreans?" I repeated stupidly.

The pictures had been taken in a little enclave on the Chinese coast so I had just assumed the people in them were Chinese. That was about all the thought I had given to their nationality. No matter how long I lived in Asia, I still saw Asian faces like a white man. Not specifically Chinese or Indonesian or Vietnamese, just...well, Asian.

But now that Archie said the people in the pictures were Korean, I thought I could see it, too. Sort of. They looked to me like Koreans who had had some kind of plastic surgery to make them look less Korean.

"Fair dinkum, mate. The crew smurfing money through the MGM are all dinky-di Koreans, exactly like your new pal Freddy." Archie cut me the biggest wink I had ever seen. "Now what do you reckon the chances are that's only a coincidence?"

I shuffled through the photos one more time, but I didn't say anything. I didn't know what to say.

29

WHEN FREDDY OPENED HIS eyes, his first conscious thought was of how completely crappy he felt. He had a headache, his stomach was rolling, and he had a taste in his mouth like he had been sucking on sweaty athletic socks. It felt like the worst hangover he had ever had. He would kill for a drink of water.

Freddy strained to remember what he had been doing to leave him with such a massive hangover, but his mind was a complete blank. So he turned his attention instead to working out where he was and how he had gotten there. Perhaps, if he could do that, he could figure out the rest.

His starting point was that he was lying in a bed, one that wasn't immediately familiar to him. He was on top of the covers and he was fully dressed except for his shoes. He had woken in a strange bed more than once in his life, of course, but he had never been lying on top of the covers on any of those occasions, or fully dressed for that matter. So where in the world was he?

Freddy rolled his head slowly to first one side and to the other, and he examined his surroundings with as much care as he could, given his slightly tenuous connection to reality right at that moment.

He was in a room he didn't recognize, and he was alone. That much, at least, was clear.

The room was a small bedroom furnished in an altogether unremarkable way. The bed he was stretched out on was very low to the floor and positioned in the center of the room's back wall. Directly opposite it was a door. Up against the wall to the left of the bed was a small sofa upholstered in some kind of cheap looking blue fabric and up against the right wall was a beaten up dark wood table. There was a huge mirror on the wall behind the table, but there was nothing at all on any of the other walls. And there were no windows.

Was he in an interior room in some cheap hotel? The thought of a hotel room tickled something in Freddy's memory and he struggled to bring it into focus. Was that it? Was he staying in a hotel and had drunk too much and passed out? Surely not. He would never have checked into any hotel this cheap looking. At least not if he was doing the checking in entirely on his own.

Freddy struggled with the thought and felt himself drawing closer and closer to something…

Then, just like that, he remembered. The suite in the Grand Lapa. The Canadian pushing his way in. The two goons out in the hallway. And finally, the hypodermic needle, the shot, and sliding down into blackness.

Now Freddy remembered everything.

But he wished he couldn't.

FREDDY GINGERLY PUSHED HIMSELF into a sitting position and was surprised to discover he didn't feel as bad as he had thought he did. He was pretty sure he could even stand up without vomiting, but he decided he would nevertheless wait a minute or two before he pressed his luck. He tried to stay as still as possible as he took stock of his circumstances.

Whatever they shot him up with obviously hadn't been meant to kill him, so maybe the Canadian didn't want him dead. If he did, what was the point in knocking him out and bringing him to…well, to wherever he was now? To interrogate him? About what? Not only did he know nothing that his brother or anyone else in the DPRK could possibly care about, Freddy was sure the Canadian already realized he knew nothing anyone might care about. Everyone who knew him understood he wasn't involved in politics, so what could the Canadian possibly want to interrogate him about?

Freddy was certain the door he could see was locked, but he figured he should at least check. He would feel pretty stupid if he eventually discovered he had been dumped somewhere in a cheap hotel and the door wasn't even locked.

He slid his body to the edge of the bed and let his feet drop to the floor. Cautiously, he pushed himself up into a standing position. The contents of his stomach stayed where they were supposed to stay, which he viewed as a good start, so he took a step. He was a little dizzy, but not too dizzy to walk, so he took another.

And at exactly that moment the door opened.

"I'M HAPPY TO SEE you up and around," Harry Pine said, "but you really don't look so good. You should probably sit down."

Pine pointed at the blue couch. Freddy just stood there and stared so Pine took Freddy gently by the arms and steered him backward until the backs of his legs hit the couch and he collapsed onto it.

"You were out for a lot longer than we expected," Pine said. "I was getting worried about you."

"What time is it?" Freddy asked.

"It's a little after noon."

Freddy struggled with the concept. All this had started at the Grand Lapa sometime late in the afternoon or early in the evening, hadn't it? Was that yesterday? Yes, surely it was, so he had been out through the night and the morning of the next day. No wonder he was so damned thirsty.

"Could I have some water?"

One of Pine's arms moved and something flew through the air and bounced on the couch right next to Freddy. He looked down at it and recognized the familiar red and blue Evian label on the small plastic bottle. He scooped it up, broke open the cap, and took a long pull of the sweetest, most beautiful water he had ever tasted.

"Don't drink it too fast," Pine cautioned.

Freddy ignored him. He tilted the bottle up a second time and drained it. Against all odds, he started feeling better almost as soon as the water had washed the sourness out of his mouth. He dropped the empty bottle back on the couch and looked at Pine.

"Where am I?"

"You don't recognize it?"

"Why would I?"

"It's the place we work out of here in Macau. I thought you might have been here."

Freddy was confused. Did Pine think he was somehow involved in whatever he was doing here in Macau? No, of course he didn't. He knew better than that.

That was when Freddy noticed Pine was grinning at him in that particularly way men grin at each other sometimes when they think they are saying something slightly sly. He couldn't imagine what Pine was on about and his eyes swept the room looking for a clue. The couch, the bed, the table, the huge mirror next to the bed...

Suddenly he got it.

"This is a whorehouse, isn't it?"

Pine made a little clucking sound with his tongue. "That's such a harsh expression. I rather prefer to call it a men's spa."

"You're running the DPRK's business out of a whorehouse?"

"You don't think the irony is rather amusing?"

Freddy did, but he wasn't about to get into a discussion about the concept of irony right that moment so he said nothing.

"Besides," Pine continued, "there are so many men's spas in Macau that I figured no one would pay any attention to one more."

Freddy could only shake his head.

"I'll give you a tour later if you like," Pine said. "You really should see what we're doing here before you go home."

That got Freddy's full attention exactly as he gather Pine intended for it to.

"Home?"

"Yes, it will be a couple or three days before you can leave, but we'll make you as comfortable as we can until then."

"Why can't I go now?"

"Well…" Pine made a show of thinking, "the transportation question is rather complicated."

Now Freddy was confused again. Transportation? No place in Macau was more than a few minutes from anywhere. How could transportation be complicated?

"We have a shipment going out toward the end of the week," Pine went on. "I'm trying now to make arrangements for you to accompany it."

A shipment? What in the world was Pine talking about?

"How long has it been since you were home?" Pine asked.

"I don't know." Freddy thought about it. "A week or so. I went out to my house to see my wife but she wasn't there."

"Not your house in Coloane," Pine smiled. "I meant Pyongyang."

And all of a sudden Freddy understood what was going to happen to him.

"You're sending me to Pyongyang?"

Pine nodded.

"But why? I haven't been there in fifteen years."

"Because you're planning to defect to the US. Your brother and the wise men can't have that, can they? You ought to imagine the embarrassment they would suffer. You should have realized they simply won't allow it to happen."

"So my brother told you to kidnap me and ship me to Pyongyang?"

"Not exactly. I actually got orders to kill you, but I can't get confirmation that your brother approves of that order or even knows about it. If I do kill you, and if he doesn't approve, it's my ass."

"So you're shipping me back instead of killing me."

Pine snapped his fingers and pointed at Freddy. "I knew you were a smart guy. I send you back to Pyongyang and it's your brother's problem what to do with you."

"So you're sending me to Pyongyang with…what? Weapons? Missile parts?"

"Don't be silly. We sell that shit. We don't buy it."

Freddy waited. He knew Pine would tell him eventually, and then Pine did.

"Money, my friend. Damn near eight hundred million Hong Kong dollars. All freshly laundered and ready to go out in the world and buy the wise men in Pyongyang whatever things they most fancy in the depths of their black little hearts."

Freddy did the math in his head. Eight hundred million Hong Kong was something like a hundred million United States dollars. He had no idea what kind of businesses Pine was running out of this whorehouse, but it wasn't hookers if he was generating that kind of income. Certainly not Korean hookers.

Drugs? Gunrunning? Christ, was it nuclear weapons? Had to be something big to earn that kind of money.

"I DON'T WANT TO go to Pyongyang."

"Who does?"

"Isn't there some alternative?"

"Sure, I could shoot you. How does that sound?"

"It might be better than going to Pyongyang."

"Actually, it doesn't really matter what you want," Pine said. "When this shipment is ready to go out, you're going with it. After you get to Pyongyang you and your brother can have a good old family reunion and he can decide what to do with you. At least you'll be out of my hair."

"I don't want to go to Pyongyang."

"Yeah, you said that. You want to go to Hawaii. Me, too, but ain't neither of us going to get our wish."

"I don't know anything about what you're doing here. I can't possibly tell—"

Pine held up his right hand like a traffic cop.

"Save your breath, man. There's nothing to discuss. This is how it's going down. I'll get food and water brought to you and get you out of here in another day or two, but that's the best I can do for you."

Freddy sighed and looked down at his feet.

"After you get there you can work things out with your brother. Just leave me out of it. I'm only a working stiff. I don't get involved in all this political shit."

And with that, Pine turned on his heel and disappeared through the door. Freddy heard two solid thunks that had to be two bolts slamming shut outside. He wasn't going anywhere until Pine decided he was. And then he was going to Pyongyang.

Freddy fell back on the couch, rolled onto his side, and buried his head in his hands.

30

I LEFT ARCHIE SITTING in Bar Cristal, crossed the east lobby of the Wynn, and headed out to *Avenida 24 de Junho* to walk the short distance back to the MGM.

It didn't occur to me until I was halfway down the driveway that this was the very spot where I had been ducking gunfire a few weeks back. I scanned the street for any sign of shooters on a motorbike and checked around for another handy Rolls Royce to dive behind just in case, but all I saw were a bus, a couple of taxis, and a few people on foot who looked anxious to get into the Wynn's casino and empty their pockets as quickly as possible.

I walked a block to the back entry to the MGM, cut through the casino to the lobby, and less than ten minutes later was stretched out on the couch in my suite, lighting a Montecristo.

Some people looked upon the act of smoking a cigar as something pugnacious, perhaps even aggressive, but in my experience the only people who thought that were people who didn't smoke cigars. People who did smoke cigars knew the truth was quite the opposite. The process of cutting, lighting, and puffing a cigar into life kindles along with it a few moments of utter tranquility. Smoking a cigar, if it is a good one, is a contemplative act, even a meditative one. I did some of my best thinking with a Montecristo in my teeth, and that was what I needed right now. Good thinking.

So I took another puff, studied the ceiling, and started putting a few things together…

Maybe I was right in the middle of some huge coincidence. Maybe Kim Jong-Nam suddenly turning up in my life and getting himself kidnapped had absolutely nothing to do with the discovery that a bunch of Koreans touched up by plastic surgery were laundering massive amounts of currency through the MGM casino.

What was the chance of that?

No fucking chance whatsoever.

I would bet my last dollar it was the North Korean government that was behind the money laundering operation at the MGM. And who else but the North Korean government would want to kidnap Kim Jong-Nam?

The two things were connected by something or somebody, even if I couldn't yet see exactly what, or who, that connection was.

That was when I saw the very first signs of an idea in the tendrils of smoke reaching for the ceiling from my Montecristo.

Maybe I could make this work for me. Maybe I could even find a way to use the connection to find Freddy.

BY THE TIME I had finished my Montecristo and watched the butt burn itself out in the heavy glass ashtray on the coffee table, I was gratified to discover those first signs had very helpfully grown into something not too far from a full fledged plan. But there was a problem with it, and it was a pretty significant problem. The plan required manpower. Not an army exactly, but not a couple of guys either. Ideally, I figured we needed about a dozen people to do it right, but six people and a little luck would probably work, too. Where was I going to get manpower like that?

The only person I could think of who might be able to round

up some bodies for me at short notice was Pete Logan. Would he be willing to help? It was Pete who had lured me to Macau in the first place, presumably to help out the FBI, so he could hardly claim to be aggrieved or give me a hard time for asking for his help now, could he? Of course he could…

I pull out my cell phone, found Pete's number, and hit the call button.

"SHIT, JACKO, THIS BETTER be good."

I could hear sounds behind Pete. I wasn't certain what they were, but they sounded familiar somehow. A restaurant? A bar? Something like that. I glanced at my watch. A little before midnight in Macau, but God only knew where Pete was so I had no idea what time it was for him.

"Where are you?" I asked.

"In bed."

I had meant what country he was in, of course, but I didn't press the point. "It doesn't sound like you're in bed."

"The TV's on."

It wasn't a TV I was hearing, I was certain of that, but I didn't argue with Pete. What did I care if he was having a late dinner with some woman or even sitting in a Bangkok go-go bar surrounded by topless dancers? I went ahead and told him why I was calling and what I had in mind.

When I was finished, he said, "Not bad, Jacko. Not bad at all."

I was so surprised Pete didn't pee all over me that I didn't know what to say.

"How many men do you think you'll need?" he continued before I could think of anything.

"A dozen to do it right."

"Not possible."

"Six would probably be the minimum."

"I can give you one."

"One?"

"Yeah. Me."

"You? Can't you send me a few Bureau guys from the Hong Kong office?"

"Uh-uh."

I thought about that. After a moment, I understood.

"When you pushed me into working for Pansy Ho it wasn't an official bureau operation, was it? Whatever this is, it's strictly your own deal."

"That depends on what your definition of it is."

"That sounds even stupider coming from you than it did from Bill Clinton when he was trying to explain away a blow job."

"Look, Jacko, Pansy needed your help and I thought you helping her might help me, so I leaned on you a little. What's the big deal?"

"You let me think this was a Bureau operation."

"It is. I'm Bureau and this is my operation. So it's a Bureau operation. *Comprende*, pal?"

This wasn't getting us anywhere and it was the middle of the night and I was tired. So I let it go. For now.

"I'll see you in the morning," Pete said. "We'll figure something out."

In the morning? That was less than eight hours away and there weren't any middle of the night flights from Bangkok to Macau.

Now the familiar background noise I had heard when Pete first answered his phone was starting to make sense. Pete was already here in Macau. Probably hanging around in one of the casinos. Maybe playing a little blackjack. But what the hell was he doing here? Watching me?

"Nine o'clock?" Pete asked before I could ask him about that.

"Better make it a little later. I want to talk to Pansy first."

"Good idea. Why don't you come out to the Venetian about noon?"

So Pete was at the Venetian…

"There's a Fat Burger in the food court on the third floor," he went on. "I seem to remember you like a Fat Burger every now and then."

I did. I hadn't had a Fat Burger since I was in Dubai, and the less I thought about having a Fat Burger in Dubai the happier I was.

"See you there at noon tomorrow," I said, and hung up.

I WAS IN PANSY'S office by nine the next morning, suitably energized by three cups of coffee and a pretty decent bagel slathered in cream cheese.

"The people who are smurfing your casino have to be operating from somewhere," I told her. "They're bringing in piles of US dollars and Euros every day and they're not keeping all that currency at home under their beds. They're picking it up somewhere before they go to the casino, then I'm guessing they take the Hong Kong dollars they get from you back to the same place they picked it up. If we can find that place, we'll know who we're dealing with, and we can figure out a way to stop them."

"So you want to put some of these people who're bringing in this money under surveillance and see where they go when they leave here?"

"I think that's the best way to nail down who's really behind the money laundering."

And of course I figured if I found the place where the Koreans were running their money laundering operations, I might find Freddy, too. I just didn't see any need to mention that part to Pansy.

"How are you going to do it?" she asked.

That was the question, wasn't it? I had three guys: Pete, Archie, and me. The MGM casino was huge. The three of us had no chance of covering it. I suppose I could have asked Pansy to give me some of their security staff, but the truth was that I didn't trust locals I didn't know. If the Koreans were tipped off, they would be gone in a moment and with them would go any chance I had of finding the source of the money or where Freddy was. No locals. I couldn't take the chance.

"All I need is for your cashiers to keep an eye out for people bringing in large numbers of $50 bills or €100 notes, and let me know when they spot somebody. We'll take it from there."

"Who's we?"

I didn't want Pansy to know that it was just me and two other guys, she would laugh, so I smiled and winked. Let her think I had the whole fucking CIA on call.

"Okay, I see," she said. "It's probably better if I don't know exactly what you're doing anyway."

I nodded again. On the other hand, it would be certainly better if I did know, but I didn't. I was making this up as I went along.

AFTER I LEFT PANSY'S office I spent a couple of hours with Gerald Brady going over plans of the casino floor and working out an arrangement for the cashiers to alert me to any out-of-the-ordinary movement they spotted in $50 bills or €100 notes. I would have been happier not even to involve Brady, but there was no way to make this work without an inside man at the casino, and since Brady was head of security he was the obvious candidate. I had no reason to mistrust Brady since Pansy obviously trusted him, and besides he already knew I was trying to run down the source of the money laundering activity and it was still going on. If Brady was a risk for warning them off, he would have already done it, wouldn't he? I told myself he would have. That helped. A little.

The plan was pretty simple. When a cashier was asked to exchange a large number of $50 bills or €100 notes, he would tell the customer that his counting machine was out of order, step back into the enclosed counting room that was behind every cashier's cage, presumably to find a counting machine that was functional, and telephone Brady with a description of the smurf. After that the cashier would return to the cage and give the smurf his chips as if everything were completely in order.

The moment Brady got the call, he would call me and give me the location of the cage and repeat the physical description of the smurf his cashier had given him. If we were in a position to pick up the smurf without being spotted, we would try to cover him until he cashed in his chips and follow him back to wherever he was taking the Hong Kong dollars he got for them. If we weren't in a good position to cover the smurf, we would let him go and wait for the next one.

See, a deceptively simple plan. Some might say simple-minded.

The problem, of course, was that when a cashier alerted Brady we had to be in a position in the casino to get to the right cashier's cage before the smurf took his chips and melted into the crowd. If we weren't close enough, we would never pick him up. And three white guys could hardly hang around the cashiers' cages of a casino for twenty-four hours a day without being ridiculously conspicuous in a sea of Chinese faces.

In other words, we were going to have to get lucky. Very lucky.

WHEN BRADY AND I were done, I went back to the suite to call Archie and read him in on the plan. After I told him about Pete and where we were meeting at the Venetian at noon, Archie thought about it for a moment. "What the fuck is a Fat Burger?" he asked.

"It's an American hamburger place. They're all over. They make great burgers, and their onion rings and milkshakes are—"

"This place is actually called the Fat Burger?" Archie interrupted before I could go all rhapsodic on him.

"Really. It is."

Archie grunted. "That's way too American for me, mate."

"I don't care. Be there at noon. It's on the third floor of the Venetian, in the far back corner of the food court. We'll be the two white guys in the middle of about a million Chinese."

"Fat Burger," Archie muttered again, and hung up.

I assumed that meant he would be there.

31

THE VENETIAN'S VAST CASINO is located at the center of a ring of indoor canals lined on both sides by enough designer shops to make Fifth Avenue quiver with jealousy. A huge domed ceiling that looks eerily like a real blue sky with puffy white clouds blowing across it rounds off the illusion. The hallucination is real enough to be seriously disorienting until you stop shaking your head and treat it as if it actually makes all the sense in the world.

Naturally, the Venetian's canals are all plied day and night by serenading gondoliers in full costume, although the gondolas are actually run by concealed electric motors and the gondoliers only pretend to row. It's like almost everything else you see in Macau. The real story is hidden away somewhere beneath the surface.

The Venetian's food court is tucked into the back of another, less distinguished wing of shops that branches off from the Grand Canal. It is a considerably less atmospheric area than where the designer shops preen behind their imitation seventeenth century shop fronts. It is actually little more than an enormous open area filled with black Formica tables and white plastic chairs, surrounded on all sides by at least fifty small food stalls. Almost all of the food is Chinese, as are almost all of the customers, and the Fat Burger's red and yellow neon sign in the far back corner stood out to me like a beacon of hope in a desert of flat noodles.

I realized right away that Pete's selection of a meeting place had been shrewd. The food court was packed, the noise was overwhelming, and the crowds were in constant motion. It wasn't a place for relaxation, it was a place to eat as quickly as possible and get back to the tables or the slots. No one would be paying the slightest attention to three white guys munching quietly on burgers among a mob of hyperactive Chinese gamblers.

Pete was waiting at a table right in the middle of the whole hubbub, and I made my way toward him through the masses of Chinese carrying red plastic trays piled with odd-looking animal parts. I could only assume the stuff was edible, but I did my best not to think about the suspicious smells in the air. I wondered if most of those Chinese felt the same way about a thick, juicy cheeseburger crammed with lettuce, tomatoes, pickles, and onions.

When I got to the table, Pete had almost finished his burger and was slurping on what appeared to have once been a vanilla milkshake. I pulled up a plastic chair and said, "I've got one more guy coming."

Pete raised his eyes to ask the obvious question and I started telling him about Archie.

"Archie Ward?" Pete interrupted almost immediately. "You know Archie Ward?"

I stopped talking and nodded. I should have guessed. Archie knew everybody in Asia who mattered and Pete mattered. Of course they would know each other.

I WENT TO THE counter of the Fat Burger and got myself a cheeseburger and a Diet Coke. By the time I got back to the table, Archie had arrived and he and Pete were yucking it up about something, but they stopped laughing and fell silent as I sat down. Apparently I didn't have a need to know whatever it was that they thought was so funny. I certainly hoped the object of their levity wasn't my plan, such as it was.

Between bites of burger, I gave them the details of what I had in mind. I related the arrangements I had with Gerald Brady to be alerted when one of the cashiers spotted somebody buying chips with an unusual number of $50 bills or €100 notes, and I explained how, with a little luck, we would pick up the smurf and stay with him as long as he was in the casino. We would watch him cash in his chips in for Hong Kong dollars and follow him through Macau back to wherever he was delivering the freshly laundered currency.

When I finished there was a little silence and I caught Archie and Pete exchanging a glance.

Pete gave one more pull at the straw in his now empty milkshake glass and asked, "That's your plan?"

"Well...yeah."

Archie shook his head. "You got two chances, mate. None and Buckley's."

Now I was getting confused. "Who's Buckley?"

"Never mind, Jack," Pete jumped in. "It's a thing Aussies say. He means you've got no chance at all to make that work."

I chewed the last of my burger and wiped my mouth with a napkin. "Okay, smart guys, then tell me what your plan is and we'll do that."

Nobody said anything.

"Archie? Pete? Anybody?" I shook my head. "No, I didn't think so. So here's where I come out. Until you've got a better idea, shut the fuck up and do what I tell you to do. Agreed?"

Still nobody said anything so I decided to take that as agreement.

"We'll start at three today," I said, looking from one to the other. "We'll spread out through the casino and cover it until midnight. When Brady calls me, I'll call both of you and give you a description and location. If one of us can get on the smurf before he's lost in the crowd, the other two can catch up and we'll set up a surveillance net."

"What do we do when he leaves the casino?" Archie asked.

”What are you going to do if the target gets into a car or onto a motorbike? What if he goes to the ferry terminal and catches a helicopter to Hong Kong?”

I shrugged. “I told you we’ll need a little luck.”

“A little,” Pete snorted. “Sounds to me like you need a whole shit load of luck.”

“What if none of the cashiers pick up anybody and Brady doesn’t call?” Archie asked.

“We’ll do the same thing again tomorrow and, if necessary, the day after that. According to the cash management reports, since this started there’s never been a three day period without money being moved.”

“Okay, Jacko,” Pete said, “we’ll do this your way. But I sure hope the little fuckers turn up before I lose all my money. There’s no way I’m hanging around a casino for nine hours without playing a little blackjack.”

Archie made a face. “Do whatever you want, Pete, I’ll be in one of the bars.”

“Wonderful,” I said, shaking my head. “I’ve only got two guys to pull this off with and one of them is a gambler and the other is a drunk.”

“Sounds okay,” Archie said.

“No problem,” Pete said.

NOTHING HAPPENED THAT NIGHT. I called Archie, twice, to make sure he was still sober, and Pete once to try to keep his mind on my game rather than his, but not a single cashier spotted any unusual quantities of $50 bills or €100 notes.

I walked around the casino for a while and peered at faces as inconspicuously as possible, but when everyone I saw started looking a little Korean to me and more or less like all the security photos, I gave that up as hopeless.

The baccarat tables were the most crowded area on the casino floor, of course. The Chinese were crazy for baccarat, and I had always suspected that was because winning at baccarat was the result of pure luck. Skill didn't come into it at all. Blackjack, on the other hand, actually required at least some minimal knowledge and attention so it wasn't nearly as popular. The slots were a big draw, too, possibly for the same reason the baccarat tables were. Then there were those purely Chinese table games like Pai Gow, Sic Bo, and Fan Tan. I didn't understand any them, and I didn't know a single westerner who did.

Every time I made a circuit of the casino floor I passed Pete working the blackjack tables and Archie sprawled out on a comfortable looking sofa in the Lion Bar. They both looked like they were having a lot better time than I was so by nine o'clock I gave up my pacing, plopped down on the couch next to Archie, and ordered a Diet Coke.

"You ready to call it a night?" he asked.

I shook my head, but before I could say anything my phone rang. I looked at Archie. This could be it…

"Hello?"

"Hey, I'm up over $1000 and I figure I ought to quit while I'm ahead," Pete said.

Archie raised his eyebrows at me in a question. I shook my head and he went back to sipping his drink.

"So you want to pack it in?" Pete asked.

"I said midnight and that's still more than two hours away."

"Yeah, but I'm ahead."

"You could always quit playing."

"That's what I'm telling you. I want to quit playing. I'm ready to leave."

"You can't quit playing blackjack unless you leave the casino?"

Pete didn't answer me, which was pretty much an answer right there.

"Oh man," I said, "I can't believe I'm stuck with these two clowns."

THE AFTERNOON HAD BEEN so quiet on the casino floor that I thought it was unlikely any of the smurfs would hit the place until it was more crowded. That was usually from the early evening on into the early hours of the morning, and so the next night we set up at six, intending to stay through until well after midnight.

Pete had managed to lose all but about $100 of his winnings back to the house before I finally called things off the night before, and he was more than a little pissed with me about it. He brushed aside my observation that he had been free to stop playing anytime he wanted. Rather he saw it as my personal responsibility that he was about $900 lighter today than he could have been. If I was going to take the blame for his losses, I figured the least Pete could do was give me credit for his winnings, if not actually split them with me, but he didn't think much of that argument.

The three of us met in the Lion Bar about six and I bought Pete a beer to smooth things over. Archie had his usual whiskey and I ordered…yes, another Diet Coke. The drinks hadn't been on our table more than a couple of minutes when my phone rang. Both Archie and Pete's heads swiveled toward me as I took it out and answered.

"Hello?"

"It's Brady, Jack. The cashiers in position 9 at Cage B just took in $10,000, all in $50 bills. Where are you?"

"We're in the Lion Bar. Right under that big chandelier in the middle."

"Okay, here's what you do. Walk straight ahead to the second marble walkway. It's got big number 8s laid out on it in a mosaic design. Turn left. There will be blackjack tables to your right and Sic Bo tables to your left. Walk all the way to the end of that walkway and to the left you'll see a line of cashiers' windows in the back wall. There are numbers over each window designating the cashier positions. I'll tell number 9 you're on your way and to stall the smurf as long as possible."

"Do you have a description?"

"Female, mid-thirties, about five foot four, short black hair, wearing jeans and a yellow t-shirt. Large black purse over her shoulder."

"Got it. Thanks."

I stood up and dropped some money on the table.

"Let's kick some ass, guys."

32

WE WALKED AS FAST as we could without attracting attention and I filled Archie and Pete in on what Brady had told me. I had plenty of time to do it. It was a long walk to the cashier who had raised the alarm.

"Female, mid-thirties, five foot four, short black hair, jeans and a yellow t-shirt," Archie repeated like a man memorizing his part in a play.

"She'll be long gone before we get there," Pete said.

"Let's spread out and go in from different directions. Maybe she'll pass one of us coming back this way or we'll spot her at a table."

Archie went left between two Sic Bo tables and was quickly swallowed up in the clouds of cigarette smoke rising from the mob of Chinese gamblers. I turned to say something to Pete, but all I saw was his back disappearing off to the right behind a roulette table. That left me to continue along the walkway and follow Brady's original directions to the cashier.

I noticed that all the tables I passed had plenty of comfortable-looking upholstered chairs around them, but not many people were sitting in them. Instead, the players were standing around the tables, peering intently, even grimly at the progress of whatever game they were trying to outwit. Comfort and relaxation isn't really part of the Chinese view of gambling. Gambling is serious work, a way to get rich, not a pastime. What did being comfortable have to do with anything?

I was walking past a casino worker pushing a teacart at a stately pace when I saw a flash of yellow off to my left. I stopped so abruptly that the elderly man walking behind me stumbled into the teacart and knocked two empty cups onto the floor. He muttered something at me in Mandarin as he brushed past. I had no idea what he was saying, but somehow I doubted it was *Welcome to our country, foreigner!*

I turned in the direction where I had seen the flash of yellow and moved as quickly as I could. The casino was so crowded I didn't have a clear line of sight for more than twenty feet in any direction so I kept my head and eyes moving back and forth in front of me, peered into the crush of bodies as well as I could, and hoped for the best.

It was only a minute or two before I spotted her.

SHE WAS SITTING IN front of a video poker machine. Yellow t-shirt, jeans, middle-aged, short black hair. She didn't look particularly Korean, and I didn't recognize her from the security photos I had seen, but that didn't really mean much. She clearly met the description the cashier had given Brady.

I walked past the woman without turning my head, moved quickly up another aisle of video poker machines, and came around behind her. I sat down on a stool about a dozen machines away and pretended to study its operating directions while watching her out of the corner of my eye. She was attractive enough, slim and feminine in her movements, and she sat primly on the stool, legs crossed, playing slowly like a woman more interested in killing time than in winning money. I took out my phone to call Archie, but before I could dial him it buzzed in my hand.

"I've got her," Archie said when I answered. "She's at a slot machine."

"I've got her, too. But it's a video poker machine, not a slot."

"I thought she was supposed to be by herself."

"She is by herself."

"Doesn't look like that to me. That guy on the next stool looks awfully friendly."

I swiveled my head back toward the woman in the yellow t-shirt who was still playing her video poker machine without much apparent interest. There was nobody on the stool next to her.

Oh shit.

"We're looking at two different women, Archie."

"But mine matches the description perfectly."

"Mine, too. Where are you?"

"I'm standing in front of a platform with a red Bentley on it. Do they sell cars here or something?"

"Nope. They're giving it away."

"They're giving a Bentley away?"

"It's the grand prize this week in some sort of progressive slot machine deal. Don't ask me how it works."

"Well fuck me dead. A free Bentley? Bloody hell."

I stood up and walked out of the aisle of poker machines into a relatively open area and looked around until I saw the red car up on a platform.

"You're about two hundred feet from me, Archie, back in the direction of the Lion Bar."

I listened to Archie exhale heavily on the other end of the phone. "Okay, mate," he said, "what do you want to do now?"

I mulled over Archie's question while I walked back toward where I had been sitting. Could we possibly keep both women covered until we figured out which was the right one? I was thinking so hard about how we might be able to do it that I didn't notice for a moment that the woman wasn't sitting in front of her video poker machine any longer. And when I did notice, my first thought was I must have gone into a different aisle of poker machines by mistake.

But I hadn't. The woman I had been watching wasn't where I had left her.

"She's gone, Archie. Call Pete and get him to come to your position. I'm going to try and find this one again."

"Roger that."

I disconnected, shoved the phone into my pocket, and walked over to the stool where the woman had been sitting. When I got to it, I wondered why I had bothered. What was I going to do, collect DNA or something? I needed to know where this woman was going, not prove she had been here. I looked around. Not a sign of her. She couldn't have gone far. I hadn't stepped away to look for Archie for more than a minute, probably less. So which way? Right, or left? I flipped a mental coin.

Right.

There was a broad walkway to the right that ran through a small flotilla of at least thirty Caribbean stud poker tables, and off in the distance at the end of it I could see an exit from the casino. I thought it was the exit that was opposite the entrance to the Wynn Macau, but I wasn't absolutely certain. If it was, and if the lady in yellow went out through there and back into the casino at the Wynn, I'd never find her.

Making straight for the exit, I kept my eyes moving back but I got no joy. No flashes of yellow. I knew I could be going in the wrong direction altogether so I pulled out my phone and called Archie.

"I'm walking toward an exit, but I don't see her. She may be outside already."

"My girl's still playing her slot, but the guy who was hustling her has hit the road."

"Is Pete with you?"

"I see him coming now."

"Okay, tell Pete to sit on her and you head for the exit that's on the other side of the Bentley sign. I'm going to…wait, I got her!"

The lady in yellow was walking crisply toward the exit from the left. I was pretty sure there was another cashier's cage off in the direction she was coming from, and that could only mean…

"She's cashed out, Archie, and she's heading outside! This has to be the right one!"

"I'm on my way."

The closer I got to the exit the thinner the crowds became so I found myself covering ground faster. It looked like I was going to hit the exit about a hundred feet behind her. But what the hell was I going to do after that?

If she crossed the street and went into the Wynn after she got outside, I was toast. Even if she didn't go into the Wynn, I didn't much like my chances of keeping up with her on the street without being made. Following people looked easy in the movies, but I had tried it a couple of times in real life and for some reason it never worked out quite the same way for me that it did for Matt Damon.

The lady in yellow reached the exit and pushed out through the big brass doors. About ten seconds later, so did I, and a moment later I was standing out on the curb of *Praceta 24 de Junho* looking toward the entrance to the Wynn on the other side.

I quickly spotted the woman walking away from me a little less than a hundred feet off to my left. Suddenly she veered off the sidewalk and climbed the steps into a bus that was parked at the curb.

Shit, shit, shit!

What was I going to now? Hail a cab and shout *Follow that bus*? And, by the way, how exactly did I say *Follow that bus* in Mandarin?

I was still trying to decide what to do when Archie walked up beside me. I pointed at the bus.

"So now we know she wasn't the right one," he said.

"What are you talking about?"

"The bus. Look at the sign on the front of it."

There was indeed a large sign taped in the front window of the bus, but it was written entirely in Chinese characters and meant less than nothing to me.

"You can read Chinese?" I asked Archie.

Archie gave me a look. "That's a junket bus," he said. "It shuttles Chinese gamblers back and forth from Zhuhai right across the border in China. Tens of thousands of Chinese day-trippers come in every day and go right back after they give all their money to the casinos. There's no one on that bus that isn't a mainland Chinese. I promise you that."

I pulled out my phone and called Pete. He answered and I quickly asked him, "Is the girl you're watching still at the table?"

There was a short silence and I knew what Pete was going to say before he said it, but he said it anyway.

"I never found her. Archie told me where she was when he lit out after you, but she wasn't where I thought he told me to look. Either I misunderstood him or she left before I got here. What happened to the one you were following?"

I told him.

"Well…shit," Pete said, and I thought that summed up where we were pretty well.

I told Pete to meet us in the Lion Bar, and Archie and I turned around and headed back inside.

THE LION BAR AT THE MGM is usually a pretty good place to hang out. It's comfortable, cool, and sophisticated, and they have a great selection of malt whiskys. Even better, it has a reputation for attracting an enticing crowd of young Filipina women.

The problem right at that moment was that I didn't feel particularly comfortable, cool, or sophisticated, and I was drinking a Diet Coke. And I was so pissed off I didn't even notice if there were any women in the place, Filipino or otherwise.

"We'll get another shot, Jack."

Pete sounded like he meant it and so I nodded. Yes, we would get another shot, but now I had real doubts this was going to work when we did. Certainly not without far more luck than I had any right to hope for.

Archie and Pete had tried to tell me how tough it would be to pick up one of the smurfs in a crowded casino and stay on them until they got to wherever they were going. Between the vast size of the casino, the multitude of exits, and the huge number of forms of transportation available once the target was outside, I now understood what they had been saying. It seemed like an impossible task to pull off with only three guys. I had let my optimism rule my good sense and now my good sense had pushed its way to the front of the line and was having a good laugh at my expense.

"What do you want to do, Jack?" Archie asked.

"I have to have a pee. Let me think about it until I get back."

I walked across the Lion Bar and went out into the casino looking for a men's room. I passed the stage where the bands worked later in the evening and turned up a walkway that according to the overhead signs led to the hotel's main lobby. I hadn't gone more than fifty feet when I saw a woman walking straight toward me.

She wasn't wearing blue jeans or a yellow t-shirt, or carrying a black purse. She was in a black pants suit and her purse was red. And she wasn't middle-aged and slim. She was young, probably in her mid-twenties, wearing glasses too big for her face, and a bit on the chunky side.

But I recognized her. She was one of the faces in the security photos. She was one of the smurfs. I had not the slightest doubt about it.

There no plan better than pure dumb luck, is there?

We were back in business.

33

FREDDY HAD NO IDEA what time it was when Pine came for him. He never wore a watch. Knowing what time it was in a place like Macau had never really seemed all that important. Judging by the delivery of his meals, he thought he had been there about two days, but he wasn't even certain of that.

"We're moving you," Pine said.

"To Pyongyang?"

"No, we're cleaning up."

Freddy's head snapped up. *Did that mean…?*

"Don't worry," Pine said when he realized what Freddy was thinking. "I only meant we're taking you someplace else for a day or two, not killing you. We'll ship you to Pyongyang when the load is ready to go."

"Load?"

"Never mind. I talk too much. I know I talk too much and yet I still do it. Funny, isn't it?"

Freddy was glad to hear Pine hadn't decided to shoot him after all at least, and he was happy too to know that he still had a day or two before he was being sent to Pyongyang. Every day he was somewhere other than Pyongyang was a day that something might happen to keep him from being sent there. Maybe he would find some way to get in touch with Shepherd and be rescued. Maybe Pine would die. Maybe he would die. Well…not that, of course.

Pine had left the door open. Freddy couldn't see anything outside except a dim hallway, but he eyed it nevertheless. It wasn't much of an escape chance, he knew, but it was something. Then two of Pine's goons came through the door and it was nothing.

The man tossed a piece of dark cloth to Pine. Pine caught it and held it out to Freddy.

"I'm going to have to ask you to wear a hood," he said. "It's for your own protection really. The less you know about our operations here, the better it will be for you."

"I don't know anything at all."

"And take it from me, you want to keep it that way."

Pine held out the hood and Freddy took it. What else was he going to do? He pulled it over his head. It wasn't uncomfortable and he could breathe fine, but the inside of it smelled funny. Like steamed broccoli. It made no sense that the inside of the hood would smell like steamed broccoli, but it did.

Pine or someone pulled the drawstrings on the sides of the hood. They tightened around his neck and he was in darkness.

SOMEONE TOOK HIS ARM and led him forward a few steps, turned him to the right, and tugged him gently forward. Freddy walked with a shuffling gait like his feet had been chained together, although they hadn't been. It was simply a disconcerting feeling to have to walk without being able to see anything and it made you walk funny.

"We're coming to the stairs."

He was surprised to hear Pine's voice close to his ear. He had assumed it was one of the heavies who was gripping his left arm and pulling him along, but apparently it was Pine.

"There are two flights. Walk slowly. I won't let you fall."

DOWN THE STAIRS, another fifteen or twenty steps straight ahead, and they stopped. Freddy heard the sound of a door opening and he felt cool, moist air on his skin and heard that low murmur that every city gives off no matter how quiet the streets might be. They started walking again and he felt the surface change under his feet from indoors to outdoors.

"I'm going to put you in a van. You'll be in the back. There's a mattress on the floor and I want you to lie down on it. Do not take off the hood. One of my men will be watching you and it will go very badly for you if you try to remove it."

Freddy had no intention of removing his hood. He didn't want to see a damned thing. But when he heard the muffled sound of his own voice coming back at him from inside the hood he nodded instead of trying to talk.

Somewhere in front of them Freddy heard a metallic creaking sound that he assumed was the doors of the van being opened. With Pine tugging on his left arm he continued to shuffle slowly forward until he bumped gently into something solid about at waist level.

"Okay, you're there," Pine said. "Let me help you up."

Pine tugged at his elbow and turned him around. With surprising gentleness, he tried to lift Freddy up into the van, but Freddy hardly budged.

"Man, you got to lose some weight," Pine laughed.

Freddy shrugged. Even if he could have made himself understood through the goddamned hood he wouldn't have been much interested in discussing his weight problem with Pine. He supposed that was the upside to being sent to Pyongyang. At least he would lose a little weight. Probably quite a bit of weight…

Pine took his hands away and a moment later Freddy was lifted from both sides, so he gathered Pine's two thugs had taken over. He felt the metal floor of the van under his butt and his legs and, when he reached out with his hands to steady himself, he felt the mattress, too. He pulled himself further into the van and rolled onto the mattress. It was actually pretty comfortable. Better than the one he had been sleeping on for the last two days.

The back doors of the van slammed, followed a few moments later by both of the front doors. The engine started and Freddy felt the van begin to move.

FREDDY WONDERED IF HE shouldn't start counting or something so later he would be able to say how far they had driven. Since he had no idea where they were starting from, however, it wouldn't mean much to know how long it took them to get to wherever they were going, would it?

He knew he wouldn't be long. You couldn't drive much more than twenty minutes in any direction in Macau, even if the traffic was heavy. The whole place was surrounded by water except for the narrow neck of land crossed by the Chinese border, and he seriously doubted that Pine would be driving across the Chinese border with a guy lying in the back of his van wearing a black hood. Besides, why would Pine want to take him into China anyway? Could the Chinese government somehow be involved with helping North Korea run their operations in Macau? No, there wasn't a chance in the world of that. Whatever the DPRK was up to in Macau, they were doing it on their own. He had no doubt whatsoever about that.

Freddy tried to work out from the sounds he could hear where they were going. There was really no point in doing that either, he knew. When he got to where they were taking him, that's where he would be. What earthly difference would it make whether he had figured it out in advance? Still, he listened and tried to guess since he didn't have anything better to do.

For the first ten minutes or so he heard nothing he was able to identify, only the normal sounds of traffic all around them. The van did seem to be moving at a good clip though, which narrowed down the possibilities quite a bit. There weren't many roads in Macau where you could drive steadily at speed rather than bumping along from one traffic light to the next. He felt the road surface change and heard the hollow sound tires make when they are crossing a bridge and suddenly he knew exactly where they were. They were crossing one of the long bridges that tied the Macau peninsula to the islands of Taipa and Coloane. But were they going north toward the Chinese border or south toward where his house was at the edge of the South China Sea?

Freddy's guess was they were heading south. He had heard traffic around them when they first started out and there wasn't any traffic to the south on Coloane. It was more likely they had begun the journey on the crowded peninsula and were now moving toward the less crowded part of Macau, not the other way around. The more Freddy thought about it, the more certain he was that he was right, but he also had to admit that his insight was of no value at all in getting his ass out of this before it got shipped to Pyongyang.

THERE WERE ONLY TWO ways out of Macau if you didn't count the land crossing into China, and Freddy had already written that possibility off. One was by air, and one was by sea. If he were being sent to Pyongyang, it would be one or the other.

Macau's port was fairly small since no passenger vessels called there at all and most of the cargo for the area went through the huge container port in Hong Kong. There wasn't much use in trying to duplicate Hong Kong's extensive facilities in Macau. Hong Kong was too close and it was far cheaper to barge cargo back and forth to the port there. Still, there was a tiny container port in Macau and it was out on the north edge of Taipa close to the airport.

Freddy had never actually been to it, but he knew where it was, and he knew that occasionally North Korean ships called there. He had always wondered why they did, since surely the amount of commercial trade between Macau and North Korea was negligible. Maybe they were the line of communications between the DPRK and Pine's operations in Macau. Maybe the DPRK moved their people in and out of Macau on the freighters making those occasional port calls here. Maybe now he was going to be one of those people.

Flying him out was the other possibility. The airport in Macau was small, too, and taking him out through the commercial side certainly wasn't going to happen. They could hardly go out on a regular flight. There were no direct flights to Pyongyang and you couldn't exactly sit in an airport lounge somewhere sipping a beer and waiting for your connection when you were traveling with someone you had kidnapped who was wearing a black hood over his head. If they took him out by air, it would have to be a private flight of some kind. Perhaps a cargo flight. That could be how the DPRK moved their people in and out of Macau. Not on ships, but on cargo flights.

THE VAN STOPPED AND Freddy heard muffled conversation followed by a creaking noise. The van started rolling again right after that, but more slowly now. It sounded to him like they had probably passed through a gate.

After three or four minutes, the van stopped for a second time and Freddy heard more creaking and finally a bang. Had they pulled into some kind of parking area, a garage perhaps, and slammed a door behind them?

The more Freddy thought about it, the less it seemed to matter one way or another. Here he was lying in the back of a van with a hood tied over his head and Pine and his muscle boys were sitting in the front of the van. He closed his eyes and sighed. Pine was going to do whatever he wanted with him. The idea that he might find a way to escape or that Jack Shepherd might rescue him was a ridiculous fantasy.

His life in Macau was over. His dream of going to Hawaii was dead. All he had left now was to hope that he wasn't dead, too.

On the other hand, if the alternative was to be shipped to Pyongyang…

34

COMPARED TO THE LADY in yellow, the lady in black was a piece of cake.

I made a quick left off the walkway, wandered around among a bunch of blackjack tables until she passed, then turned and fell in behind her. I called Archie while I walked and told him to take Pete and get outside the exit across from the Wynn since she seemed to be moving in that direction. As long as she was inside the casino I could cover her, but this time I wanted to be ready if she went outside.

And that was exactly what she did. She left through the same exit the woman in the yellow t-shirt had taken, crossed over *Praceta 24 de Junho*, and went into the casino at the Wynn. She walked straight through the casino and, with the three of us rambling after her, she went right back out again through the front door. I didn't think she was making an effort to shake off surveillance, just taking a short cut to...well, that was the question, wasn't it?

The lady in black followed the Wynn's driveway down to the double boulevard on which the hotel sits. She crossed under it using a pedestrian tunnel, rode an escalator back to street level in front of the old Hotel Lisboa, and walked north along *Avenida de Almeida Ribeiro* which everyone calls San Ma Lo. It is crowded, dirty, and noisy. Its sidewalks are jammed day and night with locals trying to make their way somewhere and tourists not going anywhere in particular.

We closed up on the lady in black a bit so we wouldn't miss her if she suddenly dodged into one of the stores lining both sides of the street. But she didn't. She crossed Senado Square, passed the Leal Senado Building, a graceful Mediterranean styled building that had been Macau's seat of government since the eighteenth century, and kept striding purposefully northward.

It was a pleasant evening for a stroll. The fog had returned with the evening air and it gave the old city a gauzy, timeless feel. Once we crossed Senado Square, the crowds thinned and we dropped back a bit. We did our best to look like three pals out for a stroll between sessions at the tables.

"I think she's headed for the Sofitel," Archie said. "There's not much else down this way."

"Maybe not, but I doubt the North Koreans are laundering money out of the Sofitel."

A TOWERING PILE OF yellow stucco far newer than anything around it, the Sofitel is directly on the inner harbor, the old waterfront that was once Macau's front door. I had stayed at the Sofitel a couple of times and liked it a lot. It's a fine hotel, although a little out of the Macau mainstream, both because of its location and because it doesn't have a big, flashy casino attached to it. Come to think of it, those are probably the two things I liked most about it.

The inner harbor isn't much of a waterfront these days. It's certainly not the front door to Macau anymore. It's not even a decent back door. The Chinese mainland is directly on the other side, and decades of aggressive landfilling by the Chinese have narrowed the harbor to not more than a couple of hundred yards of open water. Now it looks less like a harbor than it does a lazy, not particularly important river. There isn't much shipping activity there anymore either. A few ferries and some private boats come in from time to time, but that's about it. All the real shipping has moved out to the new container port by the airport.

Regardless of all that, the old waterfront and the Barra district that surrounds it are still my favorite part of Macau. It's almost all that is left these days of the exotic south China port of the fifties I first learned about in black and white noir thrillers on late night television. The Macau in those films had a seedy glamour that I would associate with Asia for the rest of my life. European men in wrinkled white suits, sloe-eyed local women wearing tight fitting cheongsams, and creaking ceiling fans slowly stirring the heavy, humid air.

Except for the Sofitel, the old waterfront is still pretty seedy, which is what I like about it. Some people preferred their world scrubbed, tidy, and vacuum-sealed. I like mine with a little dirt and a few odors. It seems more real to me that way, more worthy of being lived in.

We were less than a hundred yards from the Sofitel when the lady in black made an abrupt right turn off of San Ma Lo into a tiny lane. Breaking into a trot, we rounded the corner in time to see her disappear into a building a few doors down.

The lane was no more than ten feet wide with narrow sidewalks on both sides. Flush up to both sidewalks were unbroken ranks of four and five story buildings. They were all painted in pastel shades of yellow, pink, and blue, and they had balconies on most of their floors that were railed with intricate black ironwork.

The wispy fog had turned the ambient light bluish-white and it rendered everything in soft focus. The little street didn't seem quite real. It could have been a flat-fronted replica of a Portuguese village constructed in some slightly off kilter Florida theme park.

"Let me walk down and back by myself and grab a look," I said. "The three of us are way too conspicuous in this neighborhood."

They both nodded and it seemed to me that Archie looked amused. I couldn't immediately see what I had said that might have amused him, so I let it go.

THE BUILDING INTO WHICH the lady in black had disappeared was neat and attractive. It was only about fifty feet up the narrow lane and sat on the corner of another even narrower alley. The building was constructed of what looked like slabs of rose-colored granite, but probably weren't, and the only entrance door that I could see was around the corner on the alley. Like the other buildings in the neighborhood, it had a lost and abandoned quality to it.

I strolled by, trying to look as nonchalant as possible. The windows were all dark and not a glimmer of light came from inside the building. I passed without slowing and walked another fifty yards or so. I turned around in the shadows and walked back on the opposite side of the street.

Going in that direction I found myself looking directly at the entrance, which was modest and nondescript and consisted of nothing but a small awning fixed to the face of the building and two glass doors underneath it. I could see clearly now that the glass in the entrance doors had been painted over with black paint. It was possible the building wasn't simply dark. All the windows could easily have been blacked out for some reason, too.

To the left of the door were half a dozen Chinese characters, each about six inches tall and made of something shiny like aluminum, but right below them was a small sign in some language that looked as though it might make sense, even to me. I slowed down and turned toward the entrance. In case anybody was watching, I tried my best to look lost and confused. That turned out to be embarrassingly easy.

I had to get almost all the way up to the doors before I could make out the words on the little sign. *Pensao Ruby.*

Pensao? Was that Portuguese? Was it like *pensioné*? Was this some kind of cheap hotel?

I veered away and walked on up the alleyway toward where Pete and Archie were waiting on San Ma Lo. I glanced up at the building again as I passed, but I still couldn't see any light anywhere at all. If it was a hotel, it certainly wasn't doing very well. On the other hand, we had seen the lady in black go inside and she sure as hell wasn't sitting in there in the dark, so the windows had to be all blacked out. But what kind of a hotel has blacked out windows?

WHEN I GOT BACK to San Ma Lo, I was puzzled to find Pete and Archie looking at each other and snickering.

"What?" I asked.

Pete pointed down the lane toward the *pensao* or *pensioné* or whatever the hell it was.

"Did you see the name of that place?" he asked.

"Pensao Ruby."

That brought on a new round of snickers. I waited patiently for it to subside.

"Do you know what a *pensao* is, Jack?"

"Not really. A hotel? Something like a *pensioné*?"

"Yeah," Archie nodded slowly, "back in Portugal that usually what it means, but not here in Macau."

"Okay, guys," I said spreading my arms wide, "lay it on me."

"Well, Jacko, I think it speaks well of you that you don't know. I really do."

Archie leaned forward, cupped his hands over my shoulders and flashed a wicked grin.

"In Macau," he explained, "a *pensao* is usually a whorehouse."

35

WE WALKED OVER TO the Sofitel looking for a comfortable bar where we could sit for a while and figure out what to do next. Naturally, we found one.

It was called the Rendezvous, which seemed appropriate. It was fitted out with leopard print upholstered chairs, gold tables, and red drapes, and it looked like a French cathouse, which also seemed appropriate. Well, to be honest, I had never actually been in a French cathouse but, if I had, I was certain it would look exactly like the Rendezvous Bar. The tent card on our table recommended a cocktail they called a So Sofitel that was described as a Fresca and rosemary martini. After reading it I gave my stomach a moment to settle down and ordered a beer. So did Pete and Archie. The waitress looked annoyed that we weren't ordering something more interesting than that, but she brought us three Heinekens anyway and disappeared.

"Okay, boss," Archie said after sucking down nearly half his beer in one pull. "Now what?"

"I want to get inside."

"You want to get inside a whorehouse? If you're wondering what they're doing in there, I'm pretty sure I can explain—"

"Look, we followed a woman we know has been moving

money through the MGM back there and she didn't strike me as a hooker on her way to work. Whatever people may think that place is, my guess is it's where they're running the money laundering operation."

I also thought there was a pretty good chance that it was where they were holding Freddy, but it seemed unnecessary to mention that part at the moment.

"What do you have in mind doing about it?" Pete asked. "We're not exactly a SWAT team, you know."

"Can you get me a SWAT team?"

"Nope."

"So there you go. We figure something out among the three of us. What else are we going to do?"

That question seemed to stump everyone so we all sat and drank our beer in silence for a while.

When Archie finished his, he wiped his mouth with the back of his hand and said, "I think I ought to go in and check the place out."

Pete just laughed.

"Get nicked, dickhead," Archie laughed right back. "I'm the one to do it because you both look like cops. I look like some Ocker tourist who's full of grog."

I had to admit Archie had us there.

WE HAD ANOTHER ROUND and nobody came up with a better idea, so about ten o'clock we paid our tab and headed back to Pensao Ruby. The fog had thickened considerably while we were drinking in the Rendezvous and the little lane didn't look so romantic to me anymore. Now it looked less like a theme park in Florida and more like a setting for a horror movie, one of those where the good guys never see the fellow with the axe until he is standing right behind them.

Archie walked up the lane past Pensao Ruby, turned around, and walked back. When he emerged from the fog, he said, "Still dark. The place looks deserted."

"We know it's not," I said. "We saw that woman go in."

"That was a couple of hours ago. They could have cleared out since."

"Don't see why," Pete said. "These are peak hours for the brothel business."

Archie and I both looked at him.

"That's only an assumption on my part," he added quickly.

We watched Pensao Ruby for another minute or two, but nothing happened.

"Okay," Archie finally said, "no guts, no glory."

He hitched up his pants and headed for the front door.

PETE AND I WATCHED Archie try both doors, but neither one opened. He put his ear against first one door and then the other and listened briefly. Apparently hearing nothing of importance, Archie pulled his wallet from his back pocket, took something out, and went down on one knee right where the handles for the two doors came together.

"Best lock man I ever saw," Pete said before I had a chance to ask him what Archie was doing.

"He's picking the lock? How long is that going to take him?"

Pete didn't answer. He pointed over my shoulder and I looked around in time to see Archie disappearing through the doors into Pensao Ruby.

WITHIN FIVE MINUTE, MAYBE less, one of the doors opened again and Archie leaned out and gestured to us. As Pete and I walked toward him, he put a finger to his lips.

"Who's here?" I whispered when we got to the door.

"Nobody. I've checked the building all the way up to the top floor."

"So why are we whispering?"

Archie shrugged.

The light was dim, but it was bright enough for me to see that the first floor of the building was a single large space with blacked out windows and a scratched brown and white linoleum floor. It was empty. Not only empty of people, empty of everything.

"Then why the hell did that woman come into—"

"Look at this," Archie interrupted. He squatted down, rubbed the palm of his hand over the linoleum, and held it up for me to look at.

"I don't see anything."

"Exactly right. No dirt, not even any dust. When was the last time you saw an empty building with no dirt or dust on the floor?"

"You're telling me somebody cleaned it up?"

"There was something going on here, but they cleared out. They cleaned the place when they went."

"Why would they do that?"

Archie shrugged again. He seemed to be getting into the habit.

"You think they spotted us when we followed that woman here?" I asked.

"That can't be it," Pete said. "To clear out a place like this and clean it would take time and preparation. We only found it a couple of hours ago. Most of this was done before that. Had to be."

"Why would they suddenly clear out if they didn't know we were on to them?"

"Maybe it wasn't sudden. Maybe they were simply done with whatever they were doing here."

"What was that?"

"Well," Pete shrugged, "that's the real question, isn't it?"

Archie produced a tiny Maglite from somewhere and switched it on. A bright beam of cold white light shot out of the little flashlight.

"Lock picks and a flashlight?" I asked. "What have you got under your shirt? Batman's utility belt?"

Archie didn't answer, but he flicked the beam over some narrow concrete steps at the back of the main room. "Let's go upstairs."

"What's upstairs?" I asked.

"The third and fourth floors are divided into small bedrooms. Four on each floor with one toilet. Pretty much what you'd expect to find in a whorehouse. They've all been stripped and cleaned like this floor. Nothing left behind except some basic furniture."

"What about the second floor?"

"Come on up and see for yourself," Archie said.

ON THE SECOND FLOOR there were more blacked out windows and there was more brown and white linoleum, but in the beam of Archie's Maglite I could see something else, too. Archie hit a wall switch and two weak bulbs on the ceiling flared to light, casting the whole room in pale blue light.

Stacked almost to the ceiling on the wall opposite the staircase were piles of dark green and brown boxes that in another life I had once known as banker's boxes. Generally used for storing documents at law firms or other places that accumulate large amounts of paper, banker's boxes are thick walled cardboard containers with lift off lids and push in handles that are big enough to hold a lot of paper but small enough for one man to carry.

"They left these behind," Archie said, playing his Maglite over the stacks of boxes.

There were a lot of boxes. I counted twelve across and eight high stacked that I could see and I had no idea how far back the boxes went. There were obviously several hundred.

"Why would they leave all these files?"

"Go ahead." Archie gestured at the boxes with the Maglite. "Take a look."

I reached up and braced myself to lift down the top box on the stack nearest to me but, by the time I had given the handle on the end a tentative tug to test the weight, I knew what the answer to my question would turn out to be.

They hadn't left a lot of files behind.

I pulled the oddly light box down and shook it. Holding it in one hand, I pulled the lid off with my other.

Empty.

I OPENED A HALF dozen more boxes and checked each of them. They were all empty, too.

"I don't get it," I said. "What happened to the files they kept in these boxes? Why take all of them and leave the boxes?"

"Maybe they repackaged them somehow," Pete offered. "Took them out in something else?"

"Why would they do something like that?"

Pete shrugged. Now he was doing it, too.

Archie picked up one of the boxes I had already checked and flashed his Maglite into the interior. He lifted it up, examined the sides for markings, and turned it upside down to see if there were any markings on the bottom. When he did, a small piece of paper fell out and glided to the floor.

"Must have been caught under the flap," he said as he bent down to retrieve it.

Pete and I stepped over as Archie straightened up and looked to see what he had. The piece of manila-colored paper was about six inches long and an inch wide, and it showed jagged ends where it had apparently been torn.

"A currency strap," Pete and I said at almost the same time.

Archie turned the strap over in his hands and examined both sides. One side was completely blank. The other had wide yellow borders and across the strap, also in yellow, was printed '$1000'. There were no other markings.

"It's not a bank strap," Archie said. "If it were a bank strap, the bank's name and logo would be on it. This looks like the kind of money strap you buy at an office supply store."

I looked at the money strap Archie was holding, looked at the pile of boxes, and looked back at Archie.

"Are you thinking what I'm thinking?" I asked.

"Probably."

"These weren't any files in these boxes, were there? They were used to bring in the $50 bills and the €100 notes that the smurfs exchanged at the MGM."

"But what did they do with the currency they were exchanged for?" Pete asked. "Why not use the same boxes to take it back out?"

I didn't have a clue, so I shook my head.

"I'm more curious about why there are no bank markings on the strap," Archie said. "Banks don't deliver currency in plain straps. They deliver it in straps marked with an ID."

"Does that mean the currency didn't come out of a bank?" I asked.

"That's the way I see it."

"There was a hell of a lot of currency here," I said, waving an arm at the pile of boxes. "Where else could that much currency have come from other than a bank?"

The question hung there in the air for a moment and I thought about the possible answers to my questions, and all of a sudden I thought…

Knock knock.

Who's there?

An idea.

I PULLED OUT MY phone and flipped through the address book until I found Gerald Brady's cell number. I glanced at my watch. It was late, but guys in the casino security business were probably up to all hours anyway, weren't they? I hit the call button.

When Brady answered, he sounded awake so I didn't waste time apologizing for calling so late. I asked him if he could impound all the $50 bills and the €100 notes that had been exchanged in the casino in the last twelve hours before they got shipped out to a bank and commingled with currency from other casinos. Brady asked me what I was looking for, of course, and I mumbled some gibberish about serial numbers that I thought didn't make much sense, but it seemed to satisfy him anyway.

Brady told me that there should have been a currency pickup around five o'clock, but that all the currency that had come in after that would still be in the casino cages. He promised to have security people round up the $50 bills and the €100 notes at the end of the shift and isolate them from the next pick-up.

We had spotted our smurf about seven, so whatever bills she had brought into the casino tonight ought to be included. It didn't seem likely to me she had exchanged her currency early enough for it to have been counted and packed and included in a five o'clock pick up. Not likely, but not completely impossible either.

It probably didn't matter. I was pretty sure I was wrong anyway.

At least, I hoped I was.

36

WHEN I WOKE UP the next morning I found a text message waiting for me from Brady. It said that all the $50 bills and €100 notes from the last shift had been separated out and were being held for me in the casino's main vault.

I called Pete and Archie and I told them to meet me at the vault in an hour. After that I called room service and ordered a large pot of coffee. I figured I was going to need it.

BRADY HAD MADE ALL the necessary arrangements and we were quickly ushered into one of the counting rooms near the vault, where the three of us took seats around a smooth, blond wood table in the middle of the room. After a short wait, a small Filipino man with a big head and a sallow complexion wheeled in an aluminum cart with two shelves. The top shelf was stacked with straps of $50 bills and the bottom shelf with straps of €100 notes.

"I don't understand what you're looking for," Pete said after the man had left and closed the door to the counting room. "What are the serial numbers going to tell you?"

I walked over to the cart, scooped up a pile of the $50 straps, and dumped them in the middle of the table.

"How much do you know about US currency, Pete?"

"What are you talking about?"

"I mean, can you spot counterfeits?"

Archie and Pete looked at each other, but neither of them said anything.

"It would explain a lot," I said. "For instance, it would explain why the only notes the smurfs were bringing into the casino were $50 and €100. If what you're doing is laundering dirty cash, it's not going to be in only two denominations."

Pete looked skeptical. "Do you have any other reason—"

"It would also explain why the smurfs were bringing in these two currencies and carrying out Hong Kong dollars without making any effort to convert the Hong Kong dollars into bank deposits. After all, if you have a shitload of cash, what's the point of setting up a huge operation like this and ending up with another shitload of cash, only in a different currency? That accomplishes nothing."

"Maybe the money they were exchanging was stolen and you're afraid the serial numbers are on a hot list somewhere."

"Too much money involved," I said. "Nobody has stolen tens of millions in $50 bills and €100 notes. If they had, you'd know about it. I'd probably even know about it."

For a minute, nobody said anything.

"That leaves only one possibility that I can see," I finished. "They're exchanging counterfeit currency."

"Even assuming you're right, what are they doing with the Hong Kong dollars?" Archie asked.

"If they're not depositing it in a bank here, they have to be shipping it out of the country."

"So how do you think—"

"I have no fucking clue."

PETE PICKED UP ONE of the straps of $50 bills and turned it over in his hands, examining both sides of the bills.

"I don't see it," he said. "North Korea is a backwater. They couldn't be making currency this good."

"They could be," Archie said, "because they already have."

Archie was talking, of course, about what the Secret Service had dubbed the 'supernote'. Supernotes were American currency made with the same kind of Swiss-manufactured intaglio presses and optically variable ink that the United States Treasury uses to print genuine bank notes. They started turning up in various parts of the world during the early 1990's, and as the US Secret Service tracked the examples they seized they saw the quality getting better and better. In 2005, the Secret Service fingered Banco Delta Asia in Macau as a primary source of the supernotes and accused the bank of importing them in quantity and placing them into international circulation through the bank's facilities.

"Those were $100 bills, not $50's," Pete said, "and there was no other currency being counterfeited. Besides, didn't the crackdown on that bank here in Macau shut down the whole operation?"

"What if they only got better after that? What if they diversified into other denominations and other currencies, and we stopped finding the forgeries in circulation because they got so good they couldn't be detected?"

"So if they're too good to be detected, how are you going to detect them? How would you ever prove that any of this currency is counterfeit?"

"We need to start going through all these bills—"

"Oh, horseshit, Jack. I know next to nothing about detecting counterfeit currency and you probably know less than I do. Besides, it would take a week to examine the front and back of every one of these bills even if we did know what we're doing, which we don't."

"So you're saying we should ignore the possibility?"

"If you go around telling people that there might be huge amounts of counterfeit dollars and euros in circulation without giving them any way to distinguish real currency from the counterfeit, you're going to undermine confidence in all both currencies."

"So what do you want me to do, Pete? You want me to pretend that's not a possible explanation for what's going on at the MGM and ignore all the signs that some of this could be funny money?"

"I'm only saying it would be reckless for you to make a claim like that without proof, and without a way to separate the bad money from the good."

Pete was right, of course, but so was I, and a silence fell as we both contemplated the pile of currency lying in front of us and considered the possibilities.

After a few moments, Archie broke the silence.

"Are you guys through?" he asked.

Archie was sitting on the other side of the table with his hands folded in front of him. He looked like a priest patiently listening to a parishioner's sins before prescribing the appropriate number of Hail Marys.

"Because, if you are, I have an idea."

I LEFT A MESSAGE for Pansy Ho as soon as I got up to my suite and she called me back almost immediately.

"We need to talk," I said. "It's important."

"You've found out something about the money?"

"Possibly."

"Do I want to hear it?"

"Probably not."

I listen to Pansy's tired sigh and wondered if I was doing the right thing by telling her this.

"I'm in Hong Kong," she said. "Can you come over here this afternoon?"

"Yes, but I want you to do something first."

I explained to Pansy that I needed her to call Brady and authorize him to release to me all the $50 bills and €100 notes they had isolated from the last shift.

"I want to copy all the bills and run a computer analysis of them, which requires special scanning software. Archie has a contact at Hongkong and Shanghai Bank. They have the software and they're going to help us."

"Are you saying you think there's something wrong with the currency these people have been running through us? That it's counterfeit?"

I could hear the alarm in Pansy's voice so I chose my words carefully. I didn't want to flat out lie to her, but I didn't want to explain my suspicions quite yet either. Particularly if it turned out I was full of shit. Nobody wants to look like a fool to a beautiful woman.

"I want to do an analysis of the serial numbers. I think that might point us to the source."

It was the same line of bullshit I had given Brady, and Pansy didn't question it either. Maybe they had both realized I had a reason to avoid giving them a direct answer, or maybe they had both simply decided I was an idiot.

"I'll arrange a helicopter for you from the ferry terminal," she said. "And I'll have a car meet you when you get here and take you straight to HSBC. What time shall I tell the pilots to expect you?"

I glanced at my watch. It was coming up on eleven and I added everything up. Fifteen minutes to make arrangements to take the currency, a half hour or so to pack it and get ready to leave, and ten minutes to the heliport at the ferry terminal.

"Say twelve noon exactly? Does that work for you?"

"They'll be ready when you are, Jack. Call me on this number when you know enough to tell me what's really going on here."

"I will."

I only hoped that a time like that would eventually arrive.

37

I ROUNDED UP ARCHIE and Pete, and hurried down to the casino vault. When we got there, Brady was personally packing the straps of $50 bills and €100 notes into two leather suitcases that looked sturdy but well worn and appropriately inconspicuous. I got the feeling he might have done something like this before, but never mind that…

When Brady was finished, he called for a hotel car and personally drove us with both of the suitcases to the ferry terminal. At the heliport on the roof an AgustaWestland twin turbo helicopter was on the pad with its rotors turning.

Barely fifteen minutes later, Pete, Archie, and I were getting out of the helicopter in Hong Kong at the heliport on top of the Sheung Wan MTR station. Two of Pansy's security men were waiting there for us. They carried the cases downstairs and stashed them in the trunk of a black Mercedes S series with heavily tinted windows that was waiting at the curb along Connaught Road. They got in the front and we got in the back.

The drive from Sheung Wan to the HSBC building through Hong Kong's perpetually snarled traffic took twice as long as the helicopter flight from Macau, but by one o'clock we were in a seventeenth floor conference room and Archie was explaining in

Mandarin to a man he didn't introduce exactly what we needed him to do. The man was Chinese and bore what seemed to me to be a remarkable resemblance to a young Mao Zedong. He had a square face, a large head, a high forehead, and his thick jet-black hair was swept straight back. When Mao had taken the two cases of money and left, Archie flopped down in a chair and swung his feet up on the conference table.

"The currency reader will scan high-res images of both the fronts and backs of every note into a software program that will compare all of them with a database of comparison points and flag any anomalies," he said. "It will also trace the serial numbers and try to determine if any of them are duplications."

"How long is this going to take?" I asked.

Archie shrugged. "A couple of hours?"

I TOOK OUT MY cell phone and walked over to the windows. The sun was sparkling off Hong Kong harbor and I watched for a moment as a flock of tugboats scurried around nudging a white cruise ship into a berth at the Ocean Terminal. When I was done stalling, I located Pansy's number on my call list and hit the call button. I expected to leave another message and wait for a call back, but Pansy answered right away.

"What did you find out?"

"Nothing yet. HSBC is scanning all the serial numbers and comparing them to a data base."

"Are you looking for duplicates?"

"That's one possibility, I guess." I still didn't want to lay out my suspicions completely. "There are others."

"I can hardly wait to hear what those other possibilities are," Pansy laughed. "You really are trying to break something to me gently, aren't you, Jack? And I do love you for it."

I had no idea what to say to that so I said nothing at all. In my personal experience, getting in trouble about things I didn't say was much less likely than getting into trouble about things I did say.

"How about meeting me around four?" she asked when the silence had stretched on to the point of embarrassment.

"Sure," I said, happy to be off the hook. "We ought to have something solid by four. At your office?"

"No."

Pansy said it so quickly that I wondered what was wrong with meeting at her office.

"I'll pick you up. I'll be at the Queen's Road side of the HSBC Building at exactly four."

"Another black Mercedes S series with blacked out windows?"

"We got a fleet price," Pansy said.

ARCHIE'S ESTIMATE THAT IT would take about two hours for HSBC to process the currency we had brought to them was a pretty good one, if it had been a guess at all, and I wasn't entirely sure about that. At almost exactly three-thirty, Mao returned with both cases and a manila envelope that he handed to Archie.

Archie opened the envelope and quickly scanned the four sheets inside.

"What do you want to do with the money?" he asked me.

"Can we put the cases into the vault here until we go back to Macau?"

Archie said something in Mandarin to Mao, and Mao nodded. Archie nodded to me and I nodded back at him. Here we all were nodding like crazy and I still didn't know shit.

As soon as the door closed behind Mao, I pointed to the sheets of paper Archie had taken out of the envelope Mao had given him. "Do I have to read that, or are you going to tell me what it says?"

"It says that about five percent of the $50 bills and four percent of the €100 notes have anomalies."

"What kind of anomalies?"

"Design issues, mostly."

"So you're saying that a small percentage of our currency doesn't meet the design standards of real currency?"

"Not exactly," Archie smiled. "The problem with some of these bills is that the micro-engraving is too sharp. It's actually of higher quality than the micro-engraving on a genuine bill."

"You're telling me the counterfeits are *better* than real currency?"

Archie smiled again and nodded, and I nodded, but this time Pete jumped in before all the nodding could get out of hand.

"What about the serial numbers?" he asked.

"Some appear to be duplicates," Archie said, "but it will take a day or two to nail that down for sure."

"But you're saying there's no doubt about the design anomalies?"

"Well, the software says there are design anomalies, but personally I wouldn't feel comfortable putting my name to a finding of counterfeiting until some actual human beings who know about this stuff examine the notes the software flagged."

"I've got to tell Pansy now," I said. "I can't stall any longer. She deserves to know what we know."

"It's pretty much London to a brick the software nailed it," Archie shrugged. "I think you're safe telling her she's looking at a big whack of funny money there, mate."

THE BLACK MERCEDES WAS idling at the curb along Queen's road when I came out of the HSBC building. I crossed the narrow plaza and got in. The first thing I saw was the grim look on Pansy's face.

"Tell me," she said. "Yes or no?"

"It's a little bit of both."

"Oh God, I hate lawyers," she sighed.

"I thought you said you loved me."

"I lied," Pansy laughed. "Or at least I exaggerated a whole lot."

The driver put the Mercedes in gear and pulled into traffic.

WE MADE SMALL TALK while the driver worked his way through the traffic in Central and into Sheung Wan. When we passed the

University of Hong Kong, the car turned inland and I saw we were heading in the direction Pok Fu Lam, one of Hong Kong's most beautiful areas tucked away on a sandy bay on the island's southern shore.

"Do you want me to tell you what we've found?" I asked.

Pansy caught my eye and looked at the back of the driver's head. I got the message, nodded, and fell silent.

The car turned off Pok Fu Lam Road and passed through Kennedy Town, the far western reach of the forest of featureless high rise towers that jostled for space throughout most of Hong Kong. We tracked the coast on a road that ran along a narrow ledge between the South China Sea and Mount Davis. On the right steep cliffs fell sharply away into the ocean and on the left the dense vegetation of the mountainside reached down to the edge of the pavement. It was a wild and untamed sight, a stupefying counterpoint to the human density and structural congestion that was Hong Kong's very soul. I lowered my window and breathed in the fresh, cool ocean air. I could almost feel my pulse slowing and my blood pressure dropping.

"I like to come out here when I need to think," Pansy said, as if she were reading my thoughts.

"Where are we going?"

"You'll see."

We drove another ten minutes or so until Victoria Road abruptly swung inland. Up on our right, between the road and the ocean, I spotted what looked like athletic fields, the dark green of their carefully tended grass contrasting sharply with the gunmetal grey of the sea beyond them. The driver slowed the car when we came to a utilitarian looking concrete structure about four stories high. He turned in and I saw it was a parking garage. Then I saw the black lettering above the entrance:

THE STANLEY HO SPORTS CENTRE

Of course it was.

PANSY AND I WALKED slowly around a track made of crushed red clay that was divided into running lanes with precisely etched white lines. The sun was sinking into the ocean somewhere behind the mountains and the last light of the day was making its final stand in the sea. There was a breeze from the west which carried the heady odors of salt and dead fish, and in the distance I watched a Chinese junk moving under sail through the Lamma Channel, its sails sparkling red in the dying light. The junk looked like a child's toy trapped forever in a sea of pewter.

"Tell me now," Pansy finally said.

And I did.

"DO YOU REALLY THINK the money these people have been moving through the casino is counterfeit?" she asked when I finished.

"The early indications are that it might be, but of course it's still too soon to be absolutely certain and there is always the possibility that we will—"

"For God's sake, Jack, stop being such a fucking lawyer!"

I shut up and awaited developments.

"Do you think the money these people have been moving through the MGM casino is counterfeit?" she asked again after a moment. "No lawyer talk. Just give me a simple yes or a no."

"Yes."

Pansy sighed heavily and began making a swishing sound with her feet as she slid them over the loose clay surface of the track. It made me think of a little girl playing in the sand.

"How much have they put into circulation through us?" she asked in a voice so soft I had to strain to hear it.

"I don't know. Tens of millions certainly. Maybe a lot more."

"So what you're telling me is this. The MGM casino has put fifty or even a hundred million dollars of counterfeit currency into the international banking system for the government of North Korea."

"Yes. But it was entirely unwitting, and nobody is going to blame—"

Pansy cut me off with a laugh, although there was no humor in the sound.

"Come on, Jack? Do you seriously think anyone is going to believe I wasn't involved somehow? I can see the headline now. *Chinese Triads Use MGM Macau to Launder North Korea Counterfeit Money*. I'm finished. I am absolutely fucking finished."

"No, you're not."

Pansy stopped walking and looked at me. There was something in her eyes that I liked.

"What do you mean? Have you got some kind of plan you haven't told me about?"

I didn't, of course, but there was no way I could stand there and look into Pansy eyes and snuff out the hope I saw.

"Stick with me," I said. "That's all I can say now."

It was all I could say because I didn't have anything else to say. I had no idea what to do now. Only I couldn't tell Pansy that. Pansy reached out and put her hand on my arm. It felt warm and small and I wanted to protect her in the worst way. I would have to think of something. That was all there was to it.

"I want you to talk to Dr. Ho," she said. For a moment, I wasn't certain I had heard her right.

"Your father?"

"Yes."

"What for?"

"He can help you."

I didn't see why Stanley Ho would deal with some white guy he didn't know and who couldn't do anything for him in return, but I didn't think I ought to say that to Pansy so I said nothing at all.

"If you're going to make all this go away without anyone finding out about it," she said, "you're going to need some help."

Did I say that's what I was going to do?

"Dr. Ho has the connections you'll need."

I'll bet he does, was what I thought, but that wasn't what I said.

"Connections to do what, exactly?" I asked Pansy.

"To do…"

Pansy stopped talking and looked at me. She smiled and I couldn't help noticing that it was a very nice smile indeed.

"…whatever you might need to do to shut this down before it destroys me."

I had no idea what to say to that, none at all, so I only nodded. Apparently that was good enough for Pansy because she grabbed my elbow and gave it a tug.

"Let's go, Jack. We've got a lot to do."

Pansy turned and began to walk back to where the car was parked. She moved so quickly and with such determination that I could barely keep up with her.

38

STANLEY HO WAS APPARENTLY somewhere in Macau because by seven that night Pansy and I were in a helicopter headed back there, too. I called Pete before we took off to tell him what was going on. When I talked to Pete I actually pretended I knew what was going on and he was nice enough not to laugh. Pete said he and Archie would grab a ferry that night and meet me back at the suite at the MGM as quickly as they could get there.

They got there about nine. Somewhere along the way Archie had conjured up a liter-sized bottle of Bushmills Irish whiskey and the three of us sat and half watched ESPN while we talked and drank the Bushmills and waited for Pansy to call.

Finally, about eleven, she did.

"It will have to be tomorrow, Jack."

Pansy sounded tired. I could only imagine.

"Tomorrow's fine."

"Do you know Clube Militar?"

I did, and I didn't. "Is it that pink building by the park right behind the Lisboa?"

"That's it. Meet me there at noon."

"I thought your father doesn't move around much anymore. I always heard that since his stroke, he—"

"He is much healthier than most people think. He comes to Macau frequently and he often goes to…well, other places, too. He finds it useful that not many people know how active he still is."

I wondered if it would be rude for me to ask what exactly Stanley Ho was so active in, but before I could decide, Pansy ended the conversation, which was probably a good thing.

After that, Archie, Pete, and I finished the Bushmills and speculated on what it would be like to meet the King of Macau. I was more curious about what the hell good it was going to do me.

CLUBE MILITAR DE MACAU is an anachronism, even judging it by Macau's rather generous standards of anachronism. It is a low slung, pink and white colonial building on *Avenida da Praia Grande* that looks like a strawberry wedding cake someone left in the rain. It was a Portuguese officers' mess in the 1870's, but now it is a private club that counts among its membership the political elite of Macau, if a former Portuguese colony now completely controlled by China can be said to possess a political elite.

A little before noon the next day I strolled over from the MGM. By cutting through the casino at the Wynn and through the lobby of the Lisboa, I made the walk in about fifteen minutes. When I reached the *Avenida da Praia Grande,* I followed a black and white mosaic tiled walkway between two whitewashed balustrades and up half a dozen stairs to a pair of well-worn wood and glass doors. I half expected to find military guards on alert inside where they would no doubt demand I produce photo identification, but I was being far too American. There were no guards inside the doors, nor anybody else for that matter. The lobby had the sleepy feel of a room that was accustomed to being completely deserted.

Not having any better idea, I wandered into the bar looking for Pansy. It was a cozy little room with subdued lighting, a walnut plank floor shined to a gloss high enough to use it as a shaving mirror, and a white-painted bar with shiny brass fittings. The bartender was spiffily dressed in a short red jacket and black trousers and he had big ears and a military short-back-and-sides haircut. I pulled out one of the high-backed stools, ordered a soda and bitters, and looked around. There wasn't much to see since, except for the bartender and me, the room was completely empty.

I sipped at my drink and asked the bartender, "Do you know who Pansy Ho is?"

He peered cautiously at me, probably wondering if that was a trick question, so I tried again.

"I'm supposed to meet Pansy Ho here somewhere. Do you know where I might be able to find her?"

The young man wouldn't meet my eyes. In Macau, the name Ho was magic, I knew, but there is white magic and there is black magic and sometimes it's one and sometimes it's the other. This time it looked like it was definitely the other.

"Never mind," I said, letting the suddenly nervous young man off the hook. "I'll look around."

I dropped what I figured had to be enough money on the bar to cover my drink and a decent tip and headed back out in search of Pansy.

There was still no one in the lobby, and the first corridor I followed further back into the building turned out to lead to the toilets. I stuck my head in the dining room, but noon was far too early for lunch in Macau and only a handful of people were scattered in there, none of whom were Pansy. I had retraced my steps to the lobby again when I noticed the brass plaque mounted above a closed pair of wooden doors. It said…

SALA DR. STANLEY HO

Of course it did.

SALA DR. STANLEY HO turned out to be an airy, high-ceilinged room with big arched windows hung with gauzy white fabric, and half a dozen wooden bladed ceiling fans turning slowly overhead. It was divided into three seating areas by large green and gold rugs arrayed across the glistening hardwood floor. Arranged on each rug were groupings of comfortable looking but undistinguished couches and chairs.

Pansy was perched on the edge of a blue and green striped chair in the grouping furthest away from me. Her back was to the door and she was facing an elderly man seated in a wheelchair who I recognized as Stanley Ho. Between us and only a few steps inside the doorway two broad shouldered Chinese men in dark suits, white shirts, and dark ties regarded me with undisguised suspicion.

Pansy must have heard the door open and close because she stood, turned toward me, and called out, "Over here, please, Jack!"

I started toward her, but one of the Chinese men took a step toward me and held up one hand, palm out. The other man made a raising gesture with both hands and, in case I didn't get the idea, followed it with a demonstration of raising his own arms.

"Are you serious?" I asked him. His face remained impassive and he repeated the arm raising gesture again.

"I'm sorry, Jack," Pansy said as she crossed the room toward me. "Dr. Ho is something of a traditionalist."

"I know a lot of traditionalists, and not one of them has ever demanded a couple of goons search me before we have a conversation."

"If you wouldn't mind—"

"Actually, I do mind. I mind a hell of a lot."

"Jack, please. Don't make a scene."

"You asking me not to make a scene?" I waved one hand at the two hard guys patiently blocking my path to Stanley Ho. "What do these guys think they're going to find on me? A gun? Do they think I'm going to shoot your father or something?"

"It's not personal. My father has many enemies. There is always security around him."

Pansy stepped closer to me and lowered her voice until it was not much more than a whisper.

"Dr. Ho is an old man, Jack. He relies on routine and this is his routine. Do this for me, please."

Are all men utterly helpless to say no to a beautiful woman?

Yes.

Do all beautiful women know that and work it for everything they can get out of it?

Uh-huh.

I lifted my arms and one of Ho's goons stepped around and gave me a thorough frisking from behind. He spent so much time checking out my crotch that I wondered if he might be considering proposing marriage, but he didn't. He stepped back when he was done and the second heavy waved me forward.

Pansy and I crossed the room toward Ho. I saw him studying me as I approached and I studied him right back.

Stanley Ho had to be at least ninety and he looked it. He was wearing some kind of high collared black jacket, grey slacks, and a black flat cap with a short bill. I had heard that Ho was proud of once being famed for his skill as a ballroom dancer and that he had been particularly adept at the tango. I figured that had to have been a century or two back. Now he looked like a retired cab driver.

His wheelchair was another matter altogether. It was a conveyance designed for an emperor, not a cab driver. It was motorized, of course, and the seat, back, and headrest were all thick leather cushions the color of United States currency. It looked like a first class seat on some expensive airline unaccountably detached from the plane and equipped with wheels.

Stanley watched me carefully as Pansy and I walked toward him, but he never moved. His hands were folded together in his lap as if he were preparing to say grace. His face was waxen and puffy and there were red blotches on his cheeks, but his eyes were locked onto me and he never blinked. I could only imagine the fear those eyes must have conjured up in all sorts of people over the course of Stanley's long and active lifetime. Now they looked like two black buttons sewn onto his face.

"Please sit down, Jack."

Pansy pointed to the chair where she had been sitting when I came in. I wondered if I should offer Stanley my hand first, but he was sitting there impassively so I settled for simply nodding to him. He didn't bother to nod back.

"Jack, please," Pansy repeated, nodding toward the chair again.

I sat.

"DR. HO WOULD LIKE to hear what you have discovered about the money passing through the MGM casino."

"Haven't you already told him all that?"

"He would like to hear it from you."

So I took a deep breath and summarized what I knew as succinctly as I could. I told Stanley about my discovery that the excess funds moving through the MGM could be accounted for by a large number of $50 bills and €100 notes that had been exchanged for chips, and those chips promptly cashed back out for Hong Kong dollars. I told him about our identification of the smurfs and tracing one of them to the building that had been emptied out. I told him about our discovery of the money strap in one of the banker's boxes that had been left behind, and I told him about isolating some of the $50 bills and €100 notes collected by the casino and taking them to Hong Kong to be scanned by the HSBC's computers. Finally, I told him that the computers had identified a number of the bills as possessing anomalies, which meant they were almost certainly counterfeit.

Stanley looked at me the whole time I was talking, but no expression crossed his face. I briefly wondered if he had died of boredom.

"Dr. Ho would also like to know who you think is responsible."

Was Stanley mute, or was there some other reason Pansy was leading me through this dog and pony show like it was being recorded for later playback? I supposed it didn't really matter, so I didn't ask. I just explained to Stanley about the security pictures we had collected of the smurfs and our conclusion that they were all Koreans who had probably had a bit of surgery done to make them look less Korean.

"So you are telling Dr. Ho—"

"I'm not telling him anything. Not for sure. It's all circumstantial," I finished, "but I think North Korea is using the MGM and probably other casinos in Macau to exchange very high quality counterfeit US dollars and euros for Hong Kong dollars. Then they're smuggling the Hong Kong dollars out of the country."

I wasn't sure why I bothered, but in the interest of full disclosure I also told Stanley about Freddy, about Freddy's promise to trade important information about what North Korea was doing in Macau for political asylum in the United States, and finally about Freddy's kidnapping.

"I think they will either kill Freddy or try to take him out of Macau the same way they are sending out the currency," I finished.

Ho just sat there and looked at me. He didn't say a word. He didn't even blink.

"HOW ARE YOU GOING to stop them?" Pansy asked.

I was so completely flabbergasted by her question that for a moment I didn't know what to say.

"I asked if you know how you're going to stop them, Jack."

"Look, Pansy," I said very quietly as soon as I regained the power of speech, "I'm not the cops. You hired me to find out where this money was coming from and who was moving it through your casino. I've done that and I've told you what I found. I'm all done here."

"So you're going to walk away now? What do you think the press will do to me when they find out that the MGM has laundered millions of dollars of counterfeit money for North Korea? Don't you think all the old stories about Dr. Ho's presumed criminal connections will be dredged up and they will be used to imply that I am involved somehow? They'll ruin me, Jack!"

"Look, Pansy, I don't see what—"

"And what about Freddy? You're just going to let them kill him?"

"What the hell do you expect me to do?"

"I expect you to stop them. I expect you to keep that money from leaving Macau. I expect you to prevent them from killing Freddy because he's the only one who can say that I had nothing to do with it and be believed."

"Stop them? I don't even know how to find them!"

Pansy leaned back in her chair, crossed her legs, and offered a very small smile. I shot a quick glance at Stanley and saw his eyes moving back and forth between us. At least the old man was still alive…

"Finding them is not a problem. Dr. Ho has friends everywhere. He will ask his friends to find them and his friends will do so. After that, we will tell you where they are and you can stop them."

"Why can't he do that?" I waved a hand at the old man in his wheelchair and immediately realized how silly my question sounded, so I amended it slightly. "What I mean is why can't he get some of these same friends of his to stop them?"

"Dr. Ho cannot be seen to be involved in this. If he is, many will assume the triads are involved, too."

No shit, Sherlock.

"He can arrange to get information to you about their location," Pansy continued, "but that is all he can do. I'm sure you understand."

I didn't understand, actually, but it didn't feel right demanding that an old man in a wheelchair do something I wasn't willing to do myself.

"I need you, Jack. Freddy needs you. Both our lives are in your hands. We have no one else to turn to."

I shot a glance at Stanley. I could swear I saw the sides of the old man's mouth curl up for a second into something that approximated a grin.

Pansy had me. And Stanley knew she did.

39

IT TOOK STANLEY HO less than eight hours to deliver.

When Pansy called, Pete and Archie were with me in the suite and we were watching a replay of a Dallas Cowboys game on ESPN. The Cowboys were ahead, and we all had side bets on how they were going to blow the game this time.

"Are you upstairs?" Pansy asked me.

"I guess that depends on whether you're downstairs."

Pansy hung up without saying anything else. I guess she was downstairs.

THE DOORBELL RANG A few minutes later and I got up and let Pansy in. Everyone seemed to know everyone else already so I didn't waste any time on introductions, and Pansy didn't waste any time on small talk.

"They're not on a ship," she said. "They're on an airplane."

"Does your father know which airplane?"

"Yes. He said that a flight plan has already been filed. It's departing for Sunan Airport in Pyongyang at eleven o'clock tonight."

I looked at my watch. A little after eight. That was less than three hours away.

Pete was looking at his watch, too. "That doesn't give us much time to convince whoever runs the airport to stop that plane from taking off," he said. "Does anyone know—"

"No!"

Pansy's interruption was so sharp we all stopped and looked at her.

"If you get someone official involved, all this is going to become public. You've got to stop that plane yourselves."

"Where is Bruce Willis when you really need him?" I shrugged.

Nobody laughed, probably because it wasn't really very funny.

"IS IT A REGULAR commercial flight?" I asked Pansy.

"No," she said. "At least I don't think it is."

She handed me the piece of notepaper she had in her hand and I read what was written on it.

"It's something called Yas Air," I said, looking at Archie.

"That's an Iranian freight carrier," he answered.

"Tail number is EP-GOP. The plane is an Ilyushin Il-76TD."

"That's a Russian military transport that's been converted to civilian use. It's a big motherfucker. High wings, four engines, probably a hundred and fifty feet long."

"How are we going to get on the airport?" Pete asked. "I know Macau isn't exactly New York, but they still have security. We can't climb over the fence and go looking for the plane."

"And even if we do get to the plane," Archie continued, "what are we going to do then? Shoot the crew? They'll probably be Iranians, and if they are—"

"One thing at a time," I cut in. "Let's figure out how we can get to the plane. After that we'll figure out what to do when we get there."

Archie and Pete looked at me and waited.

"You up for this?" I asked Pete.

"Yeah," he said.

"Archie?"

Archie shrugged.

"I'll take that as a yes."

"I CAN GET YOU onto the airport," Pansy said, and all three of us stopped looking at each other and looked at her. "MGM has two Falcon 50's we use for VIPs. I could take you in as high rollers we're flying home."

"Wouldn't work," Archie said almost immediately. "When was the last time any casino in Macau VIPed white guys? Everyone would smell a rat the minute we got out of the car."

"It's still a good idea," I said, "but we don't go in as high rolling gamblers."

Everyone looked at me.

"We go in as pilots," I said. "Half the pilots in the world are Americans or Aussies. Nobody would look twice at us."

"We've got less than three hours," Pete said, looking at his watch. "It's a little late for us to learn to fly."

"We don't have to fly anything. We only need to look like we can. Uniforms and IDs ought to do it."

"We've got spare uniforms in our pilots' lounge downstairs," Pansy said. "And I can get IDs made up in fifteen minutes."

"There you go," I said. "We're pilots."

PANSY GRABBED THE ROOM phone and went to work. Within a few minutes an elderly Chinese woman appeared with a digital camera to take our pictures for the IDs and five minutes after that a selection of uniforms was delivered to the suite. The three of us started trying on jackets, pants, shirts, and hats. Archie and I found pieces pretty close to our size right away, but Peter was having trouble finding a pair of pants large enough. When he caught me watching him with a little grin on my face, he said, "Shut the fuck up."

By the time we were dressed, the elderly woman was back. She gave each of us an ID in a little plastic sleeve with a clip on it and a black leather flight case like the ones everybody sees pilots lugging through airports. We clipped the IDs to our pockets, picked up the cases, and checked ourselves out in the mirror.

"Pretty damned real looking," Pansy said. "Let's go."

Archie jacked a round into the chamber of the Glock 19 I had seen back at the Grand Lapa and put it into his flight case. Pete put a little 9mm Walther into his. It was so small I hadn't even realized he was carrying it until we started changing into our uniforms.

I went to the room safe, got the silver Halliburton case I had brought from Hong Kong, and tossed it on the bed. I slid the Ruger LC9 9mm out of its foam rubber mount, loaded the clip with hollow points from the box in the case, and screwed the Osprey sound suppressor onto the barrel. I slipped it into a black nylon holster and put it in my flight case.

"Pretty fancy rig," Pete said. "For a civilian."

"Laser sight?" Archie asked.

I nodded.

"Good," Pete said. "At least you won't shoot me in the ass."

"Not by accident at least," I said.

FIVE MINUTES LATER WE were downstairs in front of the MGM. Pansy slid behind the wheel of a silver VW van with the MGM lion on both doors, and the three of us got in the back.

We pulled out of the driveway and Pansy turned west on *Avenida Dr. Sun Yat-Sen*, heading for the bridge to Taipa. She pulled out her phone, dialed with her thumb, and began speaking rapid Cantonese in a low voice. I thought of reminding her that it wasn't safe to drive and talk on a cell phone at the same time, but then I realized that was probably the least of our problems at the moment and kept my mouth shut. For once.

I looked at my watch. Nine-thirty. We would be at the airport in about fifteen minutes. We had done well to get everything together as fast as we had, but we would still have barely an hour before the Ilyushin's takeoff time. Not much time to think of something. Even less much time to do something.

"Okay," Pete looked at me and said, "what's the plan?"

"I guess the first thing to do is to find that airplane."

"I got that part. But what do we do when we find it?"

"I have no fucking clue."

"What I thought," Pete said.

WE CAME OFF THE MILE and half long *Ponte de Sai Van* bridge and drove along the north coast of what used to be Taipa Island until Taipa was joined to Coloane Island by the massive landfill that was now covered end to end in megaresorts. Passing between the Regency Hotel and the Grand Hyatt, we picked up the *Estrade de Pac On* and headed east toward the airport.

There is only one airport in Macau and the terminal and the hangers are built on the eastern edge of Taipa while the single runway sits offshore on a narrow strip of reclaimed land. I usually took the ferry across to Macau from Hong Kong, but I had been through the airport a couple of times and was trying to remember what I could about it. It wasn't very much. There was the usual sort of glass and steel terminal building, as I recalled, but I didn't know anything about the layout of the hangers or the service facilities.

Through the windshield of the silver van I could see the lights of the terminal building ahead of us. The field was out to our left, but I couldn't see much of it through the darkness and fog. Here close to the water the fog was no longer the gauzy and romantic thing you saw in travel magazines. It looked hard and menacing, like a steel-colored wall.

"I don't think an Ilyushin is going to be parked at the passenger terminal," Pete spoke up. "It's a freight aircraft."

"This is the only road into the airport," Pansy said. "Both the freight terminal and the private terminal are on the other side of the passenger terminal. Fortunately they're right next to each other. I called our hanger and told them to tow one of our Falcons out, park it as close to the Ilyushin as they could, and prepare it for take off."

"And is it going to take off?"

"Not unless one of you guys learns how to fly within the next hour."

THE LIGHTS OF THE passenger terminal drifted by on the left. They were ghostly and indistinct in the heavy fog. Up ahead I saw another clump of buildings, but not clearly enough to make out what they were.

"How do we get out to where the Falcon is parked?" I asked.

"We always drive our pilots straight out to the aircraft so I can bring you right up to the doorway. But after that..."

Pansy trailed off. She turned her head and looked at me. I understood what she was saying.

After that, we were on our own.

PANSY BRAKED SHARPLY AND moved the van to the left side of the road. We bumped slowly along parallel to a high chain-link fence until a large drive gate appeared out of the fog. The van came to a stop at the gate and a uniformed security guard stepped out of his hut and raked us with a flashlight beam. The light found the MGM logo on the door and almost immediately the gate began to rattle open on an unseen track.

The van rolled slowly across the field and I listened to the gate clatter shut behind us.

40

I'VE ALWAYS LOVED THE way airplanes look at night when they are parked on an airfield under floodlights. They appear to exist in only two dimensions, like giant stage sets ready for the play to begin just as soon as the actors show up.

When I saw the Falcon out on the field in front of us that was exactly what it looked like. Of course, in this case, that was pretty much what it actually was. A stage set. The plane wasn't going anywhere. It was there as a backdrop. The problem was I still had no script for the drama we were going to play out against it.

The Falcon was painted white with a discreet blue-black stripe down the side below the cabin windows. The vertical stabilizer displayed a stylized version of the MGM lion that looked like a particularly untalented student of Picasso must have drawn it.

The van approached the Falcon from the rear, circled around the wing, and came to a halt next to the forward door. It was standing open and the air stairs were down. The Ilyushin parked on the other side of the Falcon, two bays down. It was, as Archie had said, a big son of a bitch. It had wide green and gold stripes down the side and the vertical stabilizer was green with some kind of logo on it that looked like a marijuana leaf, but probably wasn't. The wings hung down from a sort of hump on the very top of the fuselage and two bulky engine pods were slung below each wing. The plane was anything but sleek. It looked crude and brutal, like an angry hunchback crouching in the darkness.

We all put our flight bags at the foot of the air stairs and walked around to the driver's side of the van. Pansy lowered the window.

"What are you going to do?" she asked.

"He has no fucking clue," Archie answered for me.

I shrugged. When you're right, you're right.

"LET'S DO A WALK around," Archie said, gesturing at the Falcon. "That will give us an excuse to check out what's going on around the Ilyushin without being obvious about it."

"What's a walk around?" Pete asked.

"Pilots always walk around their aircraft and inspect it for damage before they take off," I said.

"Damage? You mean like if there's a wing missing?"

"Exactly," I nodded.

"So you want me to walk around the plane and pretend to be looking at stuff?"

"That's right, Pete, Just walk around and pretend you know what you're doing. It's pretty much the same thing you FBI guys do all the time."

Archie slapped the side of the van with his open hand. "Let's go, you clowns," he said.

ARCHIE AND PETE CIRCLED around the nose of the Falcon, while I squatted next to the nose gear pretending to examine the tire and checked out the activity around the Ilyushin. The rear cargo doors were open and from a loading platform positioned under the tail a half dozen local laborers were pushing cargo containers into the aircraft. The front loading door behind the cockpit was open as well, and a set of air stairs were pushed up to it. A fuel truck was parked under the wing. While I watched, a fueler unhooked the hose from the wing tanks and curled it back into a hatch on the top of the truck. That was a bad sign. If they were done fueling, they could take off any time they wanted.

I spent so long pretending to look at the tire that I started feeling conspicuous, so I stood up and strolled counter-clockwise around the Falcon. I tilted my head up as if examining the wings and fuselage with great care, but I kept my eyes on the Ilyushin two parking bays down. The cargo loaders looked like they were finishing and preparing the loading platform to be pulled away. Yet I still saw no sign of either passengers or crew. Either they were already aboard or hadn't turned up yet.

There was nothing inherently suspicious about the plane, even it was an Iranian airplane that had filed a flight plan for North Korea. Watching people loading cargo containers into it told me nothing at all. The question of the day was what was in those containers. Was it really the piles of clean Hong Kong dollars that the MGM had paid out in exchange for the counterfeit $50 bills and €100 notes, or was it something entirely unremarkable? There was also the matter of whether Freddy was actually on board or not. Maybe he was, maybe he wasn't.

I simply had no better idea what was really on that Ilyushin now that I was standing a hundred feet from it than I'd had before. That hundred feet might as well have been a mile. To find out we had to get on board ourselves. It was just that simple, and just that complicated.

The whole idea of getting on board seemed hopelessly farfetched. There were only three of us and we had no weapons other than our three handguns. It wasn't exactly the makings of a military operation, and it looked to me like that was exactly what would be needed to take control of an aircraft of that size.

All I really knew for sure right at that moment was that Stanley Ho had told Pansy that both the money and Freddy were on a Yas Air Ilyushin with the tail number EP-GOP. And now that aircraft was right in front of me.

I fully understood that the triads had people everywhere in

Macau, and I had no doubt they kept close tabs on what was moving through both Macau's airport and its container port, because they no doubt dipped into the passing stream here and there and extracted a bit for themselves. Whether Stanley Ho was really a triad boss himself or not, I had no trouble believing that he could reach out to people who could locate almost anything or anybody in Macau he wanted to locate.

I simply wasn't certain Stanley would necessarily tell me the truth about what he found out when he did that reaching out, even if the reason I wanted to know the truth was to help his daughter, Pansy.

WE MET BEHIND THE Falcon's vertical stabilizer where we were momentarily out of sight of the Ilyushin.

"Did you see any sign of passengers or crew?" I asked.

"Nothing but the cargo containers," Archie said.

"The money could be in them," Pete added.

"And it could be food packages from the Red Cross."

"Whatever is in there, they're about ready to close up and take off," Pete said. "We need to think of something fast."

He was right, of course, but I still had no idea what we were going do about it. We couldn't exactly rush the plane with our little popguns.

While I was still thinking about it, a white van that looked very similar to the one Pansy was driving pulled up next to the air stairs at the front loading door of the Ilyushin. Two men wearing uniforms that also looked pretty similar to the ones the three of us were wearing got out. The van drove away and the men climbed the air stairs lugging their flight bags with them.

And that was when I saw exactly how we were going to get on that plane.

"WHEN THEY COME OUT to do their walk around, let's go over and talk to them," I said. "Just pilots being friendly with each other."

"Where does that get us?" Pete asked.

"Probably inside the Ilyushin. We ask those guys if they would give us a look at the cockpit. How can they say no to fellow pilots?"

"They can say no because they're Iranians and they probably hate Americans."

"I don't think they're Iranians," Archie said. "Look."

I glanced back at the Ilyushin and saw the two pilots coming down the forward air stairs. I wasn't sure I could pick out an Iranian at that distance with any certainty, probably not with certainty at any distance, but it looked to me like Archie was probably right. Whatever two Iranian pilots might actually look like, it almost certainly wasn't like these guys looked. Both men were tall with very fair complexions and light colored hair.

"I'll bet they're Eastern Europeans or Russians," Archie said. "It's possible they don't hate you after all. At least not as much as Iranians would."

"Even if we can get them to let us into the Ilyushin, what do we do then?" Pete asked. "We can't just start searching it."

"Maybe we can. If we reason with those guys, they probably won't get in our way. They're foreigners being paid to fly an Iranian airplane ferrying cargo to North Korea. They're not going to get into a fight with us."

"But what if they do push back?"

"We can always shoot them."

"You're kidding."

I didn't say anything. I hoped I was kidding, too…but maybe I wasn't.

DUCKING UNDER THE WING, I walked up to where we had left our flight bags at the front air stairs and squatted down next to mine. I lifted out the Ruger LC9, worked the slide to chamber a round, and slipped it back into the black nylon holster. When I stood up, I clipped the holster inside my belt. My jacket was a little too big for me so when I buttoned it and smoothed it down over my side the gun was invisible.

While Pete and Archie retrieved their own weapons, I watched the Ilyushin pilots, whatever nationality they actually were, start their own walk around. I was still thinking about how to approach them when Archie walked up next to me with something in his hands that I couldn't immediately identify. I raised my eyebrows at him in a question.

"FlexiCuffs," he answered. "I always have a couple of pair with me. Never know when you're going to have to restrain someone."

"Give me a pair," Pete spoke up. "Maybe I can use them to keep Jack from shooting somebody."

"I thought we'd use them on the Ilyushin pilots, not on Jack."

"Whatever works," Pete said, but I thought he looked downright disappointed. He took a pair of FlexiCuffs from Archie anyway and stuffed them in his pocket.

WE GATHERED NEXT TO the driver's window of the silver van. It was open and Pansy looked at me expectantly.

"Guns?"

"Only a precaution," I said. "We're not really going to shoot anybody."

"Jack would like to," Pete added, "but we doubt he could hit them."

I ignored Pete and looked at Pansy. "We're going to go over and strike up a conversation with the Ilyushin pilots. I'll try to get them to take us into the plane to show us the cockpit."

"Is that when you're going to shoot them?" Pansy asked.

"Will you cut that shit out! We're not going to shoot anybody."

"So then why are you all carrying guns?"

It was a good question now that I thought about it, but I didn't really have a good answer for it. Threatening people with a gun wasn't much use if you weren't ready to pull the trigger. Whoever you were threatening almost always knew you weren't going to shoot, and they just stood there laughing at you. Unless of course they had guessed wrong, in which case the joke would turn out to be on them…

"If you see us go up the air stairs into the Ilyushin," I said to Pansy, "pull the van around and park right at the bottom. We'll probably need to make a quick exit."

Pansy nodded. "Be careful, Jack."

"Don't worry," I told her. "It's all going to be fine."

I could only hope I was right about that.

41

THE TWO ILYUSHIN PILOTS were standing by the air stairs with their backs to us.

"Hey, either of you guys speak English?" I called out as we walked toward them.

They both looked over their shoulders at us. The heavier-set one, who I could see now was about twenty years older than the thinner one, lifted his hand and gave a little wave. Probably he was the captain and the younger man was the first officer. The captain, if that's what he was, seemed friendly enough, so I waved back.

"I speak," said the pilot who had waved when we got to the bottom of the air stairs. "A leetle."

Pete, Archie, and I introduced ourselves by our first names, and we shook hands all around. The Ilyushin captain said his name was Vlad and the first officer said he was Mikhail.

"Russian?" I asked, and they both nodded.

"But you're flying for an Iranian airline?"

"Is job," Vlad shrugged elaborately.

"I hear you."

"You are *Amerikantsy*?" Mikhail asked, taking in all three of us with a big gesture.

"Canadian," I answered quickly before with Archie or Pete could say anything.

"But you fly…" Mikhail pointed at the MGM log on the tail of the Falcon and the American tail number above it, "…American registered plane?"

I tried to shrug every bit as elaborately as Vlad had. "Is job," I said.

Everybody got a big laugh out of that. We were really having fun now.

IT TOOK ME ONLY a few minutes to bring the subject around to whether our new best pals would take us on board the Ilyushin to have a look at the cockpit.

Mikhail and Vlad glanced at each other and Vlad gave out with another of his picturesque shrugs.

"Is okay," he said, "but must be fast. We leave soon."

"Sure," I said, looking at Pete and Archie, "we can be fast. Where are you headed?"

Vlad hesitated, but apparently decided it would be rude to lie to his new friends.

"Pyongyang," he eventually said after a slight but noticeable pause.

"Wow, that sounds exotic," Pete said. "Is it a fun city for layovers?"

For a moment no one said anything, but when Vlad and Mikhail burst out laughing we all joined in.

"Are you loaded?" Archie asked.

Vlad gave us a thumbs up. "Loaded and locked, as your *Amerikantsy* say."

I didn't bother to correct Vlad's misuse of the phrase. Instead we all laughed some more and nodded appropriately to indicate our deep appreciation for his wit.

"And what about your passengers?" I asked.

Suddenly Vlad stopped smiling.

"Why you ask about passengers? We cargo flight."

"I thought perhaps…" My eyes flicked quickly to Archie in an appeal for help, but it was Pete who spoke up.

"Don't you take hookers with you? How could you spend a night in Pyongyang without a couple of Macau hookers?"

Vlad started laughing again and this time he laughed so hard I thought he might hurt himself.

"Right idea," he managed to choke out between guffaws. "Next time I do, my friend. We have only small rest compartment behind cockpit, but will fit four or five."

"Will that be enough for two Russians?" Pete asked, and we all erupted into one more round of appreciative laughter.

AFTER THINGS CALMED DOWN a bit, Vlad leaned toward me and lowered his voice.

"Is true we have passengers. Two. Sick person and someone else."

"Sick person?"

That drew another of Vlad's elaborate shrugs.

"Yesterday we told by company we carry sick person to Pyongyang along with cargo and someone go along to watch him," he said, "but I not understand. Who go to Pyongyang for hospital? Important people in Pyongyang go somewhere else for hospital. China maybe."

I nodded, but I didn't say anything.

"Passengers on board since morning, waiting, which seem very strange. But what I know?" Vlad finished. "I only drive airplane."

We all bobbed our heads and looked sympathetic. Three more hard working pilots doing what we're told and not asking too many questions.

"So come," Vlad sang out, gesturing toward the air stairs. "We show you ours, and next time," he grinned, "you show me yours, huh?"

Another round of laughter, and we all started up the stairs. Vlad led the way and Mikhail brought up the rear.

AT THE TOP OF the stairs, Pete and Archie turned left behind Vlad and followed him in the Ilyushin's cockpit. Mikhail gestured for me to go in too, but I stepped back, bowed from the waist, and made a smiling 'after you' gesture to my new comrade. He smiled back and walked into the cockpit behind Archie.

Which gave me an opportunity to take a quick look back to see what I could see in the interior of the Ilyushin…

A narrow passageway led past a compartment with two closed doors, and at its end was what I assumed had to be the cargo area. I took three fast steps along the passageway and peered toward the back of the aircraft. As I expected, I was looking into the cargo area, a single vast open space probably sixty feet long, ten feet wide, and ten feet high. There were no windows at all. On both sides of the long compartment, fold-down metal seats lined the fuselage. No cushions, no seat belts, no view, no inflight entertainment. It looked like a giant, metal lined bowling alley. It also looked like a lousy way to travel.

The steel deck plates had embedded container tracks for easy roll on and roll off of shipping containers, and in the dim glow of the interior lighting I saw that only three containers had been loaded. They were roughly in the center of the space and had been locked down to the tracks with restraining bars to keep them from shifting in flight.

Only three containers on this giant aircraft? Had to be the money. What else could it be?

I glanced back at the closed compartment. Whoever was on board was in there. Nowhere else they could be. A sick man and an attendant? We would see about that.

I moved quietly back up the passageway and stepped through the open door into the cockpit.

MY MOUTH OPENED IN surprise as I glanced around. The cockpit looked like a set for a cheesy space movie filmed on the cheap back in about 1950. The controls and instruments were all big, clunky, and old-fashioned looking. After all the modern airplanes I had been in, their cockpits filed with flashing LEDs and clean microelectronics, there was something downright antediluvian about it. If Noah had built a flying ark, I would bet the cockpit would look exactly like this.

Archie and Pete glanced at me as I came through the cockpit door and I made eye contact with each of them in turn and nodded slightly. I had no idea what they thought that meant, but it seemed to satisfy them.

Vlad was in the captain's seat on the left and Mikhail was in the co-pilot's seat on the right. Vlad was rabbiting on about something and pointing out instruments in what sounded like an incomprehensible imitation of English. Both of the pilots' seats were ratty and dirty and their green cloth upholstery was worn and ripped. The throttles were in the center console between the two pilot seats, and somebody had dumped a short-handled sledgehammer on the deck right behind them. I sincerely hoped a sledgehammer wasn't an essential component for the Ilyushin's inflight operations.

I slipped past Archie and positioned myself directly behind Vlad's seat. Pete mirrored my movements and put himself behind Mikhail's seat. I stretched out my right foot and quietly slid the sledgehammer out of reach. When it was far enough back, Archie bent down and silently scooped it up.

I caught Pete's eye and Archie's, and I nodded again. I unbuttoned my jacket and slid the silenced Ruger out of its holster.

Taking a deep breath, I leaned forward and dug the silencer into Vlad's right ear. Out of the corner of my eye, I saw Pete doing the same to Mikhail's left ear with his Walther.

That was when the cockpit got very still.

42

"YOU ARE HIJACKING US?" Vlad asked in a voice that I thought was remarkably steady under the circumstances. Perhaps he was used to having a gun in his ear. "You are taking over my plane?"

"You can't be serious, Vlad," I said. "Nobody would hijack a piece of shit like this."

"Close the cockpit door," I said to Archie.

If our two Russian pals starting making noise, I wanted as much protection between the passenger compartment and us as I could get. Archie didn't even look behind him. He kicked out with his left foot and the door clunked shut behind us.

Vlad started to turn in his seat, probably to see if this was all some kind of crazy Canadian joke, but I pushed the snout of the silencer harder into his ear.

"Eyes forward, Vlad! Put your hands behind your seat." I glanced to my right. "You too, Mikhail. Same drill."

"Who are you?" Mikhail asked.

"Nobody really. We're just some guys."

Pete took the Walther away from Mikhail's head long enough to bat him across the ear with the barrel. He didn't do it very hard, but he made his point well enough. Mikhail quickly shoved his hands behind the co-pilot's seat. Pete pocketed the Walther, pulled out the pair of FlexiCuffs that Archie had given him, and strapped Mikhail's wrists to the safety harness bracket. Mikhail would stay there until somebody cut him loose or he could figure out how to pull the seat out of the floor.

"Come on, Vlad, don't give me any trouble," I said. "I don't want to hurt you."

Very slowly Vlad moved his arms back until they were crossed behind his seat. I glanced at Archie and he stepped forward, took out another pair of FlexiCuffs, and lashed Vlad to the matching bracket on the back of his seat.

"Now here's the deal, guys," I said when they were both secure. "We're going to search your cargo and have a talk with your passengers. We think the cargo is stolen currency and one of the passengers is being kidnapped."

Vlad and Mikhail shot a quick look at each other.

"We only fly plane," Vlad said. "We know nothing."

"I understand that," I said. "And if you cooperate, we'll cut you loose when we're done and you can be on your way."

"But you will take the cargo, yes?"

"It's stolen, Vlad."

"You are the police?"

"Not really. But we're here to get it back for the people it was stolen from."

Vlad gave out with a snort so loud that I wondered if he had been heard back in the passenger compartment.

"I not idiot. You just stealing."

"No, we're not. The people your cargo was stolen from hired us to get it back without involving the police, and that's what we're doing."

I slipped my Ruger into its holster and gave Vlad a pat on the shoulder.

"I know you only fly the plane, Vlad. You don't have any stake in this. Keep your mouth closed while we talk to your passengers and check your cargo. After that we're out of here and you'll never see us again. But if you do anything to warn your passengers, there's likely to be a lot of shooting. Call me crazy, but I wouldn't want to be sitting here strapped to a seat if people behind me start firing automatic weapons."

"Automatic weapons?" Mikhail squeaked. "Who the hell are you guys?"

"I already told you," Archie said. "We're just some guys."

WHEN WE LEFT THE cockpit I raised a finger to my lips for silence and pointed at the two doors in the side of the passenger compartment. Walking as quietly as I could, I moved past the doors to the cargo area and Archie and Pete followed me.

"Here's what I want to do," I said keeping my voice low. "I'm guessing Freddy is this sick man that they told Vlad about, and I'm also guessing they've drugged him to make him appear sick and keep him under control. The attendant would have to be a guard and he's probably armed. We can't go charging in there like some whacked out SWAT team or somebody's going to get shot."

Pete glanced over his shoulder at the narrow passageway that led back to the front of the aircraft. "I don't see how we're going to sneak up on them."

"We're not. This pilot getup fooled two real pilots and I'm betting it would fool whoever is in there with Freddy, too. I'm going to knock on the front door, walk in, and introduce myself as the pilot. While the guard is looking at me, you two are going to come in the back door and take him down."

Pete looked skeptically at me. "An American pilot on an Iranian airplane? Nobody will ever believe that."

"They don't have to believe it. They only have to think about it for a few seconds. That will distract the guard long enough for you two to come in through the back and take him."

"Let me do it," Archie said. "There are Australian pilots everywhere, probably even in Iran. Besides, we Aussies are much less threatening blokes than you Yanks."

I just looked at Archie.

"It's our accents," he shrugged. "Everybody loves 'em."

ARCHIE WENT TO THE forward door of the passenger compartment and Pete and I positioned ourselves by the rear door. I placed my left hand on the handle, pulled my Ruger with my right, and turned on the laser sight. I looked at Pete. He raised the 9mm Walther in a two-handed grip, barrel up, and waited.

I turned my head toward Archie and nodded.

Archie knocked on the front door with one hand, turned the handle with the other, and entered the passenger compartment.

"G'day!" I heard Archie bellow as soon as he was inside.

"Who the fuck are you?"

The voice came from inside the passenger compartment. It sounded familiar to me, but that didn't make any sense. Could it be Freddy's voice? No, of course not. That wasn't Freddy. But then whose voice was it?

"I'm your pilot, mate," Archie said. "Wanted to tell you—"

"The fuck you're the pilot, man. What is this?"

I heard scuffling noises that sounded to me like someone pushing himself up out of a seat and moving across the deck toward Archie.

I looked at Pete and mouthed, "One, two, three…Go!"

I twisted the knob and jerked the door open.

Pete leaped inside screaming, *"Freeze! Freeze! FBI! On your knees! Get on your knees!"*

I was right behind him.

A NARROW AISLE RAN the length of the compartment. There were four rows of seats, two seats in each row, and all four rows were lined up along the other side of the fuselage. The seats were covered with blue cloth that looked old and worn. They might have been seats discarded by some discount airline in Europe a decade or two ago.

Freddy lay curled in the fetal position across the two seats in the back row, his feet hanging out into the aisle. He looked dead.

Halfway up the aisle to where Archie was doing his pilot imitation at the front of the compartment, Harry Pine had stopped walking and was looking back over his shoulder.

I watched the red dot from the laser sight on my Ruger dancing on Pine's face and stole another glance at Freddy lying across those two seats in the back. He looked like a dead fat kid. *If Freddy was dead,* I told myself, *and if this dirt bag had had anything to do with killing him…*

I felt my finger tightening on the Ruger's trigger and yelled at Pine, "What the fuck are you doing here?"

Before Pine could say anything, Archie pulled his Glock out from under his uniform jacket, took two quick steps, and jammed the muzzle into Pine's belly.

"On your knees!" he screamed. *"Hands on your head! Do it now!"*

Pine was half smiling as he slowly sunk to his knees and laced his fingers together on top of his head. It didn't look to me like he needed any instruction on assuming the position.

"That's Freddy on the back seats," I told Pete. "See if he's alive."

Pete slid back past me and put his fingers on Freddy's neck. He pulled up his eyelids one at a time and checked his pupils. "It looks like he's been drugged, but he's certainly alive."

"What did you do to him, Pine?" I snapped.

Pine ignored the question. "I've got to give you credit, Jack," he chuckled instead. "I have no idea where you came from or how you found us, but I guess you must be as clever as most people say."

Pete looked at me. "You know this guy?"

"He's been turning up everywhere I've been in Macau. He said his name was Harry Pine and he has something to do with reviewing construction contracts."

Pine was on his knees now with his hands on top of his head, but he was still twisted around watching me with that silly half-smile on his face. I took a step forward, cocked my arm, and whipped the barrel of the Ruger across this cheek. His head snapped to the side and a thin line of blood appeared where the front sight had dragged across his face.

"I asked you what you did to Freddy."

Pine shook his head a couple of times and blinked his eyes rapidly. "I just shot him up enough to keep him quiet until we get to Pyongyang."

"What did you use?"

"Rohypnol. I gave him two milligrams in liquid form. He'll be fine, but when he wakes up in North Korea he won't remember much about how he got there."

I must have looked to Pine like I was going to stroke him with the Ruger again because he quickly added, "If you don't believe me, look in my backpack. It's under the seat over there. I've got a couple more doses for him if he wakes up too soon."

"Get the backpack, Pete," I said without taking my eyes off Pine.

43

PINE LOOKED AT ME and I looked at him.

"I still don't understand what you're doing on this plane, Pine, if that's even your real name."

"Probably not," he grinned. "Look, Jack, I work for the Koreans, but I'm no big time spy or anything like that. I'm only an errand boy. I do the Koreans' grunt work. I handle banking and look after some companies. You might say I direct traffic. That's it really. Nothing very interesting."

I jerked my head to where Freddy was sleeping peacefully across two seats. "I thought kidnapping was supposed to be pretty interesting work."

"That was a one-off for me, man. I didn't have any choice. They wanted me to kill him, but I'm no killer. So I'm taking him back to them instead. It's better than being dead, isn't it?"

"Why were you following me around Macau?"

"I wasn't really following you, Jack. I only wanted to find out more about you. You're an interesting man. I wanted to get to know you better. I thought we might even become friends."

"You wanted to know if I was on to you yet, didn't you?"

"Well…yeah. That, too."

"How big is this counterfeiting operation?" I asked. "Do you have more money to move or are you done?"

"Now don't put me in a bad spot here, man. You have to know I can't answer that. It would be my ass."

I cocked my arm back to slam Pine with the Ruger again, but Archie reached over with his free hand and held my elbow.

"That's not going to help," he said. "Besides, it doesn't matter what he says. Your interest is in rescuing your friend and returning the MGM's money to Pansy. Now you can do both. Leave the rest to other people."

"What other people?"

"You don't really want me to tell you that, do you, Jack?"

I shook my head. No, I probably didn't.

PETE CAME UP BEHIND me and dropped a dark green backpack on a seat. He pulled a small metal box out of it and held it out so I could see what was inside: a clear glass vial and two hypodermic needles.

I looked at Pine. "This is what you gave Freddy?"

"Yeah."

"How long before he comes out of it?"

"Four or five hours."

I examined the vial. The label read Flunitrazepam.

"That's the generic name for Rohypnol," Pine explained before I asked. "And that's really what it is."

"I can think of a good way to make sure," I said. "Get his asshole up and put him in a seat."

Archie kept the Glock leveled at Pine's midsection while Pete stepped past me, jerked him up, and shoved him into a seat.

I looked at Archie. "You wouldn't happen to have another pair—"

"I always have another pair of everything," Archie said, dipping into a pocket with his free hand and producing a pair of FlexiCuffs.

I took them, pulled Pine's hands together behind his back, and cuffed them to the seatbelt anchor.

"You taking Freddy with you?"

I nodded.

"You going to get me in all sorts of shit, man."

"I'm counting on that actually."

"You going to let us fly out after you've got Freddy?"

I nodded again.

"To Pyongyang?"

"Yep."

I took the vial and one hypodermic out of the box Pete was holding, pulled the tip off the needle, and pushed it through the top of the vial.

"You don't have to use that shit on me to prove it really is Rohypnol," he said. "I give you my word."

I lifted the vial up to the light and slowly pulled back the plunger of the hypodermic, but I didn't say anything.

"Okay," Pine sighed. "Shit, I guess I can use the sleep anyway."

He eyed the hypodermic as I continued to fill it.

"Don't OD me, man. Too much of that stuff can kill you."

"You say you gave Freddy two milligrams?"

Pine nodded.

"So you get three."

"Whatever, man."

ONE OF THE ADVANTAGES of Flunitrazepam is that it works fast. I pushed up Pine's sleeve and injected him without making any effort to be gentle about it. Five minutes later his chin was on his chest and he was off to wherever people like him went when they were asleep.

I pulled up the armrest between the seats, lifted up Pine's feet, and curled his body into a shape across the two seats similar to the shape in which Freddy snoozed on his seats. The FlexiCuffs didn't stretch far enough for me to make him particularly comfortable, which was fine with me.

"Let's get Freddy down to the van," I said. "We need to see how much money is in those containers and figure out some way to get it off by ourselves."

"What are we going to do with the pilots?" Pete asked.

"We're going to cut them loose and tell them to go ahead and make their delivery in Pyongyang as scheduled. Only they'll be one passenger and a little cargo short when they get there."

"That's going to go pretty hard on this asshole," Pete said, patting Pine on the shoulder.

I smiled.

WE GOT FREDDY OFF the seats where he was sleeping and carried him down the air stairs, although with some difficulty. He was all dead weight, and he was a great deal of dead weight. It was quite a struggle, even for the three of us. When we got to the bottom of the steps Pete looked at me and said, "Remind me of this if you ever see me reaching for another Big Mac."

Pansy had pulled the silver van to the bottom of the Ilyushin's steps like I asked her to, so we tucked Freddy up in the back and climbed up the air stairs again. We walked past the passenger compartment to the cargo area where the three containers were sitting strapped down right in the middle of it.

All we had to do was figure out a way to get the money off the Ilyushin, and we could cut Vlad and Mikhail loose and send them on their way to Pyongyang. Taking the money off wasn't going to be any easier than it had been taking Freddy off. Probably a lot harder.

The containers were the problem. Containers are a highly efficient way of shifting freight when you have access to the specialized equipment required to move them, but they aren't so efficient when all you have are three guys working with their bare hands and a van sitting at the bottom of a set of air stairs.

"The money wasn't thrown into the containers," I said. "It's packaged up somehow. Let's get one of these suckers open and see what we've got."

THE THREE SHINY ALUMINUM containers were each about eight feet wide, five feet high, and five feet deep with two recessed handles on both of their long sides. I fiddled with the handles on one side of the first container and Pete attacked the handles on the other side. I managed to figure out how to work mine first. When I twisted both at the same time, one in a clockwise and the other in a counter-clockwise direction, the two panels forming the side of the container separated. One swung up and the other swung down, giving free access to the interior of the container.

I bent down, peered inside, and saw neat stacks of uniformed cardboard cartons, each about a foot wide, a foot high, and eighteen inches long. I pulled one out and tested the weight. Not too bad. We could do this.

"Okay," I said, "the freight doors are open and the reloading ramp is still down. That's a break. Somebody go down and get Pansy to pull the van around to the bottom of the ramp. We'll take these boxes out of the containers, push them down the ramp one by one, and load them into the van."

Pete looked skeptical. "You think they'll all fit?"

"We won't know until we try. Besides, what choice do we have unless we get somebody else involved and have them pull the containers off?"

"Get the van, Pete," Archie said. "Let's go to work."

BY THE TIME PANSY brought the van around and Pete directed her with big gestures to line it up perfectly with the bottom of the loading ramp, Archie and I had already stacked a dozen of the cartons at the top.

"I'll keep the boxes coming," I said. "You push them down and Pete can load them into the van."

The first five boxes slid down the ramp exactly like they were supposed to. Pete scooped each one up and loaded it into the back of the van. Then one didn't slide down like it was supposed to, and everything changed.

THE SIXTH BOX HIT a rough spot on the ramp, spun over the side, and dropped eight feet straight down to the concrete parking apron. It hit on one corner and broke wide open. Pete hurried over to it to collect the loose money before it attracted anyone's attention. He started to bend down, but all of a sudden he stopped and just stood there looking at the broken box.

"Jack!" he called up. "Better come down here and take a look at this."

I stopped pushing boxes and Archie stopped hauling them and we both walked down the ramp and stood next to Pete. We joined him in looking down at the piles of Macao Tourist Office brochures that had spilled out of the broken box. After a moment of stunned silence, I spoke up.

"Pete, you check the boxes you've already put in the van. Archie and I'll check the others up in the plane."

WE WERE STILL PULLING boxes out of the containers and tearing them open when I heard Pete trudge up the loading ramp.

"They're all the same," he said when he got to the top. "Tourist brochures."

Archie and I straightened up and looked at each other. All of the boxes we had opened were the same, too. Identical stacks of Macau tourist brochures. No currency of any kind. Not a single note.

"Somebody took the money before it was loaded onto the plane," I said. "Then they filled the containers with this stuff so their weight would be right."

"So you figure Pine was pulling a fast one on his bosses?" Pete asked.

"It wasn't Pine. Pine was flying back to Pyongyang with the containers. If he had switched out the money, he wouldn't have wanted to be within ten thousand miles of those containers when they were opened."

Archie cleared his throat, and Pete and I looked at him.

"I've heard stories," he said, "that the triads run the freight business here at the airport. The crews that do the loading and unloading all pretty much belong to them. They also control a lot of the printing business in Macau. It's possible they even do the printing for the Macau tourist office."

Archie didn't say anything else. He just stood there looking at me with a half smile on his face, waiting for me to get it.

It took me a moment, but then I did.

I WALKED BACK TO the loading ramp and looked down at the van and the boxes of tourist brochures that Pete had opened and dumped out on the concrete. All I could do was laugh and shake my head. Archie came over and stood next to me, and he laughed some, too.

Pete didn't laugh. He just shook his head and looked mystified.

"I guess I don't get it, guys," he said. "Where did the money go?"

"Somebody arranged for it to be switched for these boxes of tourist brochures before the containers were loaded onto the plane," I said.

"Yeah, but if it wasn't Pine, who else could have done that? We only found out a few hours ago ourselves that the money was supposed to be on this airplane."

"That's right," I nodded, "and how did we find out it was supposed to be on this airplane?"

"Pansy told us."

"And how did she find out?"

"Well, her father…"

Abruptly Pete stopped talking. He looked at me, he looked at Archie, and then he looked down at the broken boxes scattered underneath the plane.

"Oh hell," he said.

And then he started laughing right along with us.

THE END

AUTHOR'S NOTE

It is a tricky business for a novelist to combine real people and places with imaginary ones, so I want to make this absolutely clear: THE KING OF MACAU is a work of fiction. Although some of its characters are based on people who actually exist, those characters do and say things here that, as far as I know, none of those people have ever done or said in real life. Most of the places described here are real, too, but those places have never actually witnessed any of the events that occur in this narrative.

I make this stuff up, folks. I hope it all feels real to you, I really do; but it isn't. That's the simple truth of it.

• • •

I want to express my thanks to Peter Caprez, the general manager of the JW Marriott in Bangkok, and all the staff in the Marriott's executive lounge there for giving me a place to hide from the world's nosiest and most frustrating city while this book was finding its feet. The endless cups of good coffee and the wonderful food that kept miraculously appearing from somewhere were just a bonus. The real treasure was being made to feel so protected by Pat and all the ladies of the executive lounge. Without your help, I doubt this book would ever have been written.

I am also deeply in the debt of the many people who helped me get to know Macau well enough to make it the basis for this book. The people I am referring to here can be divided into two quite distinct groups. There are those who would no doubt be pleased to see themselves mentioned, and there are those who most decidedly would not.

The people in the first group include: Quentin Gore-Rowe, David Wong, Brady Hiscox, Normandy Madden, Ruben Tuck, and Yves Duron. An equal number of people are in the second group, and all of you can stop holding your breath now because I am not going to tell anyone who you are.

Then there are some other people I need to thank, too. Julia Gibbs, Eric Rosenkranz, Rob Carnell, and Pintuporn Needham did the tedious work of proofreading successive drafts of the manuscript until it was finally fit to show its face in public.

I owe you all. Without your help and your support, THE KING OF MACAU might have turned out to be THE QUEEN OF CLEVELAND.

THE AUTHOR

Jake Needham is an American screen and television writer who began writing novels when he realized he didn't really like movies and television very much. He has since published ten popular international crime novels set in the cities of contemporary Asia.

Mr. Needham has lived and worked in Hong Kong, Singapore, and Thailand for nearly thirty years. He is a lawyer by education and previously held significant positions in both the public and private sectors that he has no intention of telling you about. He, his wife, and their two sons divide their time between homes in Thailand and the United States.

Please visit Jake Needham's official website at www.JakeNeedham.com to learn more about Mr. Needham and his novels.

THE BOOKS IN THE
JACK SHEPHERD SERIES

Jack Shepherd #1

"*LAUNDRY MAN* becomes a crazed ride of financial misconduct, dirty money and misuse of power as Shepherd's investigations draw him into a twisted conspiracy involving Burmese drug traffickers, American intelligence agencies, and Chinese military groups."

– The Malaysia Star

Jack Shepherd #2

"*KILLING PLATO* shifts the Eric Ambler style of spy novel into a cynical post-Cold War world of financial crime, casual murder, and spiraling conspiracies. Needham's prose is never overwrought. The threads of the plot trail out beyond the novel straight into the evening news."

– International Noir Fiction

Jack Shepherd #3

"Needham's tale of Thailand on the brink has a sense of old-fashioned elegance like the casual grace of a perfectly tailored English tweed jacket. Not a word too many, not a word too few, and a society simultaneously brutal and graceful is wonderfully illuminated."

– The Bangkok Post

Jack Shepherd #4

"One of the distinctive strengths of Needham's novels is that he has the urban landscape of Asia down cold. He sketches it in sharp, sure strokes with language that is at times richly poetic. In his power to bring the street-level flavor of contemporary Asian cities to life, Needham is Michael Connelly with steamed rice."

– The Bangkok Post

Jack Shepherd #5

"What you will not get is pseudo-intellectual Asian literature, sappy relationship writing, or Bangkok bargirl sensationalism. This is top class fiction that happens to be set in an Asian context. As you turn the pages and follow Jack Shepherd in his quest for the truth, you can smell the roadside food stalls and hear the long-tail boats roar down the Chao Praya River."

– Singapore Airlines Silverkris Magazine writing about the Jack Shepherd series

15818471R00185

Printed in Great Britain
by Amazon